*H*is eyes riveted her to the spot. She lowered her hands to her sides.

Unshielded now.

Without disguise.

His stare drained her of her will. While he undid his coat and cuffs, she studied the moonbeams on the carpet and wished she could appear as cool as he, as aloof, not anything to be captured. But she was human, hot-blooded, her emotions teetering on the edge. If he didn't make a move soon, she would disgrace herself.

He was the only man who'd ever turned her head, and she had silenced her needs for too long.

How easily they fell into bed together.

How effortlessly he inflamed her blood and made her forget that *he* had forgotten her.

"You're incredible," he whispered, his hands everywhere at once. "I wish the light were better so that I could see you."

She laughed, cradling his face to return his kisses. "I like the dark."

"Then I do, too. I missed you."

"Prove it."

Also by Jillian Hunter

THE SEDUCTION OF AN ENGLISH SCOUNDREL
THE LOVE AFFAIR OF AN ENGLISH LORD
THE WEDDING NIGHT OF AN ENGLISH ROGUE

THE WICKED GAMES OF A GENTLEMAN
THE SINFUL NIGHTS OF A NOBLEMAN
THE DEVILISH PLEASURES OF A DUKE

WICKED AS SIN

A Wicked Lord at the Wedding

A Novel

Jillian Hunter

BALLANTINE BOOKS • NEW YORK

A Wicked Lord at the Wedding is a work of fiction. Names, characters, places, and incidents are the products of the author's imagination or are used fictitiously. Any resemblance to actual events, locales, or persons, living or dead, is entirely coincidental.

A Ballantine Books Mass Market Original

Copyright © 2009 by Maria Hoag
Excerpt from *The Wicked Duke Takes a Wife* by Jillian Hunter copyright © 2009 by Maria Hoag

Published in the United States by Ballantine Books, an imprint of The Random House Publishing Group, a division of Random House, Inc., New York.

BALLANTINE and colophon are registered trademarks of Random House, Inc.

This book contains an excerpt from the forthcoming book *The Wicked Duke Takes a Wife* by Jillian Hunter. This excerpt has been set for this edition only and may not reflect the final content of the forthcoming edition.

ISBN 978-0-345-50394-7

Cover design: Lynn Andreozzi
Cover art: Alan Ayers
Cover lettering: Iskra Johnson

Printed in the United States of America

www.ballantinebooks.com

9 8 7 6 5 4 3 2 1

For Aunt Eleanor, who is nothing like the Eleanor in this story. But any woman who makes her husband take an IQ test before she agrees to marry him, and accepts only after he beat her by one point, is a heroine in my book.

I love you.

Chapter One

LONDON
OCTOBER 1816

The baron's mind was not on the masquerade ball. His brooding thoughts overshadowed a face that even in its undefended moments had been described by his admirers and adversaries alike as cruel.

His dance partner complained repeatedly that he was not in step. It was true.

Lord Sebastien Michael Boscastle, 1st Baron Boscastle of Wycliffe, was contemplating how to lure London's most notorious gentleman to his bed. He hadn't decided on the exact strategy he would use. But after three months of waiting for an invitation, he had decided that he'd waited long enough. Indeed, it tested his patience to walk, hop, and turn about until the two of them were reunited in the ridiculous figures of the country reel. Only then, as they met, was he completely engaged.

He couldn't say the same of his partner.

Of course it didn't help that the gentleman who had captured London's imagination happened to be his wife. She'd captured him seven years ago and held his heart to this day. Everyone understood that the husband ought to maintain the upper hand in a marriage. Still, his wasn't the sort of problem he could discuss with the other officers at his club. God forbid anyone else found out.

The fact that his wife had scandalized the Polite World during their six unstable years as a married couple was a consequence he'd been hoping to deal with on the quiet. Whether they had been officially estranged or not, it stung a man's pride, however, to hear that his wicked beloved had appeared in bedchambers all over town when she had studiously avoided the one bed in which she belonged.

His fingers flirted with the voluptuous curves of her breasts, then slid down her side, to her hip. She broke away. They made a circle. The next thing he knew, he was holding hands with a sweaty young colonel.

He shrugged in apology.

The colonel blushed.

The dance ended.

Sebastien bowed, searching for his wife as he straightened.

She was instantly encircled by chattering guests. He battled his way through the crush to her side. Unruffled, she gave him a smile that indicated she had the situation under control.

He wished he could say the same.

To look upon his comely baroness was to see a tall, curvaceous woman who visited libraries and attended parties, who had written one or two political pamphlets, and who wore rather outrageous costumes but who did not indulge in low gossip.

Perhaps because everyone was gossiping about her.

All the talk at the costume ball marking the last fortnight of London's Little Season was of the scoundrel known as the Mayfair Masquer. His escapades had invigorated a year remarkable only for debts and hailstorms. His elusive celebrity had captured the town's imagination at a time when Society desperately needed a distraction.

The ladies who braved Lord Trotten's *bal masqué* that foggy October night professed alarm that his sightings had become more frequent. Their escorts vowed to protect these cherished gentlewomen in the event that the blackguard appeared in one of their boudoirs.

Which meant naturally that these gallant young defenders of virtue must first be ensconced behind the closed doors of their helpless damsels' bedchambers in order to catch the fellow in the act.

In the act of what exactly was not understood.

The saucy rapscallion had rifled through one or two desks, a writing cabinet, and several chests of drawers. He had taken nothing of value. Yet he offered the invaluable gift of entertainment, a spark of mischief, to create an amorous mood for those so inclined. He symbolized danger, yes, but also desire.

"He stole a kiss from me while I was sleeping," one widow remarked.

"How would you know, if you were asleep?" asked an obviously envious younger lady.

The widow smiled. "My cheek still burns."

"You are lying," the young lady said in a seething voice.

"She isn't," said the indolent rake who lived off the widow's largesse. "I have only to lie beside her and I feel myself catch fire."

None of the Masquer's alleged victims could describe him in helpful detail to the police. In fact, their reports so wildly contradicted one another that he could have been a dozen different men. To add to his air of mystery, varying accounts indicated that over the course of his exploits he had grown several feet in stature.

His physique had broadened. He had grown a beard. No—his clean-shaven jaw was unmistakable. He had a dimple in his chin.

The first three ladies who claimed to have sighted him exiting their windows said he had left a peacock feather on their pillows. Soon after it became the rage to pin a peacock plume above one's heart to show support for . . . well, one couldn't say.

Was it wrong to harbor a secret tendresse for a wicked gentleman who truly had committed no harm? England was recovering from a devastating war. She needed romance.

So far every one of the Masquer's devoted victims had once been acclaimed by Society for either her beauty or sexual appeal. A fading blossom could not help perking up a little when the sun of public notice shone upon her again. To be chosen, after all this time, when one had settled for insignificance was more flattering than a lady could admit.

The single point on which everyone seemed to agree was that this intruder struck in the late evening hours, when shadows drifted across time and dreams could not be discerned from waking truths.

In those mists of magical perception he appeared and assumed whatever form a woman might most fear, or wish for. The delicate of heart could only shiver in wonder.

What would he do? What did the unsuspecting want him to do?

He had to be stopped.

Didn't he?

"I don't think he exists at all," one inebriated young blood had the stupidity to announce across a crowded antechamber where a lively conversation on the topic had broken out. The remark promptly ostracized him. He lacked imagination.

Impostors. Pretenders. Lovers and rivals.

Only two guests at the masquerade appreciated the delicious absurdity of this speculation. One was the husband of the Mayfair Masquer. Aside from this dubious distinction, Sebastien also held the secondary honor of being the only gentleman at the ball masquerading as Lord Whittington. The other guest in the know was his wife and distracted dancing partner, Eleanor. Costumed as Whittington's beloved cat, in a knee-length black cloak that swirled around tight broadcloth trousers and jack boots, she trod the floor with a gamely dignity that cast all the requisite princesses and pretty shepherdesses in a pale light.

He hadn't taken his eyes off her all night. And not just because her beauty becharmed him.

He'd kept her in view because he didn't trust her not to get into trouble.

His lovely wife had stirred up a cauldron of the stuff while he was gone. She also happened to be the only woman who had ever stirred him. The light shed from the chandelier above enhanced the milky hue of her complexion. How innocent she looked, how subdued—until one caught the devilish twinkle in her eye.

Sebastien appraised her in grudging amusement. Who would have guessed that his wife had sent so many other ladies into a swoon? Not that anyone had to convince him of her appeal. He could barely refrain from finishing the dance and whisking her off to a private spot. He hungered for her in whatever masquerade she chose. Whether she would admit to reciprocating his passion was uncertain at this point.

Until tonight, he hadn't pressed the issue. But he needed her. Hang the masquerade. To hell with her faux mission. He wanted to be her husband again.

She didn't seem to need him, though.

Her amber-brown eyes regarded him with a confidence that heated his blood. He remembered how enamored of him she'd been when they had met in Spain. They had been married a little over six years ago. He'd been away from England for three. But in the years since they had shared a bed, he had not touched another woman. Unfortunately in the few months since he'd been home, he hadn't found the words to explain why he'd abandoned her, either. If her trust in him was gone, he could only blame himself. And vow to do better if she'd give him half a chance.

If she wouldn't, well, he would have to resort to other means.

After all, it wasn't a crime to covet one's own wife. Nor to seduce her. His pulses fired in anticipation. She'd stolen his heart. He had broken hers.

"You need to pay attention." She looked away. "It's almost time."

"I am paying attention," he retorted, as if they both didn't know where his thoughts had wandered.

"Are my whiskers coming off?" she whispered.

He tucked a tendril of her hair back under her cap. "No. But—" He drew a breath, tortured by the yielding softness of her breasts against his arm.

What kind of man wanted to make love to a woman with a coal-black nose and broomstick whiskers?

"I don't know how you bear it," she said absently. "It's driving me quite mad."

"I know the cure," he said in a deep, suggestive voice.

"I'd shave twice a day," she added, wriggling her nose.

"You'd . . . what?"

"The whiskers. I want to scratch at them so badly I could scream." Her voice was provocative and innocent at the same time. "That is what you were talking about?"

"Not exactly."

Her eyes glinted through the openings of her black silk mask. "Is it too much to ask that you keep your mind on this assignment?"

"Is it too much to remind you that *I've* been put in charge?" he replied with a fleeting sense of victory. "I happen to be your superior."

"No, Sebastien," she said. "You surrendered that authority years ago."

"Well, I want it back."

"I'm not going to discuss this when we have work to do."

"Are you telling *me* how to carry out this preposterous mission?" he asked softly.

Her lips curled into an alluring smile. "Are you able to stop staring at my tail long enough to succeed?"

"I wasn't."

"You were."

His gaze wandered over her shapely form. "Fine. I was."

"I knew it," she whispered.

"And I will again," he promised her with a grin.

"At least wait until after we've gotten the letter."

"Now that sounded like an invitation."

The band launched into another set.

She danced around him, agile, evasive. "Behave yourself, baron."

"It *was* an invitation." His blue eyes burned with confidence. "And, by the way, I accept."

He realized that she doubted him when he swore he'd make up for not being a decent husband. But had she fallen completely out of love with him?

Chapter Two

If anyone had asked Miss Eleanor Prescott to describe her life on the day she met a lean, black-haired infantry captain named Sebastien Boscastle, she would have answered that she had stepped into the pages of a fairy tale.

It hadn't mattered that until then she had been passed off on dour relatives or sent to gloomy boarding schools, her destiny taken out of her hands by the well-meaning. It hadn't even mattered that she had no inkling what her destiny might be.

She recognized her fate the instant she looked up into the sultry blue eyes of the infantry officer who entered her father's hospital station on that sweltering afternoon in Spain. He was the reason she'd braided jasmine in her hair early that morning, even though she'd never bothered before.

"Have you been injured?" she'd asked, aware by his unabashed grin that there wasn't a thing wrong with him.

He took off his black bicorne hat. He had thick

ebony hair and strong, sun-burnished features. The epaulettes of his scarlet infantry coat rested upon broad shoulders. He was tall, even taller than she was, and his spare frame filled the makeshift wooden station with understated power. A saber hung at his side.

"Do I have to be injured to talk to you?"

His deep, teasing voice gave her chills of delight.

All the officers flirted. It was one of the reasons her father, Dr. Jason Prescott, a senior regimental surgeon in General Sir Arthur Wellesley's army, had argued that she shouldn't leave school to join him. Assisting at surgery was hard, heartbreaking work.

But even her father hadn't been able to refuse when she had been dismissed from Mrs. DeLacey's Academy in Knightsbridge with a letter of regret claiming that she had no academic potential at all. She lacked the social grace to become a debutante. She couldn't stay put in a chair long enough to even call herself a wallflower.

The day she met Sebastien, her dismissal became a blessing instead of a disgrace. What did it matter if there were donkeys and dirty wagons in the background rather than a coach and four?

No godmother at a fancy ball could have created a stronger magic. The dire predictions of her undesirability vanished. She knew about Sebastien from campaign gossip. The officers' wives whispered that he was brave, and good-natured, which made him the worst kind of temptation. It was common knowledge in London that a Boscastle recognized no competition, and once one of his infamous family set his mind on a love conquest, the rest was history. Passion, these experienced ladies warned Eleanor in knowing whispers, appeared to have been passed through his breed's ancient bloodlines.

"Seduction is a strategy to men like him," the lieutenant general's niece informed her, not bothering to hide her envy. No matter what anyone said, Eleanor was impressed that he didn't seem to be intimidated by her father's reputation. It took nerve to enter a medical shelter for no other reason than to flirt with her.

But then, he could probably sense from the way she agreed to talk to him that he had caught her interest.

"Is there anything wrong with you?" she asked again, realizing that one of them should break the spell of staring at each other.

"There might be," he said wryly.

She tried not to encourage him by laughing. She might have been able to resist his blue eyes. His easy charm targeted the chink in her armor. "Where?"

He cleared his throat. "It's my—my breathing. It's stopped."

"This sounds very serious," she said, biting her bottom lip. "It might even be contagious. I think we ought to find my father."

He stepped in front of her, looking abashed, but oh-so attractive. "I'm a fraud," he confessed without warning.

"I thought so," she said quietly.

He reached down toward the cot for his hat. "I suppose you want me to leave?" he asked awkwardly.

She sighed. She wished he'd waited a little longer to admit the truth, which left her with no choice but to pretend she was offended. "It's a good idea. I'm meant to be packing my father's instrument case. And if you aren't in any pain—"

He straightened. There was a smudge of dirt on his cheek. She wouldn't have noticed it if she hadn't been studying him so intently.

"But I am in pain," he insisted, his blue eyes sincere. "I have been since I noticed you at the general's dinner party the other night."

She swallowed a laugh. "That was *you* behind the screen?"

"I thought I was rather subtle. But, well—I probably wasn't thinking at all."

"Didn't you knock over the tea urn the same evening?"

His grin deepened. "You noticed that, too—you noticed *me*?"

"I'd venture everyone in the hall did," she said with a giggle. "Although all I saw of you was the back of your head."

"I would like you to see more of me—no, I meant—" His eyes glinted with rueful humor as she started to laugh in earnest. "I don't usually knock things over."

"I imagine that's a good trait in an officer."

"My name is Sebastien Boscastle, Baron of . . . of something or other."

"Are you a good baron or a bad one?"

"Why don't you judge for yourself?"

"How?" she asked, laughing again at the glint in his eye, and the silly question. He had to be a good officer because she'd heard his promotion universally praised. His company stood in awe when he strode past. She was overwhelmed by him herself, and not because she hoped to move up in the ranks.

But a bad baron was another thing. She envisioned dark-hearted warlords battling one another in medieval civil wars and bearing fainting brides up to impenetrable castle towers. There was no question that this man could hold his own as a warrior. But as to whether he was wicked enough to abduct a lady, well, it was unlikely she would ever know.

"How am I supposed to judge you?" she asked, folding her arms. "There isn't a castle close by for you to besiege. Not an English one, anyway."

He leaned his head toward hers. She knew right then that he wasn't going to ask her to come outside and watch him shoot an olive from a fellow officer's hat to impress her.

"May I offer evidence?" he asked, his smile darkly inviting.

She sighed. Her heart pounded at the leashed sensuality in his eyes. He wouldn't dare to kiss her. She would never let him. But somehow she heard herself asking, "How?"

His lips slowly pressed to hers. So far, so good. Sweet. Quite unlike a kiss one might imagine a wicked baron inflicting. She felt awash with a ridiculous sense of relief. Then something changed. Slowly that first kiss transformed into a potent eroticism that she never wanted to end. Her illusion of safety fled. His firm mouth demanded entry into hers. She unfolded her arms. Her fingers felt the hilt of his saber.

Hard. Cold steel.

His tongue teased at hers. He was holding her— no, suddenly *she* was holding his upper arms. Mercy. No wonder those stolen brides fainted. Not all of them could have fallen unwillingly. She should never have flirted with him in the first place. His tongue delved deeper into her mouth. Her mind spun. So this was what all those warnings meant. A woman bewitched lost her power to see what was right in front of her. His hands molded her to his hard body, a novel delight she could not deny. But in the next instant those strong hands conjured urges and aches that no lady would *ever* admit aloud.

He stopped.

A benediction, she told herself, which didn't explain why she felt bereft or why the dust motes that quivered around them glimmered like proof of magic. She backed away from him. She had never felt this disarmed before.

"Tell me," he said, his grin vulnerable and yet assured. "What do you think?"

She stared up into his hard, beautiful face. "I haven't decided."

"When will you let me know?"

Her father walked into the station at that moment, his gaze shrewdly appraising. "If it's a prognosis you want, Boscastle, then as the senior surgeon I regret to inform you that it is rather dire for young rogues."

Sebastien blinked. "Am I known to be a rogue, sir?"

"Do you have an injury?" the older man asked frankly.

A flush crept across Sebastien's broad cheekbones. "Well, I got hit last week by—"

"Yes or no?"

"No, but—"

"Then get out. You have a sterling reputation. Let's not ruin it."

"Yes, sir. My apologies, sir. And to Miss Prescott."

He glanced from Eleanor to her father, pivoted, and walked straight into the other soldier who had been waiting outside for Dr. Prescott and the ever-desired glance from his dark-haired daughter. The heavyset subaltern from Surrey drew up his shoulders to stare around Sebastien's taller figure.

"Get out of here," Sebastien said in an undertone. "She's mine, and I'm pulling rank."

The subaltern stumbled back against the tent stake. Eleanor dropped her father's chisel into his case.

Mine. What nerve. What a bold-hearted man.

She's mine.
And he was hers, too.

At first, they tried to hide their attraction to each other. But if she needed help unloading her father's supplies or help sitting in an ambulance wagon, Sebastien found a way to assist. When his company marched to another village, he lingered to make sure she hadn't fallen too far behind. The French troops had assaulted several women on the campaign. Sebastien vowed no one would lay a hand on Eleanor.

They met a few times at the river, too, right before dawn. She carried a passport that enabled her to leave camp. He was an officer. He helped her carry buckets of water back and forth to her father's shelter. Often they wouldn't see each other for days, although Sebastien managed to keep an eye on her.

"I think you should stay in England after we get married," he once said, when she was leaning back against an olive tree.

He was kissing her face. His knuckles drifted from her jaw, across her collarbone, to the inside of her cloak. The next thing she knew he had thrown his coat on the ground and had drawn her down underneath him. She was exhilarated, shaking, about to fall and no force in the world could save her.

"You have some gall," she breathed between kisses that beguiled her like black magic. "You never even proposed to me."

"I know your answer." His hands stoked the

instincts she kept trying to subdue. She wasn't in control. She wasn't sure how far she would go. But when his fingers caressed the tender hollow between her thighs, she was his, wracked with longing, her instincts trampling everything she had been taught about virtue and men no one could resist.

He resisted her. "Not here," he whispered roughly. "Not like this."

Years later they would compete to prove which of them was the stronger one. But on that day, Sebastien won their first battle of wills by proving that her body wasn't all he wanted. He pulled her to her feet and back into his arms. Her legs shook while he stood as solid as the tree behind her.

"Listen to me." His voice barely penetrated her thoughts. "I'm not going to be alone with you until after we are married because the next time I won't be able to stop."

She pressed her face to his chest. If she listened hard, she could hear his heart beating against her cheek. Wild. Strong. Stronger than she wanted to be.

He drew her cloak around her shoulders—to shield her from his desire or the morning damp, she wasn't sure. "What if I make you pregnant and get killed before we're married? I don't want you to be a campaign wife, either."

He was right.

She was practical. Her father had raised her in a world that was not always kind. And yet she dreamed about Sebastien every night after their encounter at the river. She lost herself in hot, misty visions of what they would have done had he not been stronger than her.

They tried to avoid each other. It didn't work.

He invented excuses to talk to her. No soldier had ever suffered as many inexplicable medical ailments as Sebastien did that summer. He made medical history. The pungent scent of witch hazel might have been the most prized aphrodisiac. When Eleanor dabbed it on his face, he had to clench his fists and hope to God she couldn't tell his whole body had turned to stone. But, hell, the woman could have slapped pond slime on him for all he cared.

She listened for his name to be called after every battle, sometimes so immobilized by dread she could not breathe. She lived for the moments they met, at a memorial service, a dinner, or during the rare moments when General Wellesley appeared in camp to rally spirits.

Desire grew glance by glance. So did trust. One meaningful stare, a few words, one smile at a time, Sebastien Boscastle and Eleanor Prescott fell deeper and deeper in love until neither of them bothered to deny it.

Soon, no other officer in the company dared to flirt with her. One dark look from Captain Lord Boscastle kept his competitors at bay.

He pursued her with the same unfaltering determination that had earned him his early success. An infantry officer, he knew the danger of early fire. There was always a perfect moment to make a definitive move on the field. And so he captured her, having been her captive from the instant he had seen her face.

And then one day he came to her with a lost child, a distraught boy of three whose father had been killed on the field. The boy's mother had disappeared a few hours after viewing her husband's body. The soldiers were searching a ravine where she might have been ambushed.

"I can't stand this anymore," she said as she knelt to wipe the boy's grimy face. He was shivering, too tired to sob, his body limp in Sebastien's arms.

Sebastien stared down at her. "I want you to go back to England."

His hand closed over hers, protective and strong. That same night the boy's aunt came to claim him, and Sebastien staked his claim on Eleanor by asking her father's permission to marry her.

When she stood later with her father and Sebastien in the lamplight, she had to comment upon Sebastien's arrogance.

"You still never asked me."

"Well, he asked me," her father said in his blunt manner. "And I've accepted."

Sebastien. A good officer, a good man. A bad baron at times, to judge by the way he'd chased her.

The only time he shocked the camp was right after a grueling battle, when he persuaded a barber to carve Eleanor's initials into his buttocks. She begged him to keep it secret, but news of Boscastle's amusing misdeed spread through the regiment until it reached her father, who only shook his head and said it was fortunate he hadn't gotten sepsis of the arse.

"And I thought you were the sensible one," she said as they trudged alongside a line of artillery wagons a few days later.

Sebastien smiled with the confidence she adored. "Did I ever tell you that I want a large family?"

Hot, grumpy, and happier than she'd ever imagined, she shook her head. He'd given her water from his canteen, but what she craved was cold lemonade.

"Well, I do. And if we have a son first, I want to name him Joshua, after my father."

"He isn't still alive?" she asked, waiting quietly for his answer. He'd never talked to her about his family.

"He was murdered."

"Oh." She hadn't expected that. She managed to act as if she heard that sort of confession every day. In fact, she did. As a surgeon's daughter, she listened to men confessing the saddest and most poignant stories anyone could imagine. And from her father she'd learned that being trusted was an honor, so she kept their stories to herself. Trust meant everything.

"I didn't know," she said.

"The man who killed him was never caught." He looked at her intently before adding, "Yet. One of us will find him."

"Us?"

"My three brothers. We'll find him sooner or later."

She didn't press him to elaborate. Every time they talked it felt natural to share things they had never admitted to anyone else.

"I was an utter failure in school," she confessed. "I couldn't hold still long enough to read an entire book."

"You don't hold still now." He hesitated, mischief in his eyes. "Except when I'm kissing you."

"Which is certainly more exciting than reading about the Battle of Pharsalus."

"But Pharsalus was fascinating. The men in my company all know Pompey's battle cry—'Herculēs invictus.' "

"You aren't making fun of my unfinished education?"

"Not at all." He looked as innocent as Lucifer before his fall. "What would I want with a wife who knows more about Caesar's cavalry than kissing me?"

A smile tugged at the corners of her mouth. "I do know one thing."

"That my kisses excite you?"

"No. That Caesar won his battle, and Venus helped."

" 'Venus victrix,' " he said, breaking into laughter again. "Don't you think it would sound a little silly for the British infantry to charge into battle invoking the goddess of love as their inspiration?"

"Love is a war, Sebastien."

A goat rambled up between them, nibbling the tail

of his coat. For several moments he succeeded in ignoring the animal. "In that case," he said, finally nudging the goat away, "I've already lost, haven't I?"

So had she.

"If we have a girl first," she said, smiling at the thought, "we'll call her Elizabeth. That was my mother's name."

"Elizabeth it is. And we'll name the next pair John and Olive."

"John and Olive," she said, shaking her head.

He stared straight ahead, so confident of the future that she believed it, too. "That's a good start. Now all we need to agree on is nine or so more names."

"Nine?" she asked, incredulous.

"To make it a baker's dozen."

"Thirteen?" She'd been an only child. She couldn't imagine thirteen of anything, not of cats or dogs, dolls or children, and by the time she caught the bedevilment lurking in his eyes, she realized he could probably talk her into anything if she didn't stop him.

"Where would we put them all?" she wondered aloud over the the wagons creaking and the dogs barking at the sheep ambling behind them.

He glanced at her with that stern, indulgent look that said he would take care of everything. "I have a small country house in Sussex. It's in poor shape, but with a little time we could make it a good home."

She stopped in her tracks to stare at him. "You've thought this through."

"And it has a library." He grinned. "Where you'll read to our children."

She laughed again, losing ground to his persuasive warmth. "You're so arrogant. I still can't believe you won over my father. Maybe you should have asked him how many children he'd like."

He smiled. "I can picture it now. I'll sit at my desk and examine estate accounts while the children listen to *Gulliver's Travels*."

"Do you really have an estate?" she asked skeptically.

"We will after the war. It's not much to speak of now, only a white Palladian house with old Venetian windows. The park is five or so acres of oak wood where smugglers used to hide their goods."

"It sounds quite lovely."

"The woods have been taken over by wild deer."

It sounded more than lovely. It sounded like the home she had secretly craved while her father vanished from medical assignment to assignment. She couldn't deny she'd relished the adventure of finally joining him, but what Sebastien described suddenly made her want what she had never known.

When she glanced up, he was standing in front of her, his eyes as dark as indigo, a hint he was about to kiss her. Her bones softened until she was surprised she had the strength to stand.

"Don't," she whispered, when she wished he would, and she had backed against the wagon, not to escape, but to wait.

He bent his head. Her lips parted involuntarily. There was no way he would kiss her with drummers, staff-soldiers, and their wives openly watching. But if he did, it wouldn't matter. Love offered hope. And she loved this man who had grown up knowing that the person who'd murdered his father had gone free. She hurt inside as if his anger had become her own. Or maybe this was how it felt when you let another person into your heart.

He laughed easily in those days and battled hard. He was strong-minded enough to match wits with Eleanor, his intensity a counterbalance to her unbridled energy.

A month later when he was shot five times, once in the thigh, shoulder, neck, and twice in the back, she knew that he should not have lived. Something beyond her father's skill had saved him. Four of Sebastien's closest friends had died at his side. An act of grace had saved him.

She was grateful that he had survived. She had prayed to God. And she had bargained with the devil, not knowing what she had to offer either of them.

Yet her first thought during his recovery, when his hollow blue eyes opened and stared past her, was that her wish had only been half-granted.

Sebastien Boscastle *had* died during battle, and his ghost had been returned to her.

They were married a few months later in early May of the following year at her aunt's home in

Dover. Sebastien had been given an indefinite leave, but he didn't talk to Eleanor about the war or their future in England.

Her father took her aside right before the wedding ceremony. "Be strong. You've seen this happen to men before. Some injuries need more time than others to heal."

But when Sebastien and Eleanor exchanged vows in her aunt's parlor, a premonition of dread stole over her.

Who was he? What had happened to her cynical rogue?

Did she know him at all?

His firm mouth captured hers, a kiss that could have been a promise, or even a farewell.

She felt tears stinging her eyes, but she couldn't cry, even though the small assembly of guests would understand that a bride could weep a little in happiness on her wedding day.

He withdrew from her during their wedding reception, and she had no idea how to comfort him. He drank too many glasses of champagne and picked a fight with a junior officer who'd given her a harmless kiss.

She'd never known Sebastien to lose his temper; he had always seemed aware of his physical strength and refused to abuse it.

But that afternoon she saw her own fears reflected on the faces of his friends as they pulled him away from the other man.

"What are you doing?" they questioned him, joking through their concern. "Your bride is going to toss you out before your honeymoon."

Her father quietly asked Sebastien if he were in pain, but he only shook his head, looking as distressed at his violent outburst as everyone else.

"It's nothing," Eleanor's aunt said. "Weddings have a way of undoing some men. This will blow over before you know it."

But when Eleanor noticed a fleck of blood from the fight he'd started, on her husband's perfectly knotted neckcloth she knew it signaled bad days to come. His earlier wounds hadn't even healed completely.

"After all," her aunt added, "the Boscastle men have a reputation for wicked turns. Passion does not necessarily express itself in lightness."

A dark and passionate man Sebastien proved to be.

He spent their entire wedding night bringing her pleasure. Patient. Intuitive.

His hands and mouth left her breathless, so replete that no woman could have asked for more. Her body burgeoned with wicked urges as he unbound her. One pearl button, one lace string, one layer of white silk and one inhibition at a time. She almost fainted when his hands swept over her bare shoulders and breasts.

"You," he whispered as he leaned over her, stealing kisses, her breath, every thought that rose in her mind, "are the most beautiful, the most exciting, the *only* woman who has ever existed."

" '*Venus victrix*,' " she said, smiling up into his face.

He frowned in amusement. "If you like," he answered after a puzzled silence that indicated he had no idea what she was talking about.

Something cold crossed her heart. "What happened to you today?"

"Don't ruin this." He didn't want to talk about it. Truthfully, neither did she. She'd never seen him drink. She told herself that the advice of her favorite aunt and not alcohol meant this marriage would last forever.

She closed her eyes while he undressed. Curiosity, however, one of her many flaws, overcame her. She sat up to help him, to watch. She'd removed many a man's shirt in surgery. But no man had ever tightened her throat with desire or tempted her to touch him for the sheer pleasure of it.

She winced when she saw his scars. But he only smiled when she traced her fingers down his neck and across the muscled ridges of his back. "Those stitches don't look half bad. And—" Her gaze dropped to her initials, carved neatly into his hard buttocks. "And as for those other scars, you'll be embarrassed if you ever end up in bed with another woman."

"As if there's any chance of that," he said with a smile, and scooped her into his lap.

The next thing she knew, he had lifted her to straddle his knee. His hands locked around her bottom, a good thing, too. She felt that pleasant faintness again. She lowered her face to his shoulder.

"Not a mark on this lovely body," he whispered,

and slowly feathered his fingers down her breasts and belly.

"No one is going to carve *your* initials on my backside."

"He wouldn't live long if he tried."

His hands roamed over her body. Her gaze drifted over him until it stopped at the mysterious hollow between his legs. His heavy shaft rose from a shadow of dark hair. He seemed so comfortable with his sexuality while she, pinned to the spot by his presence, could barely force herself to breathe.

He pulled her down beside him. She clenched her thighs at first when his fingers stroked her folds. Then he whispered, "My wife," and the need that those two words awakened swept away her last defense.

His touch scorched her like smoke. He breathed a deep sigh into her neck. Her husband. She lifted herself to his ministrations. Heaven. She closed her eyes, felt the painful sweetness of his mouth at her breasts. "Oh," she said, unprepared for the deep ache that pulsed in her belly.

More. She couldn't ask. But he knew. He squeezed the bud of her sex as he licked the circles around her tight nipples. Another finger worked into her sheathe, stretching her open. Wetness seeped from her body. She heard him groan in pleasure, inhaling deeply as if her scent excited him.

Suddenly she couldn't keep herself from moving. This felt good. But her greedy body knew he could give her more.

"I need . . ."

He smiled.

"Oh, you do. You're the wettest thing I've ever touched."

His dark, sexy voice undid her. She shook, pushed herself at him, practically sobbing for what his wicked smile promised.

She was certain she would die of pleasure as his hard body hovered above hers. His calloused palms rubbed upward from her ribs to her swollen breasts, caressing the tips he had sensitized with his mouth. His dark eyes devoured her.

"I love you," he said.

"I love you, Sebastien."

Her hips moved sinuously, inviting him. She felt his erection press between her thighs. The air they breathed erupted into fire. He pushed inside her. Damp heat and discomfort interwove. She wrapped her arms around his waist. He groaned. She stopped caring what she ought to do and let desire, instinct, take its course.

She was happy. And she thought he was, too. He even laughed like he used to, as she drowsed against him, whispering, " '*Venus victrix*,' " in her ear. "I don't know how I forgot. My memory some-times—"

She kissed him before he could finish. "I suppose Herculēs can't be expected to remember everything and be the bravest soldier in battle."

He rolled away from her, his smile rueful. "I'm not a soldier anymore."

She heard a quiet knock at their door during the night. She thought nothing of it. He'd told her to expect he would be officially called to his assignment soon. But on their wedding night?

He was gone before she woke the next morning.

And if the man she had married ever returned, it would not be to an unsophisticated bride.

Chapter Three

For the first three years after their wedding night, after Eleanor settled in London, Sebastien made irregular visits home to his wife. But then he became more involved in his work and another three years passed during which they had no contact at all. When he returned to London this time to stay, he knew it was naïve to hope her feelings for him hadn't changed. He had disgraced her at their wedding. His behavior during their following years of marriage wasn't anything to be proud of, either. If he'd been a better man, he might have done her a favor and not shown up at their wedding at all.

In retrospect, he really did appear to have been a bastard.

However, from what he'd gleaned from intelligence sources over the last year, Eleanor had gotten her revenge in an unbelievable way. He might not have visited her, but he'd had contacts in London who kept him aware of how she was.

He stood on the doorstep of his Belgrave town house for a full minute before making his presence known.

Did he knock or simply open the door? He owned the damned house. His wife still lived here. He had been following her alarming activities for several months and had maintained her finances through his London solicitors for the six years of their marriage.

True, he could have written ahead to tell her to expect him. But part of him was afraid she would have bolted if he'd given her warning of his return.

He took off his hat.

Two hot-eel vendors had slowed on the pavement to stare at him. One nudged the other. His dark scowl sent them scurrying down the street.

He reached decisively for the doorknob. The door was locked, a sensible thing when a lady lived alone in a crime-plagued city, he assured himself.

He lifted the heavy brass knocker. After an interminable silence he heard footsteps hurrying to answer the door. He glanced around. Was it his imagination or had the dust-collector slowed his cart to observe him? Was his return such a momentous event that it attracted the notice of strangers?

He half-smiled at the dust-collector, who did not smile back.

The door opened. Relief and disappointment briefly overshadowed his anticipation. His short, balding butler studied him with respectful suspicion for a moment before masking all expression and bowing to allow him entrance.

"My lord," the butler said. "I did not realize—"

"Who is it, Walbrook?" a melodious voice inquired from the vestibule to Sebastien's right.

He stepped around the genuflecting Walbrook, the tidy line of traveling bags in the entry hall. He wasn't sure if he'd caught Eleanor on her way out or in from some entertainment. But one thing was certain. He understood by the shock on her oval face when she stepped forth that he was the last person on earth she had expected at the door.

He cleared his throat. In truth, he was probably as discombobulated as his wife. *He* had expected more. A shriek of delight. A tearful hug. A wife rushing forward to greet her husband after an inexcusable separation. She was beautiful, elegant, frozen in place. He was not sure what she would have done had he not swept forward and crushed her in a desperate hold. She had little choice but to allow herself to be embraced.

"Eleanor." He couldn't help himself. His hands swept down her nape, her back, to the soft curves below. He realized that another servant had joined the chambermaid on the landing. But he was holding his wife, in his own house, and it wasn't a dream. He closed his eyes for several moments of bliss—half-convinced by her stunned silence that he could step back into the position he had eluded for the last six years. No questions asked. No answers given.

Wasn't that the English way?

The master is home. The wife is beside herself with joy. Let's not embarrass ourselves with a display.

All is well now that his lordship is here.

Not exactly.

"I'm home," he announced unnecessarily, as if her lack of enthusiasm meant she was too overwhelmed by emotion to react.

As it turned out, she *was* overwhelmed. But not with the, "Sebastien, I have wished for this moment so desperately that I cannot speak," sort of emotion. It was more of the, "Heaven help me. The rotter has actually come back. What am I supposed to do with him?" shock of a woman who considered herself virtually a widow.

His old deerhound had galloped forth to get down on all fours and growl balefully from the bottom of the stairs, as if Sebastien were a ghost. Even Eleanor's personal maid, Mary Sturges, many years in faithful family service, entered the hall to regard him in chagrin before apparently remembering her place and welcoming him back with wan enthusiasm.

Considering his history, he should not be offended that his wife and small domestic staff did not expect him to stay. To be fair, he'd been in France longer than he had ever been home. He'd barely lived in London at all. The pattern of his household had arranged itself around an absent master. But from the instant of his return, he began to perceive that his presence discomforted everyone.

Had he been missed?

Not if one were to judge by his dog.

Nor by anyone else, either, he quickly decided.

"Sebastien," Eleanor said with a stilted smile, still not moving. "I had no idea you were back in England."

"I should have written."

Her eyes darkened in mordant agreement. "Well, yes."

"I didn't think—" He released her, aware suddenly they had a small audience of servants and that she was dressed in a light traveling mantle.

He motioned to the bags on the floor. "Are you going away?" he asked with a frown.

Suddenly he wondered whether she *had* known he was coming home. Maybe he'd caught her trying to escape. That he would not permit. She had to at least give him a chance to redeem himself.

She leaned her head back. The faintest blush tinged her pale cheekbones. "Yes, I—"

He kissed her then.

He didn't want to hear she was leaving. Or that he might be too late. His arms locked around her waist, unbending her an inch at a time until she was forced to yield or make an unseemly fuss. Her mouth tasted as cool as English rain, but the flicker of surprise in her eyes reassured him she had not forgotten the passion they had once known.

Too brief. He savored the faint pressure of gloved fingertips above his wrist, the warm surrender of a woman's body against an unfair strength.

He let her go before she could draw another

breath. Her hand dropped from his wrist. Then she laughed as if embarrassed by either his kiss, or her own indefinable response.

"I'm going away for a fortnight," she said after an awkward pause.

"To?"

"Brighton. With the duchess and her boys," she explained, recovering from their embrace with enviable aplomb. "She thinks a brief spell of sea air will be good for them."

"It won't be good for me," he said without thinking.

"I beg your pardon."

He laughed. He didn't care what the servants thought. He wasn't asking the staff to bear his children or share his life. "What I meant," he said, "is that you're leaving just as I've come home. And I am disappointed."

She shook her head. He waited for her to invite him to accompany her. Instead, she said, "Well, you understand why I can't disappoint the duchess. Are you planning to stay here while I'm gone?"

"No." He glanced around the hall at the servants who stood waiting like a row of wooden soldiers. "I have other arrangements." And at her clearly relieved nod, he felt compelled to add, "For now."

She shot him a look. "Then I suppose I will see you—"

"When you come back from Brighton," he said firmly. "You aren't leaving now?"

She stared past him to the door. "Mr. Loveridge should be here at any minute."

"Who?" he asked sharply.

"The duchess's secretary," she replied.

"Oh, yes. Loveridge. I've heard the name."

An uncertain silence spun out between them. A few minutes later he watched as she was whisked away in the Duchess of Wellington's comfortable traveling carriage.

What irony. Three years ago she had stood on this exact spot and watched him go away for the last time, offering an explanation for his departure as hollow as hers now sounded. She had known little about his work, only that he'd been discharged from his Peninsular company five years prior at the Duke of Wellington's personal request.

She and his London household staff believed that he served in some covert intelligence capacity.

He'd chosen not to elaborate on this flattering misperception.

In darker reality, after Sebastien had been wounded in Spain, incapacitated in spirit longer than body, he'd been handed the ignominious honor of hatching insurgent plots at strategic French ports. While the soldiers in his regiment had gone on to glory at Waterloo, Sebastien had been relegated to the taverns of Le Havre or Honfleur, intercepting messages between barmaids and lusty patrons that only occasionally bore significance.

His superiors thought they'd enacted a kind deception. He was no longer fit for the battlefield. He might easily hold a rifle and shoot it. He just hadn't recovered enough to reliably make out who he was firing at, a considerable liability for a frontline infantry officer. He could, however, commit necessary evils and leave no trace.

He delivered payments and caught war criminals. He offered bribes.

Sometimes he started riots. He discovered he still harbored the Boscastle talent for hell-raising. Every so often he would make a double agent permanently disappear, and not always in a pleasant manner.

The price he'd paid to regain his pride was not anything he intended to reveal to Eleanor.

She was disillusioned enough by the way he'd treated her without giving her more reason to mistrust him.

Still, who would have guessed that his neglected wife would have sought a secret life of her own? That he would return, not to the light-hearted English girl who had whispered on her wedding day that she couldn't survive without him, but to an adventuress who had not only survived in his absence but who had thrived?

A wife who had become a private agent in subterfuge to the Duchess of Wellington?

He had come back with every intention of becoming the husband Eleanor thought she had married. But clearly his beloved had filled the void he had left with mischief of her own.

What a crafty revenge.

He'd wanted her to miss him. To forgive and

become his wife again. Instead, they had become competitors.

He stood on the steps until the ducal carriage swept her from his view. How the deuce could he impress her now? Should he run after her like a besotted fool and demand she return?

He glanced around. An assembly of street vendors stood on the corner gawking at him.

"Go away," he said grumpily, turning to the house.

His courtship of Eleanor had been take-no-prisoners passionate, an officer who had fallen in love with a surgeon's daughter in Spain and chased her between battles with merciless determination.

But he'd been a nitwit to assume that having won her once, she would belong to him forever.

He had expected he would have to start all over again. To prove he would not disappear from her life this time.

He had been looking forward to wooing his own wife.

But what he had not anticipated, and what became startlingly evident in the following three months, was that he not only had to prove himself a better husband, he also had to prove to Eleanor which of them was the better man.

Chapter Four

Eleanor's voice, playfully scolding, brought him back to his present dilemma, the masquerade.

"You *aren't* paying attention," she whispered, pursing her lips. "You haven't heard anything I've been saying."

"Of course I have," he lied.

He stared at her mouth. He wasn't really listening to her now. He had as much desire to chat as he did to dance.

His senses, too long deprived, begged for relief. He had barely touched her since his return, and he was as primed as a pair of dueling pistols. He'd waited for any encouragement to bed his beautiful wife.

He pretended to appear attentive. He even inclined his head to act as if his life depended on her next words. For a final taunting interval the dance brought her against him. He had missed the sensual fragrance of her skin, the warm pleasures it invited. No matter how grim his assignments had been, thinking of Eleanor had made him smile. He'd always intended to come home to her. He probably should have let her know that.

"I *am* paying attention," he said in dark amusement. "Don't worry. This is child's play compared to what I'm used to doing."

"So you've said." Her eyes studied him in cautious speculation. "Are you ever going to reveal the gruesome details?"

"No," he said, determined to maintain his silence on the matter. If she ever learned the dark and dirty nature of his ignoble missions, she would run shrieking out of his life forever.

"Why can't I know?" she asked.

"I think a little mystery makes a man more appealing," he said flatly. And if that didn't make him sound like an ass, he didn't know what did.

Her soft mouth curled below her half-mask. She had the loveliest smile he'd ever seen, if one could overlook the whiskers and the fact that she was frustrating the hell out of him.

"A little mystery is all well and good," she replied. "But you, my shadow lord, are the Holy Grail of mysteries."

"You don't have to go on a hunt for me," he said with a grin, whirling her gracefully through the line. "I've no intention of being a missing husband again."

"Husband or arrogant guardian?"

"It seems you need a bit of both." And he meant

it. She had no idea how resolved he was to have her.

She faltered a step, her eyes glittering. "I've managed quite well alone."

"You've managed to land yourself in an incredible mess."

"You mean being back in your arms?"

He chuckled, drawing her into his body. "You might have eluded the best detectives in London, madam, but there's no escaping me."

She lifted her hand to straighten the sash that lay across his chest. "I never went anywhere, Sebastien," she said in a soft voice that stirred guilt and longing inside him. "You could have found me whenever you wanted."

His throat tightened. She had a siren's touch. He wanted to know it all over his body again. She also had a tongue as sharp as a Toledo steel sword. Her words cut.

"Is Will here?" she asked, her hand slipping to her side.

He ground his teeth; his gaze raked her in unhidden demand. If she felt the steamy heat that smoldered between them, she showed no sign of letting it wilt her. Barbed tongue, beautiful body, guarded heart. He might have to revise his strategy and take her by nefarious means instead.

He glanced across the room at the harlequin standing alone in front of a high marble fireplace. He wasn't sure whether her cousin Will had encouraged

Eleanor's quest for excitement, or if it was the other way around. He only knew the misadventurous pair had to be reined in. "He just came in from the garden."

Laughter and conversation welled in the sudden void of silence as the orchestra ended their set. Sebastien released her with reluctance. He noted that she resisted looking around to acknowledge her cousin. How self-composed his wife had become.

Was this what befell a woman who had learned to live alone? He realized he had changed. It was reasonable to assume she would not have remained the uncomplicated person he had married. To be honest, though, he had never considered that love in absentia could present this intriguing predicament.

How did a man earn back his wife's trust when that wife had become a man about town?

"Any moment now," he muttered. "If something goes wrong, you mustn't give in to panic."

She gave his arm a condescending pat. "Nor you, my lord. I shall bear full responsibility in the event we are caught. Blame it all on female madness. The duchess will find a way to get me safely out of the country."

"Excuse me?"

"I have everything under control, Sebastien."

"As long as you believe that, darling, I won't disillusion you." He stared down at the slender hand that claimed his arm. "Not in public, anyway. In private, it's every man for himself. Even those who only aspire to manhood."

He waited for her to react. Another man would have risen to the insult.

Instead, her eyes locked with his in unspoken assessment. He realized he hadn't affected her at all. Then her lips parted, and the sheerest of sighs escaped her.

It might have been a sigh of exasperation.

But his blood still heated, his pulses raced in male resolve.

He had a chance.

He knew it.

No matter how impenetrable her shield of coolness, they had made vows to each other. The instant she weakened, which she would, he'd seize the advantage.

"Follow my lead," he instructed her, withdrawing his arm from her charmingly assertive hold, the matter decided, at least in his mind.

"As you say, Sebastien."

He nodded. That was more like it.

It was an evening to impress her, to demonstrate his profound experience in subterfuge. He wasn't going to brag. She would soon understand how a professional handled covert matters. Even frivolous ones like pinching old love letters for a demanding duchess.

Confident that the course of his own true love would run smooth, he was irritated when he turned to discover a portly gentleman bedecked as King Charles the Second, in a black curly periwig and knee breeches, positioned in his path. Sebastien could have pushed the annoying fellow aside as rudely as he'd presented himself. Regrettably the same could not be said of the deep-bosomed, low-bodiced Nell Gwyn who cheerfully brought up her sovereign's rear.

A gentleman did not roughhouse a lady, although certain exceptions applied.

Eleanor slowed to chat with them. Sebastien hesitated to intervene. She knew her game. Did she need help?

It did not appear so. She gave no indication that she had anything better to do than exchange meaningless pleasantries with a couple they would never encounter again.

"Darling," he said, in the lightest of censures, as if at any second the ballroom would not go up in smoke at her cousin's hand.

"Darling," she said, smiling up at him ingenuously, as if the world could erupt in flames and she would manage to escape unscathed. "Do you remember Major Dunstan and his wife?"

"I *knew* that face looked familiar." He paused. The couple looked no more familiar to him than the footmen who had refilled their champagne flutes. Sometimes his memory lapses seemed to be a blessing. At others they posed an embarrassment. "One never forgets old friends or—"

"—those made during our travels," Eleanor said quickly. "How unremarkable our stay in Bath would have been without the major entertaining us with his pithy jests."

He glanced at his wife in reluctant gratitude. He resented that she understood his problem; *he* wanted to rescue her, damnit, not the other way around.

"We are relieved to see you home, and in such good form," the major's wife said, shouldering in front of her husband for a better view of Sebastien.

He bowed over her heavily powdered décolletage. One good sneeze and the friendly beldame would take out his eye. "And how good to see that you are"—he floundered for an apt description—"fit for a king."

Eleanor smiled, taking a subtle step back. He restrained the impulse to grab her by the tail and keep her at his side.

"The major and his wife have written frequently to ask when you were coming home."

"How gracious of them."

"A gentleman cannot sire an heir while he's away," Major Dunstan said jovially.

"True," he said. Sebastien slanted a meaningful look at his wife. She had lowered her gaze, but for a moment her eyes had been shadowed.

"Then what are you doing here, my lord?" the major-king asked with a sly wink at Eleanor.

Sebastien shook his head, wondering the same thing himself as Eleanor rattled off some vague response.

As far as the rest of England knew, he had served honorably in the British infantry under Wellington's command until battle injuries had forced him to fulfill his duty in a quieter capacity. One assumed from appearances that he had returned home to fulfill his next role as a privileged member of Society—the begetting of heirs.

Of course, appearances deceived. Not that he wasn't eager to do his duty.

But what lay beneath the appearances of this particular marriage would have shaken Society to its hollow marrow.

Well, the fact that he now worked for the duke's home agents probably would have only raised a quizzing glass or two.

But that he and his elegant wife had become rivals in a heated race of personal intrigue? That while Sebastien had been carrying out subversive assignments for the duke in obscure French ports, his dearly beloved had earned a place of notoriety in London's history that neither of them could live down?

The duchess considered Eleanor to be her best spy.

Espionage? Sebastien had to smile.

The weapons Eleanor employed were but emotions and grand gestures. The battlefield of fidelity she defended on behalf of the duchess was not fought on some foreign soil, but here in the bedrooms of England.

How the bloody hell had this transpired?

How during their separation had his beloved become the man who scandalized the whole of London?

Sebastien had learned of her involvement only because he worked in British intelligence.

From what he gathered, the Duchess of Wellington, a neglected wife in her own right, had taken Eleanor under her wing. The duke and duchess both held Eleanor's father, a surgeon of uncommon skill and compassion, in the highest regard.

Presumably the duchess's affection for Dr. Prescott had been transferred to his daughter, who had developed some uncommon skills herself.

How the two ladies had cooked up the Masquer scheme, Sebastien wasn't sure.

He supposed the pair of them had masterminded this nonsense over tea—the sort in which one adds liberal splashes of sherry to the pot. He could picture their plot growing more outrageous with every sip until one had convinced the other that their plan bore merit.

Their purpose, as he understood it, was to find a series of twelve letters written to various women across England by a lady who claimed to have been cast aside as the duke's mistress. Her name was Lady Viola Hutchinson, and she now resided in either Belgium or Ireland. This disgruntled authoress hadn't been sighted in quite some time. But the threat of her letters being made public had apparently provoked the duchess to take action.

Wellington did not give a damn what anyone said of him. He had won a brilliant war. He was busy in Paris doling out portions of the world to its powers as one would a tasty Christmas pudding. He had been accused of infidelity before. He'd even been named in a lawsuit.

When Sebastien told Wellington what he had learned, the duke bellowed to let the blasted letters be published. Why did it matter what a spurned lover said? Let the accusations fly like arrows. He'd shrugged them off before. No doubt he would again.

His wife, the Duchess of Wellington, decided otherwise. She would tell the duke to his face if he'd bother to listen. These letters affronted her dignity. She had her children's reputation to consider. Why should her boys grow up believing their brilliant papa had committed adultery? The alleged sins of their father would *not* be weighted on their young shoulders.

Thus, motivated as only a caring mother could be, not merely content to be the wife of a warrior, she had commissioned her faithful friend, Lady Boscastle, to assist her in retrieving these scandalous missives.

Sebastien, upon learning of this scheme, had hastened to intervene as quickly as he could. Quite frankly, he'd been looking for any excuse to return home. Although he and Eleanor had drifted into their estrangement, he had never stopped thinking of her as his wife. He disliked the idea of her involved in any type of intrigue, even this tea-cup sneaking about. He hadn't realized the potential danger she risked until arriving back in London. And he had lied, baldly, when he told her that his superiors had ordered him to monitor her affairs.

But, unexpectedly, instead of stopping her, he had

become involved himself in her questionable intrigue. In the course of the past few months, he had leapt from a window into a cart to impress his wife. The police had chased him through alleys.

Instead of persuading Eleanor to give up her folly, she had convinced him to help her.

And still she had kept him at arm's length, a temptress who would soon find herself taken.

He frowned, his thoughts returning to the masquerade. Nell Gwyn had just nudged him in the ribs.

"Is your wife afraid of him, my lord?" she asked quietly.

He blinked. One of Nell's beauty patches was sliding down her chin. He observed its descent in concern. "Afraid of—"

"You know who," Eleanor said with a conniving shiver, pressing Nell's beauty spot back in place. "That rascal who is terrorizing all the bedchambers of London."

Major Dunstan tapped his scepter against Sebastien's sash of office. "What do you say, my Lord Mayor, if we combine our authority to put this Mayfair Masquer in the Tower?"

Eleanor's eyes widened in alarm. "You don't think he's here, do you? Good heavens." She glanced across the candlelit room. "Not one of the guests?"

She stared up helplessly at Sebastien, pressing closer to him. Even though he knew this feminine plea to his masculinity was an act, his masculinity responded. His theory had always been to take what was offered, and offer apologies afterward. He faced a considerable amount of taking and apologizing to even out their marriage.

"Perhaps we should go home, after all," she added. "I never dreamt that the miscreant would be so brazen as to appear at a party. I believe my knees might buckle."

"I'll be sure to catch you," he said gallantly.

She gave him an ironic smile. How brave she was to tease him. "What a comfort you are, dear heart."

"I'll do anything to protect you from the Masquer, my precious pearl," he replied.

"I doubt he presents a danger to you, Lady Boscastle," Nell Gwyn said, sizing up Sebastien from the corner of her eye. "It's hard to imagine the plucky devil getting past his lordship's guard."

"He has more pluck than any of us can imagine," Sebastien said with an unwilling laugh.

The lady cocked her head. "Do you have a personal association with him?" she asked shrewdly.

He grunted. "Not as personal as I might—"

"My husband knows him as little or as well as anyone in London," Eleanor broke in promptly. "And he admires him, as I do."

He sent her an appreciative smile. "My admiration for him knows no bounds. Nor does my desire to see him retire for his own sake before he strikes again. I should love to meet him alone in the dark and convince him to cease his dangerous adventures."

"You'd have to be quite persuasive," the major remarked.

"Take my word on it," Eleanor said. "He is."

"This all sounds a little wicked," Nell said, pursing her lips in speculation.

Eleanor tapped her tail against her thigh. "Wicked is his lordship's middle name."

"I'm enjoying this conversation immensely," Nell confessed. "Why have we waited so long for our reunion?"

Her husband scowled at her. "Hoist up the ear trumpet, dear. Didn't you hear? His lordship's just come back from France."

Sebastien glanced over at the fireplace, then back at Eleanor. Major Dunstan had lowered his vizard to inspect her gray-striped doublet and close-fitting black breeches, or rather the ample curves accentuated by the snug wool.

"What a novel costume," he remarked.

Sebastien loudly cleared his throat and frowned at Eleanor. "Do you want me to fetch your cloak?"

"I'm quite comfortable," she said. "Are you feeling a chill, my lord?"

"I could be warmer."

"Perhaps you should stand by the fire," she suggested.

"But then who would be here to protect you?" he asked quietly, shifting his stance to remind her he had reclaimed that duty.

"The good major, possibly," she answered.

He let the comment pass, aware that she was trying to provoke him. His interference in her work for the duchess had not helped heal their estrangement.

"Would you like a cup of hot tea?" she asked solicitously.

He gazed at her. "Not unless you're offering to go home and boil it for me."

She turned.

It was time.

Straightening to follow his wife, he gave a faint nod to the harlequin waiting beside the fireplace.

A basket of oranges gripped against a wrinkled pair of bosoms obstructed his path. "What do *you* think the Masquer wants?" Nell Gwyn breathed, her obsession with the man who was his wife grating on his nerves.

He shrugged, counting backward. "Only he can answer that."

Five.

"Do you know that at least one description of this villain could match your own?" she asked, edging a little closer.

He curbed his exasperation. "Say it isn't so."

"Oh, yes. Well, as far as I can remember. How tall are you, if you don't mind me asking?"

"*Four.*"

She giggled. "You're ever so much bigger than that."

"Mrs. Dunstan," he said in mock reproach, "do not tell me that a lady of your good sense ascribes heroism to this character's acts?"

"Well, one feels a certain sympathy for the rogue."

Three.

She attempted to squeeze her husband to the side

to continue the conversation. "I will admit only this—if the ladies of London are hesitant to venture out after nightfall, it is only because they hope he will visit them in the privacy of their homes. I—I wish he would come to my bedchamber, my lord. I would give him whatever it is he seeks."

Two.

"Madam." He touched his heart, a perfect gentleman embarrassed by this candid confession. And—where the hell had Eleanor gone?

"Cat giving you the slip?" Major Dunstan asked with a shrewd glance at the black-trousered form weaving across the ballroom, tail swishing across her backside.

One.

A series of deafening cracks and impressive flashes of red-gold light erupted from the fireplace. Smoke followed in tendrils that writhed toward the chandelier like unleashed demons.

Nell Gwyn shrieked, flinging her basket in the air. Her oranges flew into orbit.

Before Sebastien could escape, she feigned such a dramatic faint that he was obliged to catch her in his arms. The instant she appeared to be steady on her feet, he thrust her back at her partner, who had not uttered a word, his face chalk-white under the sausage ringlets of his long black peruke.

Swearing to himself, Sebastien picked up several oranges and plopped them back into her fallen basket.

It was tempting to waste time reassuring the

bewildered guests that they were in no danger from this illusionary pyrotechnic peril, as convincing a display as it was. Sebastien had practiced similar effects a few times himself in empty brandy kegs when he'd hidden aboard French schooners and had required a distraction to jump overboard.

Still, he should have known better than to dally admiring the amateurish trick.

Before the smoke thinned, he realized Eleanor had taken the opportunity to escape. As should he.

À bon chat, bon rat. It took a good rat to outwit a good cat.

He cut a path across the ballroom to the door behind the corner stage where the orchestra had burst into a deafening rendition of "Rule Britannia." He'd lost an opportunity, hoodwinked by his wife. While he had been gathering oranges, Eleanor had sneaked off to search Lady Trotten's bedchamber for the next letter in the missing collection. So much for impressing her with his professional wiles.

Truthfully he could not care less about a handful of scribblings describing an affair that may or may not have even occurred. He'd rather dazzle Eleanor with his bedroom skills than his ability to set off little bombs. He intended to make up for six years of neglect, as her husband and lover.

What remained uncertain was whether he could persuade her that he deserved the chance to try.

Chapter Five

꧁ ꧂

A change of plans. Sebastien congratulated himself for having the foresight to exit the small door behind the musician's stage, thus circumventing the crush that Eleanor would meet outside the ballroom. From there, he anticipated it would be easy work to find the letter. He soon discovered that Lady Trotten did not keep her private belongings in the bedchamber she shared with her husband. She maintained a separate suite at the opposite end of the hall. It was a good thing he'd learned to anticipate these unexpected detours. No doubt Eleanor was still searching the wrong chamber.

It took him an additional thirty-five seconds to pick the brass lock to a darkened anteroom furnished with a massive velvet chaise lounge that sat upon four lion-clawed feet.

Encircled in the far corner by three standing mirrors, the couch was clearly placed to invite moonlight encounters. One would hope, however, that whatever trysts her ladyship enjoyed in that corner were waiting for a more convenient moment.

At least, more convenient to the man who'd broken into the room.

No sooner had he slipped into his tunic the letter, designated as the one desired by its broken crimson seal, than he realized he was not alone in her ladyship's room.

Neither was her ladyship. She was steering a man to the couch. Lovely time for her to conduct an affair.

"Je vous en prie, madame," her enthusiastic lover gasped as he stumbled onto the chaise, so flattened beneath her generous form that all Sebastien could discern of him was one outthrust arm and a stockinged foot.

"I have no idea what you're saying," she whispered breathlessly. "But please don't stop. I know our countries have been at war. Let's make peace on our own terms."

Sebastien leaned against the wall, sighing heavily. Well, wasn't this delightful?

If he failed to meet Eleanor at their agreed-upon time, he would never hear the end of it. She would accuse him of being an amateur.

He waited for several moments behind the dressing screen, trying to ignore the cries of passion that rose from the couch. At one point Lady Trotten's lover screamed that she had killed him. Sebastien resisted the urge to look.

In an hour or so, he hoped to be suffering a similar turmoil himself. His wife had to know how much he wanted her. And he thought she wanted him, too.

But then again he wanted her enough for both of them.

"Your breasts are like Anjou pears," the adulterous man beneath Lord Trotten's wife gasped as he resurfaced for air. "Your belly is an orchard of ripe offerings, a meadow of fertile pleasures, a—"

"Do speak in French," she moaned. "And hurry up. My husband thinks I'm changing my shoes."

Sebastien glanced up instinctively as the door opened to admit a silent black shadow. The eyes of the shadow caught his.

He smiled.

She moved toward him.

He shook his head in warning, waited until Lady Trotten gave another insensible groan, and stole from behind the screen to join Eleanor at the door.

Moments later Lord Whittington, Lord Mayor of London, and his faithful cat, descended the main staircase arm-in-arm. Lord and Lady Boscastle had been separated for years by circumstances beyond their control. The ton understood the significance of an early departure. Who did not sigh in pleasure to see the tall, dashing baron and his loving wife reunited at last?

Lord Boscastle thanked their cuckolded host for a marvelous time, and walked his wife sedately to the carriage parked on the next street. Eleanor's cousin was hunched over the coachman's box, his harlequin masquerade disguised beneath a brown serge cloak and the reins looped over his wrists.

"You're three minutes late," he exclaimed as they

approached. "I thought I was going to have to rescue you."

Sebastien snorted. The day Will Prescott rescued anybody would be one for the history books. The young actor was as thin as a twig and half as intimidating, with barely a stubble of beard to prove his manhood. He quailed at the sight of fake blood on stage. He'd had nightmares since childhood. But he was Eleanor's family and constant companion. Sebastien felt a reluctant fondness for him even if he suspected that she was the one who took care of Will, despite his claims to the contrary.

He climbed the steps after Eleanor and closed the door.

The carriage trundled off at a neat pace before either of them had a chance to sit.

Eleanor removed her cap, her dark red hair tumbling free. Sebastien smiled to himself as she dropped back against the seat and began tugging impatiently at her trousers. He wondered how long it would take her to realize she was trapped. And that he was willing to help her if she would only ask.

"I recovered the letter as promised," he said, pretending not to notice her predicament until her indignant gasps grew too loud to ignore. "Is anything wrong?" he asked.

"You closed my tail in the door!"

"I didn't—" He glanced down, grinning slowly. "Did I?"

She collapsed to the floor of the coach, flinging him

a look. "Are you going to sit there with that awful smirk while I struggle to get it free?"

"You only have to ask if you require my help."

"I thought I was asking."

"It's an honor," he said, leaning over her. "After all, how many times is a husband asked to extricate his wife's—well, it's probably better not described."

"No." She swallowed as he bent his head to hers. "It's better untrapped. This is very uncomfortable."

"I can imagine."

"It's tempting to believe you did it on purpose."

He tutted. "Should I ever have the pleasure of trapping you, it won't be in a carriage racing through the streets of London."

"I hope that isn't a threat?" she asked softly, falling still.

He chuckled. "When have you ever known me to resort to physical force?"

"Sometimes I think I've never known you at all."

"I intend for that to change. Assuming that you'll give me a chance to prove myself."

Her lips tightened in a beguiling smile. "I'm hardly in a position to do anything else."

Ah, an opening.

Or was it wishful thinking on his part?

Damn if it mattered in the end. A man learned to put his foot in the door and make a place for himself.

"Sebastien," she whispered uncertainly.

He took a breath. Her soft mouth tempted him.

He leaned closer to kiss her at the inopportune moment that Will turned the corner on two wheels.

"Hell," he said, and caught her under her arm, steadying her against the bouncing motion of the carriage. She started to laugh. For a moment he contented himself to hold her. Then slowly he lifted his other hand, stroking his fingers down her face, her throat. Her eyes darkened, holding his, drawing him to her.

"Dear me," he said quietly. "You have gotten yourself in trouble, haven't you?"

"I realized that on my wedding day," she said.

"Ah. It comes back to haunt me. I'd hoped you would forgive and forget."

"Sebastien, please. We can discuss our ill-fated wedding at another time."

He pulled off his mask and went down on one knee, running his hand from the captured appendage to the seat of her trousers.

"I think I perceive the problem." He patted her rump consolingly. "Your tail is attached to your costume. One clearly goes with the other."

"How astute of you."

Her champagne-scented whiskers tickled his nape for several tortuous moments, and her breasts, whose shape he would never dream of describing as Anjou pears, pressed against his shoulder. Desire for her beat through every blood vessel of his body. She was his, and yet he was afraid he had lost her.

"What *are* you doing down there?" she asked in a hesitant voice.

He contemplated her hindquarters before glancing up again. "I was thinking how peculiar life is."

"It's hardly the time to turn philosophical," she said with a frown.

He grinned.

This was the closest encounter they'd had in years. She was literally a captive audience, in a position he had dreamed about, and even though it wasn't a situation conducive to lovemaking, he hadn't come through hell to give her up without a fight.

He shook his head in bemusement. "In all the years we've been apart, I constantly wondered how you passed your time."

"And now that your curiosity has been satisfied?"

He regarded her with a thin smile. "My curiosity hasn't been satisfied at all. I have more questions than ever about your activities, although I'll confess that during my worst moments I never pictured you in this situation."

"No? Then how did you picture me?"

"I suppose I was afraid that I would have rivals for your affection. Gentlemen who considered an absent husband not a liability but a lure."

She blinked as he slipped his hand around her bottom. "I've been at no man's mercy until this moment," she said. "Your imagination deceived you."

"I'm relieved to hear that," he said after a pause. "However, I never imagined that my wife was involved in any manner of subterfuge. Or that my rival was to be you."

"But once you found out—"

"I rushed back to your side, alarmed for your safety." He gave the length of wool a tug. "You're free," he said, tossing her squashed tail into her lap. "You can get up."

She rose from her uncomfortable crouch, studying him in—well, he couldn't decide what that look on her face meant. He decided he'd done a reasonable job of concealing his own thoughts considering that he'd not only wanted to liberate her tail but to remove the whole damned costume and have his way with her.

She settled back against the squabs. "Thank you," she said guardedly.

He shrugged, staring out the window so that he wouldn't be tempted to take her in his arms again until they got home. A man who couldn't control himself in a moving carriage could hardly hope to assert control in more important matters. "It was nothing," he said. "Any husband would have done the same."

Chapter Six

❦ ❧

But he wasn't any husband.

And she did not wish to be any wife.

Eleanor felt her heart pounding in countertime to the hoofbeats against the cobbles. She stole another peep at his angular profile. The night shadows suited his dark countenance. She had exerted all her willpower to keep from crumpling in his arms. She clasped her hands together, quickly looking away as he turned his head.

Too late.

His brooding glance met hers. A pleasant languor stole over her. She had not felt this helpless in years.

She forced herself to stare back into his fathomless blue eyes.

A flame of excitement caught in the air between them before he finally looked away.

She unclasped her hands, the blood flowing back stingingly through her veins. She had lived without him. She could do so again.

And yet she had seen desire in his eyes. What was he waiting for? How long could she continue to pretend that while the wounded part of her wanted to order him out of her life, the other part simply wanted—him? Years of his unexplained absence, of hoping for word to assure her that he was even alive. She had been lonely and furious. She understood that he did not wish to admit what kind of work he had done.

But what kind of man had he become? What dark deeds *had* he committed in the Crown's name?

Did it make a difference?

Could she resist him?

Cynicism had sculpted intriguing creases in his face. She couldn't keep from staring at him at the ball tonight. Sebastien had never been a shy man. Nor one who kept secrets. Now she sensed something calculating about him. Even his laugh held an edge that had charged the evening with an unexpected thrill of anticipation. He had flirted with her, yet kept a distance.

His eyes studied her with uncompromising intimacy. His smile promised and denied at the same time. Sometimes she was positive he wanted her. At other times, she wasn't sure who he even was. He wasn't the man who had chased and caught her in Spain.

He was far more dangerous.

But then again, according to the London newspapers, so was she. But she wasn't really. Her monstrosity was a myth. While certain people in Society might attribute dangerous motives to the Mayfair Masquer, the truth was that her other identity balked at even swatting a fly. She fed stray cats in the street. Granted, she carried a pistol during her undertakings for the duchess. Heaven only knew what would happen if she needed to use it. She had never deliberately hurt anyone or anything in her life.

Sebastien had. But his actions had been such a protected secret that even the duchess's contacts couldn't uncover them.

Eleanor hadn't tried to stop him when he'd accepted his nefarious assignment in France shortly after their wedding. It was obvious that he was relieved to be back in action and that he couldn't stand feeling useless. What else could she do except let him go?

But since then, she often wondered what it had cost him to return to service. And as to the exact nature of his work, whenever she asked him, he replied, "I prefer not to talk about it."

"Are you a spy, Sebastien?"

"Not exactly," he would answer with a mordant laugh that made her think he was doing something worse.

"Well—are there other women involved?"

"Not in the manner you're thinking."

"What does *that* mean?"

"It means there are certain government concerns of which a lady should not be aware."

She had never been much of a lady, she wanted to shout. She was certainly strong enough to accept whatever the truth was.

How many ladies had held their bare hands over

the perforated intestines of a surgeon's patient in a midnight emergency? Or had assisted in numerous bloodlettings? Or who loved to play with leeches?

Or, the very worst, who wanted to grab her husband by the shoulders and kiss the devil until he begged for mercy?

No, she had never been much of a lady in Society's sense of the word.

She made a better gentleman.

"We're almost home," he said genially. "And about time, too. I've waited forever for this night."

She narrowed her eyes at his cheerful announcement. He'd been back in London for three months and hadn't spent more than an hour or so in their town house. The way he acted one would think that their attendance at the masquerade tonight signaled the resumption of wedded bliss.

"I think we ought to go straight to bed," he added, in case she had misunderstood him.

"I *am* tired," she admitted, lowering her eyes. "I could sleep for a week."

"I found the evening to be invigorating."

"But you just said that you—"

"Yes. I did. *We're* going straight to bed. We've waited long enough. We're reacquainted, partners in this mission of yours. It *is* time, don't you agree?"

Her throat closed with a pleasant sense of panic. She wondered what he would do if she refused him outright. Had she deceived herself into thinking he would quietly accept a rejection?

Or that she would be able to deliver one?

His smile acknowledged her uncertainty.

Perhaps this wasn't her husband at all. Perhaps he'd had an evil twin hidden away that no one knew about. He had brothers he'd never discussed. Maybe one of them had snuffed out Sebastien, stolen his title, and returned to London to wreak havoc.

The carriage wheels hit a rut. She cursed Will inwardly for his reckless driving, then bounced forward. Sebastien's muscular arms enclosed her. He murmured soothing words in her ear. Before she could assure him she was fine, he seized the advantage. His mouth covered hers in a dizzying kiss.

Or had she kissed him first?

She suspected she had, which did not bode well for her planned revenge. Up until then, they had both shown remarkable control. She hadn't wanted to break first.

Her thoughts dissolved. Male power dominated her. Not an evil twin. This *was* the man who had taught her everything she knew about love and loss. Wasn't she supposed to teach him a lesson? Didn't he need to know that he couldn't pop in and out of her life with impunity?

The carriage rounded another corner. Sebastien's body steadied hers while her senses spun; her pulses throbbed in painful need. He exploited her response. He drew her closer, crushing her breasts to his chest, kissing her shoulders, promising her she wouldn't be sorry that he'd come home. Her head dropped back as his hard mouth demanded more than she'd intended to give. At the very least he could tell her why he'd gone.

"We're almost home," she murmured.

"Thank God."

His mouth captured her helpless moan. She melted into reflective submission, her hope for a forceful response less likely by the moment. With artful seduction he kept kissing her until it was torment not to ask for more. Finally she placed one hand around his neck and sank slowly back. He bent over her. His thick erection strained against her stomach. Her body responded eagerly to his potent sexuality.

He trailed his gloved fingertips across her collarbone, into her neckline, between her swollen breasts where her heart fluttered. A stinging flush rose to her skin, his caresses incendiary, a flagrant beguilement. She lifted her head to stare up into his strong-boned face.

No safety there. His eyes glittered down at her with an elemental desire that laid her heart bare. Her husband, a man she did not recognize, but hungered for all the same. He had hurt her.

"I have never kissed a woman with whiskers before," he said softly.

She had to laugh. "And I've never kissed a rat."

"Then we must be very desperate."

"Or married," she said, wriggling back into a sitting position.

He sat back, his expression watchful. "You'll be glad to get out of that costume when we get home."

"That depends," she said after a pause.

His brow lifted. "On?"

"On what I shall be getting into."

"We'll find out soon enough." His rich voice resonated in the dark confines of the carriage. "We've just turned off Brompton Road."

She glanced over his shoulder to the window. That *was* the old tavern on the corner. Surely she could last a minute or so more. But she could not fend him off indefinitely as she had the past few weeks.

What to do? Engage? Escape? But to where? The marriage laws, as deeply rooted in Anglo-Saxon autocracy as he appeared to be, provided no feasible escape from living with her husband.

Why he had waited until tonight to pursue his marital rights seemed irrelevant. She suspected she'd given him more than a little encouragement. He slid back against her. She opened her mouth to object, then stopped at the naked longing in his look. Raise the drawbridge. Call out the guards.

His hand cupped her chin. "Elle," he said gently, using his pet name for her. "You still want me."

"Yes," she whispered. "And I want a gold-wheeled carriage, a palace in India, a hundred servants at my beck and call. I want wine with every meal and—in my father's words—things that are not always good for me."

"I'll be good for you." He stared at her in conviction. "And good to you. Please say that you want me."

The carriage slowed.

"Very well," she said. "I want you in the way that you probably mean. But even more I want to know that you won't walk in and out of my life again and expect me to wait, or to be the same."

"I realize that now." He paused. It seemed too easy. "Is that all?"

"Well, you have to prove it."

"Can't I have you now and offer proof later?"

She shook her head in exasperation. The carriage rocked to a stop. Her cousin's footsteps scuffed against the cobbles. She and Sebastien sat for another moment, regarding each other in heated silence. Her every female instinct craved his hard-sculpted body in her bed again. But her heart sought retribution for his neglect.

"Welcome home," she said.

Then she picked up her tail with as much dignity as she could muster, and left before he could say anything to stop her.

Chapter Seven

❧ ❧

He watched her dive through the carriage door her cousin had opened and stride across the pavement to their Belgrave Square town house. He sat back with a sigh of pent-up desire. What pitiful male arrogance to expect she'd want him back without certain demands met on his part. A woman needed explanations and apologies. Damn if he could find the words to make her understand why he'd stayed away so long.

He shook himself and stepped outside into the night. His gaze shot to the figure lurking at the back of the carriage.

"Is she upset with you?" Will asked, materializing from the misty shadows.

"I didn't hear the door slam," he said. "Let's hope she left it unlocked."

Will held up a conciliatory hand. "Look, she's my cousin, as close to me as a sister could possibly be. But that doesn't mean I can influence her behavior, and if you don't mind me saying—"

Sebastien looked around sharply. Two horsemen

trotted toward the carriage, then suddenly crossed the street. He stepped in front of Will, instinctively guarding him.

"London is unsafe these days," Will commented after several moments elapsed. "A gentleman is afraid to walk to his club after dark."

"What with this Mayfair Masquer breaking into bedrooms?" he asked wryly.

Will lowered his voice. "I don't think we were ever in any actual danger."

Sebastien grunted. "Lighting bombs in a crowded ballroom is not what I consider to be a harmless pastime. And just because I went along with this tonight doesn't mean I'll do so again."

Will stared down at his feet, looking for all the world like a chastened schoolboy. Wisps of straw-blond hair escaped his bell-trimmed hat. His rice powder had smeared, white chalk merging into triangles of black boot polish. "Perhaps you should leave finding the rest of the letters to her. If only to prove your love."

Love.

Sebastien gazed up at the elegant white stucco town house. Candlelight flickered behind the third story bay window, illuminating the ironwork balcony. "Even a man in love needs leverage, doesn't he?" he mused.

"I hope you're not seeking my advice. I don't have the guts to ask the most desperate of debutantes to dance."

Sebastien laughed. "No. Only to set her dress on fire with your gunpowder theatrics."

"Did I do a decent job?" Will asked, his grin widening.

Sebastien tactfully avoided an honest answer. "You looked after Eleanor while I was away. Nothing else matters."

"It's your turn now."

His mouth twisted into a droll smile. "Well, wish me luck."

Eleanor peeked out through the bedroom curtains to the lone figure in the street. Will had trundled off into the night, presumably to get his beauty rest for rehearsals tomorrow at the theater.

She wondered if Sebastien was going to stand there forever.

Had he changed his mind? Had she frightened him off?

She turned from the window in utter exasperation and went to her dressing table to remove the last of her whiskers.

What an impossible man to predict.

Had all that kissing and heavy breathing been a prelude to a passionate evening or to another night of twiddling her thumbs in the dark? Thumbs that were dying to undo his costume and reacquaint themselves with the lovely muscles of his chest, his shoulders, his other parts.

She pulled off her hat and her cap, purposely

dropping them in the middle of the floor. Let Lord Boscastle comment on what a little sloven her ladyship had become. She tugged off one of her jackboots, threw it over her shoulder, and clumped back to the window.

Only one more peek, she promised herself.

Just one. Maybe he would look up and remember she was waiting for him. Maybe he would even remember that they were married and he'd promised he would never go missing again. Husband and arrogant guardian, her left foot.

Oh! She thought she could make out his tall, mist-enshrouded figure hurrying off in the direction of the square. Was he running after something, or away?

"Coward," she whispered. "You aren't brave enough to face me."

She shook her head, backing away in rueful disappointment. Now where had he gone? To sleep on his beloved boat?

Well, in her opinion if he'd left her again, he belonged at the river with the rest of the rats in London. She bent to remove her other boot, disgusted with herself for hoping tonight would be any different.

But it *had* been different. She hadn't imagined the heat that had flared between them in the carriage.

"Here," a silky voice whispered over her shoulder. "Let me get that for you. I don't know how you managed while I was away."

She twisted, lost her balance, and fell—flustered—

into his arms. He lifted her effortlessly, enfolding her in his steady grasp.

"I didn't hear you come in," she said in an embarrassingly low voice. "I thought you'd gone down the street."

"Whatever for?"

"It wouldn't be the first time I've waited for you in vain."

He clasped her hands and led her toward the bed, agilely sidestepping the hat, cap, and boot she had left on the floor. He didn't comment upon the mess, but she saw his brow lift.

He looked up at her with a smile she had dreamed about. "I thought you might want a few moments to prepare," he said after a heavy silence, his gaze piercing her.

"For—?" Not that she couldn't guess what he meant.

His strong hands settled on her shoulders. "For us to be man and wife again."

What a beautiful sentiment.

What gall.

Still, a bolt of heat streaked through her body. She didn't care if she were dreaming or not. He stood like a tower of Damascus steel—hard, beautiful to behold, tempting to touch.

"But you're still dressed," he added with a *tsk* of disappointment.

She stared at him in fascination. What was happening to her resolve? She knew how unreliable he was. And yet . . . "I wasn't sure you were coming back. I watched you from the window."

"At least you've taken off your whiskers," he said with a teasing grin.

She glanced inadvertently at the cheval glass behind him. His reflection was all she could see. Masterful, dark, and wicked. He was really home.

He guided her by the shoulders, his voice deep and lulling. "I don't mind being of service in these matters."

"So you've said," she whispered, bracing her hand against the bedpost.

"You always were a perceptive woman," he murmured.

"You were easy to perceive once. I can't say the same now."

"My motives are quite straightforward," he said.

"Even if your methods of achieving them are not."

"Dearest, you have developed such a suspicious mind."

She laughed at that. "Well, you know what they say. 'An idle mind is the devil's workshop.' And you left me idle for long enough."

"But your devil is back," he countered. "And he has several surprises planned for those idle hands of yours."

Her breath caught.

She nodded slowly. "All right. I'm game."

A smile crossed his face. "I thought you might be."

"Aren't we sure of ourselves?"

"I have so much to make up for."

"What—"

"Let me show you." His hands wandered down her back. "Hold still."

And a moment later he had not only untied the myriad black laces that crossed her back, but also those of the corset beneath. The distinct popping of intricately stitched threads broke the silence that had fallen. She was too startled to protest.

Another ruthless tug or two, and she stood naked under his pleased scrutiny.

"My goodness." She stared down at her ruined costume, the cat's tail curled in a little question mark at his feet. "Wasn't that a subtle overture?"

"Don't you think we've waited long enough?"

"I certainly have," she said, looking up at him frankly.

"Thank God for that."

His eyes riveted her to the spot. She lowered her hands to her sides.

Unshielded now.

Without disguise.

His stare drained her of her will. While he undid his coat and cuffs, she studied the moonbeams on the carpet and wished she could appear as cool as he, as aloof, not anything to be captured. But she was human, hot-blooded, her emotions teetering on the edge. If he didn't make a move soon, she would disgrace herself.

He was the only man who'd ever turned her head, and she had silenced her needs for too long.

How easily they fell into bed together.

How effortlessly he inflamed her blood and made her forget that *he* had forgotten her.

"You're incredible," he whispered, his hands everywhere at once. "I wish the light were better so that I could see you."

She laughed, cradling his face to return his kisses. "I like the dark."

"Then I do, too. I missed you."

"Prove it."

He laughed, kissing her face, her lips, the points of her breasts until the damp heat in her belly turned to steam. His head lifted, a challenge smoldering behind his slumberous smile. "What do you want?" he asked slowly.

"I don't know anymore."

"You're still my wife," he said, his hand sliding around her waist. "That hasn't changed."

Man and wife. A license to love as well as to lust after each other. As for the rest of their vows, she had no idea whether he had kept them, or what they meant to him now. She would address that matter in due course.

From the instant she had kissed him in the carriage, she'd realized she would have to come to a compromise with herself. She could make them both miserable by pretending she did not desire him. But how much better to show him what he had missed.

She had missed him so much. Every hot male inch of him. His musky scent. His low-pitched voice. The deft hands that moved over her body with a magician's power.

"Elle," he whispered, deep kissing her again as if this were their first sexual encounter. His long fingers combed through her hair. His body settled against hers, his place marked, her surrender assumed. "Do you think anyone in London will notice if we stay in bed for a week?"

"You've been gone for—"

"—three years, and that's only if we don't count the other three when I rarely saw you." His honest stare discomposed her. "So you see—I'll need more than a week alone with you to make up for my neglect." He shaped her bottom with his large hands. "Perhaps if we start with what comes to us naturally, the rest will fall back in place."

No. *No.* Wait. She refused to grant him what remained of her heart as eagerly as she did her body. The first three years of their marriage had been utterly bereft. Seeing him at the odd interval only made her miss him more. And while she might not have found contentment during the three later years of his absence, she had found her balance. No hills. No deep valleys. A safe footpath in between.

"Get on your back, Sebastien," she said with a resolve that, judging by his expression, surprised him as much as it had her.

He rolled onto one shoulder, lifting his hands in laughing surrender. "What do you have in mind?"

"I haven't decided."

"That sounds . . . promising. Spontaneous."

"It does, doesn't it?"

"Well, I'm yours." He crossed his hands behind

his neck, regarding her in expectant silence until her throat closed, and she realized that she had to do something to give her threat credence.

Still, for all she had hoped for this moment of passionate revenge, the Eleanor of her powerful fantasies possessed stronger nerves than she of the vulnerable flesh.

He lifted his brow, the superior male not only calling her bluff but reasserting his dominant place. Her gaze surveyed his nude body, a source of inspiration if ever she needed one. He had certainly risen to the challenge that she offered him. She pondered her next move, although his musky scent and overwhelming maleness certainly distracted her from cool strategy.

He levered onto his elbow, his face smug. "If you'd rather I take the initiative—"

With renewed determination she slid down between his outstretched thighs and raised onto her forearms beneath his erect staff. Her veins tingled in warm anticipation. She might not possess a wealth of sexual experience, but she had a keen memory for detail, and a maiden she was no more. She'd had ample time to reflect upon the few things he had taught her.

And what she lacked in knowledge, she made up for in all the lonely hours of her imagination. Still, she would have liked a little time to reacquaint herself with the sinuous grace of his body—and its uninhibited response—to her beguilement.

"Please," he said, dropping back onto the bed with a moan. "Eleanor, please, for the love of God," he said, rough breaths interspersed between each utterance. "*Please.*"

"Is that please as in yes or in no?" she asked with the eagerness of one who enjoyed her wickedness more than was wise.

"Yes—as in I will go down on my knees to thank you every day for the rest of my life. Please take me in your mouth."

He shook, from his shoulders to the calves of his legs, his hard body responding dangerously, inviting her efforts to arouse him. All that strength at her command.

It was tempting to misuse this temporary power.

But why not? A license to lust. And if she pushed him too far—a provocative thought. She had a wildly excited husband at her command. She was willing to pay whatever price he demanded in return.

Her tongue darted like a flame. She licked her way from his tight sac to the heavy purple knob of his sex. His hips jerked. His muscles relaxed, then tightened again. He knotted his fingers in her hair and tugged, not hard enough that she felt pain, but so that she understood he wanted more.

"Have mercy on me, madam." His voice rasped pleasantly at her nerves. Revenge might be more sweetly served than she'd hoped. "Don't make me spill into your mouth on our first night in bed together."

She raised her gaze in acknowledgment, conceding nothing, holding his gaze for a satisfying moment. At his burning look she lowered her head to resume her campaign until she sensed he would break. It was then, at the moment she sensed victory, his body taut, dangerously still, that he suddenly caught her beneath her arms and threw her gently onto her back.

"You're overpowered," he said simply.

"You—"

"Time to give the devil his due."

Her heart pounded, as if seeking to escape from her chest. In a simple act of unfair domination she had become his captive. Or had she? True, his large hands had locked around her wrists like shackles.

But she had to admit there was certain advantage to having provoked Sebastien to this point. They could have been two strangers who had met at the masquerade.

No confidences had to be shared.

No promises made. Tomorrow they might be estranged again.

Tonight they belonged to each other.

"How can you be more beautiful than I remembered?" he mused, his husky voice warming her all over. "And even softer."

"I'm not as soft as I look. Not anymore."

"No?" He swallowed. "That's all right. I'd rather you didn't break easily."

She wanted to ask him to reveal more of what he felt. Instead, she allowed a moment to pass. "Your body is harder," she whispered. "I might have bruises all over me in the morning. And I noticed a few lines around your eyes. Not many, but . . . they are becoming."

"If you find them so," he teased, "then I won't fret the next time I look into a mirror."

His hand smoothed the muscles between her shoulder blades, caressed her ribs then her hips before skimming across her belly. She seemed responsive, but he sensed she was holding part of herself back. He suffered no such restrictions.

She'd made him so hard that every drop of blood in his body had apparently rushed to his cock. He buried his face in the curve of her neck. He let his hand wander lower, lower, into heat, into the creamy hollow between her thighs. He spread her folds and pushed two fingers into the slick passage. Was she still only his?

She moved her hips as if to guide his fingers deeper, as if every instinct he possessed would not have found the way without her help. She was so silky wet that he could sink inside her and drown.

"Hurry up, Sebastien." Her hips lifted from the bed.

"Why?" He pressed the palm of his other hand hard against her mound. She inhaled sharply, her eyelids fluttering. He leaned down and kissed her mouth, capturing the little moan that escaped her. "I'm not in a hurry."

"Well, I am."

He laughed. "I'm not the kind of man who loses his girl at midnight, either."

"Did you bring a slipper?"

"The same one you wore before."

Every night for the past year, as his soul had come back to life, he had thought of her. He'd been prepared for tears and anger, for the bedroom door bolted in his face. He had searched his mind for ways to appease her, for excuses as to why he had not behaved like a husband. Trust Eleanor to take his intentions by the throat and shake them into such an uproar that he couldn't tell seduction from surrender.

He surrendered.

But so would she.

"I don't want to wait," she whispered, pulling one hand free to walk her fingertips up the length of his shaft. He flexed his back, his blood pulsing in need. How he had missed her, missed not only sex but the intimate moments of laughter they had shared afterward in the dark. He craved that closeness again. He'd never been this comfortable with anyone else.

"Not yet." He kissed her ripe mouth. "Soon." He sank another finger inside her, stretched her until she whimpered. "I might have to make room first," he teased. He bent his head to her plump breasts. "What do you think?"

"There's only one way to find out."

"You're wrong." He drew one pointed nipple into his mouth, suckled hard and heard her groan softly above his head. "There are several ways, in truth. I doubt we'll explore them all in one night, but we could try."

"You mustn't say such things, Sebastien."

"Fine. As long as I'm allowed to do them."

She panted lightly. She scratched his shoulder again and strained and swore that she would never forgive him. And when he felt her arch, her back taut, he released her hand and held her through the climax that shook her. Her uninhibited release drove the limits of his control to a mindless edge.

His desire for her intensified. He fought to subdue his most elemental instincts. If he unleashed them all at once, he feared he might lose his sanity, frighten her by revealing his darkest needs.

"Give me another chance," he said, his body anchoring hers. She looked so beautiful, so completely wild, that when she straddled him a few moments later, he resolved to give her the pounding of her life. But then she lifted her bottom and sank down upon his swelling erection with such unmerciful slowness that a groan broke in his throat. She was taking every inch of him into her body, sheathing him in fire. Sensation overwhelmed him.

"I think the slipper still fits," she whispered in a husky voice.

"Do you think you can keep it on for the entire ball?" he asked, inviting her to try.

She shivered as he thrust upward, giving her a little more incentive. "I suppose it depends on whether you're dancing a minuet or a country reel."

"It doesn't matter to me. As long as we're together at the end." He stared up at her for several moments, drinking in every detail of her seductive beauty. Her soft mouth curved in the familiar smile that twisted his heart. And while his own body hungered for completion, he wouldn't protest if she hoped to use her sensuality to teach him a lesson. He welcomed her aggression, a punishment he well-deserved. Let her prove he could not ignore her again without a price.

She raised herself again and slowly eased down on his shaft, whispering, "You're the one who's different. I don't know who you are."

He grasped her hips. "Your husband," he said, and surged with all his strength inside her.

Chapter Eight

❦ ❦

She lay against his outflung arm, sated, her mind fully awake. Sebastien slept beside her, his breathing slow and steady. A pleasant sound when one had gotten used to lonely peace. Still, she also had grown comfortable sleeping alone, having tea and toast in bed, reading until dawn when she liked. A husband took up an unseemly amount of space. Suddenly everything in the room appeared to shrink.

"I will not love you again, Sebastien," she whispered, studying his lean backside. Had his scars completely disappeared? Her initials? She sat up, straining her eyes for a better look.

His deep voice startled her. "I won't give you a moment's peace until you do."

She flushed guiltily, pretending she hadn't been studying his muscular torso and buttocks. "You're deceiving yourself if you think it's going to be that easy."

He turned onto his shoulder, his tone neutral. "I never expected it to be easy. Nothing else in my life is."

"I hope that isn't a ploy for my sympathy."

"Not at all. Merely a statement of fact which should be interpreted to mean that I don't intend to give up."

"We have probably lived apart long enough to warrant a legal desertion," she said, combing her fingers through her tangled hair.

"I visited you when I could."

"You came and went so at whim that your own dog no longer recognizes you."

He pursed his lips as if contemplating her viewpoint. He did not fool her for a moment. She'd caught that wolfish gleam in his eye again. Her husband was heat and danger. Love and all the risks it entailed. She would never allow herself to care as much or cry over him again. It wasn't possible to fall in love with the same man twice, was it?

He said, "As long as that dog recognizes no other man as master I shall not have cause to object."

She settled back down beside him, absently pulling a sheet over his bare behind. "The dog rejecting you is the least of my worries."

"Perhaps, but I feel rather like a father whose own child does not recognize him on his return."

Silence dropped between them.

She stared into the dark. He does not remember that we lost a child, she thought. How else could he have made such a careless remark? She swallowed, suddenly feeling cold. She'd hoped he might. Neither of them had realized that she'd become pregnant on their wedding night hours before. He had been eager to set sail for France after their disgraceful ceremony. She hadn't known where to send him a letter informing him of the news.

She had miscarried in the middle of the night before anyone except her lady's maid knew. Certainly it wasn't Sebastien's fault, but she blamed him for not being there to grieve with her all the same.

On his return, four months after the day they'd married, she waited for him to ask why she looked as if she'd been crying for an entire week. Or why all her corsets had been piled on the bed for the seamstress to alter.

He didn't appear to notice. And when she finally broke down and told him, he looked so bereft, so guilty, that she wished she'd kept it to herself.

His visits home became less frequent over the next three years. Eleanor's intuition told her that even if his physical wounds had healed, he hid a deeper pain inside. By their first Christmas together she perceived that her husband seemed more intent on reproving his worth to his commander than on caring that she needed him, too.

She stopped looking forward to his leaves. His desire for her had grown so cool that even on summer evenings she wore her warmest woolen shawls to keep from shivering. More than once in the night she would touch his body, and he would turn away, pretending to be asleep. The next morning he might be gone; she had to wonder whether he had taken another lover because he no longer found her desirable. When they had first fallen in love, he touched her every chance he could. Then, after three years, he didn't come home at all. And still she loved him.

But at some indefinable point in the past year she had stopped imagining him in her future at all. Even his voice grew fainter in her memory, like an echo, until one day she woke and she could hardly hear it at all.

She'd felt panic. What did it mean?

She decided she had fallen out of love with the Sebastien she had married. It was like mourning a death, not only his, but that of the woman who had been waiting for him to come back.

She never wanted to feel that pain again.

A warm hand at her shoulder brought her back to the present. A shock sizzled down her back. A handsome stranger was lying in her bed.

"Do you mind trading sides with me?" he asked politely. "I prefer to sleep closest to the door."

"What?"

"If it doesn't inconvenience you."

Inconvenience her? His arrival disarranged every aspect of her life. "But . . . as you like." And as she slid over his body, she saw another smile cross his face. "Is that better?"

He stretched out with animal grace, glancing across the room at the furnishings, as if studying his next move on a chessboard. "Yes."

"Why do you have to watch the door?" she ventured after a pause.

He hesitated for such a long time that she thought

he wasn't going to answer at all. "I've made a few enemies."

Her skin prickled. "Surely none that would follow you here to Mayfair."

He turned his head to regard her. The dark honesty in his eyes made her a little afraid. "Probably not. But some habits are difficult to break. I don't always sleep well at night."

"I sleep like the dead myself."

He laughed gently. "Then you have a clear conscience."

Didn't he?

"Go to sleep," he said, his voice compelling. "You're in no danger, I promise."

Was *he*?

Her eyes felt heavy. Drowsiness weighed down her thoughts. She could not stop from curling against him when he reached for her. His hard body offered warmth and comfort. His hands stroked away her resistance. "We could have done better tonight," she whispered with a little sigh.

"Then let's try again."

She laughed at him. "The letter, man of a single mind. We took twice as long as we should have. I should not waste time getting the next one on the list."

"The St. George Street address?" he asked thoughtfully.

"Yes. And I've got a plan of the house."

"I could find the rest of them alone."

She opened her eyes, his self-assurance raising

her suspicions. If he hadn't weakened her with his wonderful lovemaking, she would never have lowered her guard. "This is between me and the duchess. A female affair, if you wish."

"The duke does not think so," he murmured.

"I do not work for the duke," she said in annoyance. "I have made a promise, and I will keep it."

His voice dripped sheer male condescension. "Sweetheart, it is an amusing game you have played. I'm impressed at your ingenuity and dedication. But these matters are best handled by a man."

"The Masquer is a man."

"I meant a man of experience."

"It's clear what you meant."

"And"—laughter lurked in his deep voice—"you are most decidedly a woman."

"At least you and I agree on that fact."

He shook his head, quick to reassure her. "All I meant is that you and the duchess should observe your roles as nature has defined them."

She bit the tip of her tongue. Nature had not finished defining either lady, in Eleanor's modest opinion. "Have I failed you as a woman?" she asked in her most dulcet voice.

"Dearest." His gaze drifted over her.

"Then?"

"I cannot disappoint the duke," he concluded, the situation, at least in his mind, relegated to his superior talents.

Which warned her that she had to move quickly to locate the remaining letters. Her friendship with the Duchess of Wellington, their shared love of intrigue, had given Eleanor an enormous feeling of satisfaction. The two women had forged a bond based on their mutual loneliness. She was *not* surrendering her authority without a good fight. No matter how wickedly potent her husband proved to be. Nor how politically influential the Duke of Wellington became.

She'd made a pact with the duchess. She was an agent and she would be paid for her work.

His hand slid beneath the sheet and languidly caressed her breasts. Obviously she had also made a pact with the devil on her wedding day. "What do I have to do to win you back?" he asked silkily.

"Let me sleep on it."

"Do you know what a country offers when it loses a war?" He kissed her forehead. "Recompensation."

She was suddenly fully awake. "This is an affair of the heart. Not of state. Don't muddle the issue."

"From ancient times," he went on, as if she hadn't spoken, "the bond between man and wife has been understood as a sacred—an *unbreakable*—partnership."

Ah. She knew where this was leading. She thought it high-minded of herself not to point out that they were actually man . . . and man.

"You're referring to the days when peasants were enslaved?" she asked with a dismissive smile.

"I'm referring to Roman law."

"Well, Rome wasn't built in a day." She smoothed

an imaginary wrinkle from her pillow. "And neither is a good marriage. Enslave me at your own risk."

The twitch of his sensual mouth suggested he was tempted to do just that.

"Perhaps we will come to a better understanding in the morning," he said sagely.

"Will you be here in the morning?" she could not resist asking.

He paused. "Perhaps not," he admitted. "I have business matters that have been ignored. But whether I am here when you awaken or not, I guarantee that I shall be back before you miss me. And don't worry about delivering those letters to the duchess."

"I'm not worried about the letters." She looked at him from the corner of her eye. "You are another thing entirely."

"Your husband is home. Being my wife is all you need concern yourself with."

She wriggled away from his tempting warmth. "Good night, Rat."

He chuckled. "Sweet dreams, Cat."

Chapter Nine

❧ ❧

Sebastien wished to be fair. He understood that he was demanding more of Eleanor as a wife than he as a spouse had given in return. Considering his past omissions, he thought it damned generous of her to take him back into her bed with such fervor. Still, having reclaimed his rights tonight, he had no intention of abdicating his tenuous hold again. Her masquerade as the duchess's agent during their prolonged separation rendered his need to assert his place all the more expedient.

His wife a notorious figure, written up in newspapers across England? He would put an immediate stop to this mischief.

He stared down at her sleeping form. She had donned her nightrail and fallen into a heavy slumber. How easily one could miss the subtle wickedness that illuminated her face. Who would ever guess what an adventurous nature those classical features concealed?

He wondered what the ton's breathless ladies

would think if they could see their midnight intruder now.

He snorted in amusement. He didn't know what to think himself. He had bedded the man of their dreams.

With a heavy sigh, he slipped out from the sheet she'd pulled over him and left the bed. He needed to do something, walk, drink a bottle of brandy, hit his head against a post to keep from taking her again.

After three years of absence from home and abstinence, his sexual appetite had turned him into a voracious beast. He couldn't possibly explain his period of celibacy to her. Nor the missions he'd undertaken to regain his self-worth.

A gentleman would rather be thought unfaithful, disinterested, absorbed in duty, or even dead before he would admit that he had struggled to feel like a man again.

He stepped over the crumpled garments on the floor, realizing that his wife had become rather untidy in his absence, and that he needed a fresh change of clothing if he was to wander about the house.

He returned to the bed. The rise and descent of Eleanor's breasts beneath her muslin nightrail absorbed his attention for several moments. Had he ever fully appreciated her?

"Eleanor," he whispered, leaning over her. "I hate to disturb you, but I've left all my other clothes on the boat."

"Why didn't you bring them with you?" Her eyes opened, glinting in guarded awareness. "Or weren't you intending to stay?"

"I assumed I still had some clothes here." He paused. "Unless you gave them away."

When he'd arrived in London this last time he had sailed into the Thames on an ugly but seaworthy shallop. He hadn't kept the boat a secret from his wife, but he had made it clear she should stay away from the wharves. He maintained the boat as a retreat in case a dark mood descended, or one of his more unsavory associates from the past wanted to contact him.

"Look on the left side of the wardrobe." She rolled back into his place with a deep sigh, burying her head beneath her pillow.

"Thank you." He grinned, restraining himself from patting the part of the lumpy bedclothes that protruded invitingly. "You may sleep there until I come back to bed."

The pillow lifted. She released another disgruntled sigh. "Are you going out?"

"No. Only downstairs for a brandy and—I thought I might try to make friends with Teg."

"Don't start him barking at you again."

He turned toward the triple armoire that stood like a small-scale fortress beside the fireplace. Decorative turrets topped the two side doors that flanked a central linen cupboard.

He had been absent for such a length of time that

he had forgotten which clothes of his remained. Asking her to help him again would only remind her how long it had been.

He opened both doors at once. As expected, Eleanor's dresses occupied most of the wardrobe. He did not recognize half of them. Whether that was due to his faulty memory or her extravagance, he couldn't say.

He went through her apparel thoughtfully, trying to recall whether they'd been together when she had worn a particular garment.

An aquamarine taffeta evening gown. Pretty. He'd never seen her in it. One made of rose muslin. He vaguely recalled a breakfast affair, or perhaps a boating picnic. He'd only paid attention to her, not to the event.

Then, ah, *this* he would have remembered Eleanor wearing. A gown of pearl-white watered silk with a heart-shaped bodice that he thought fetching until he noticed the small wine stain—or perhaps it was something else—that marred the deep-cut Belgian lace neckline.

He rubbed his thumb across the stain as if he could make it disappear.

An unpleasant sensation burned the back of his neck. He glanced at his wife's reflection in the cheval glass that sat in the corner.

She was a pristine creature, the surgeon's daughter, a lady who had always been fastidious in appearance. She had carried a spare pair of gloves when she dragged him to the theater to see Will perform. He could not imagine her spilling wine on such an expensive-looking dress. And keeping it, too.

To what sort of function would she dress so winsomely and drink wine? Had this been an act of the Mayfair Masquer? Or that of a wife whose husband had been away too long?

"Sebastien," she grumbled from the bed in drowsy complaint. "Must you make so much noise?"

"Sorry," he said, closing the door with a brisk click.

Her face appeared from beneath the pillow. "That's the right side of the wardrobe, by the way."

"I realize what it is," he retorted in annoyance.

"Well, I told you to look on the left."

"I remember what you said. I was curious about your clothes. Do you mind?"

"I mind your noise."

"It's not as if you have a man hiding in here, is it?" he inquired half-seriously.

"Yes, I have dozens of them," she answered. "How could you be a spy when you're so indelicately loud?"

"I never said I was a spy."

"You never said anything," she muttered.

He opened the door of the central cupboard, and, yes, he knew it was neither left nor right.

But now, suddenly, he decided he wanted to go through her drawers, examine her apparel piece by piece. One could learn any number of secrets from what a person kept in a cupboard, and hadn't at least two of these drawers been his?

Muffs, garters, ribbons, and a black velvet domino.

He closed the drawer and went on to the next. In it he discovered a white christening gown carefully layered between some tissue and dried flowers.

It caught him unaware. He touched the gown gently. Had this been meant for the child she had lost?

Suddenly his hands seemed too heavy to hold such a delicate garment. He had not been able to talk about it when she had told him. He was afraid to talk about it now. Women conversed. Men conquered. Would they have other children?

"*Sebastien,*" she pleaded.

He swallowed, then knelt to wrest open the last drawer, at last unearthing a pair of his own linen drawers and stockings. These slung over his shoulder, he stood again.

The left side of the hanging wardrobe seemed rather bare compared to the right, but the presence of three shirts, two of muslin, one of lawn, reassured him that he still held a place, albeit musty and unused, in his wife's wardrobe if not in her heart.

But . . . those were *his* shirts, weren't they?

Lapses of memory notwithstanding, he was positive he had never appeared in public in this last ruffled piece that spilled lace all over the front.

A fresh doubt provoked him as he sat down on the stool to dress. Had the Mayfair Masquer worn that shirt, or had another man?

He was seized by the impulse to reawaken Eleanor and ask.

Had anyone else shared her bed while he was gone?

Perhaps he wasn't ready to face that, either. Another husband might not have cared.

Yes, infidelity occurred all the time in the sophisticated world of the *haut ton*. But Sebastien had never particularly aspired to the low morals of aristocracy.

In terms of his wife, his feelings tended toward an unabashed basicity.

She belonged to him.

If he had not been here to protect her before, he would do so now. The centuries-old arrangement gave him a chest-thumping sense of stability.

He went down the hall into the private drawing room to brood over a brandy and heard a disturbance in the street. He put down his glass and listened—a horse whickering, footsteps approaching, a cheerful knock at the door. This late at night?

Who was so confident of a welcome?

He rose from his armchair to investigate. It was probably Eleanor's cousin again. Perhaps the Duchess had sent Will back with a message. Or a demand for the last letter the Masquer had recovered. He would put an end to these nocturnal escapades once and for all.

No sooner had he gone downstairs to the door than his deerhound shot out of the shadows and set up a furious barking at his feet. He might have praised the dog had Teg's protective instincts meant to warn his master against the visitor.

Sebastien reached down. The dog bared his teeth in a growl.

Obviously Teg perceived *him* to be the threat.

"Fine, you traitorous mongrel. See if Will scratches your belly and feeds you choice morsels of his beef-steak at breakfast."

When he answered the door, however, it wasn't Eleanor's cousin and close friend who stood with his slender shoulders hunched in his usual self-effacing pose.

It was a man he'd never seen before—one who stared back at him in a surprise so genuinely awkward that for an instant Sebastien felt himself to be the encroacher, and not the other way around.

Chapter Ten

❧ ❦

Sebastien folded his arms, shifting into an aggressive stance. The two men appraised each other in a silence that turned so cold it could only herald a killing frost. Nothing could survive a chill this deadly except suspicion. Love would wither. It was the sort of hoarfrost that would strip everything from the vine, leaving only thorns that pierced trust and destroyed all but the strongest instincts.

"Who are you?" he demanded, straightening another inch to stare down the uninvited man.

"Nathan Bellisant," the younger gentleman answered, his voice uneven. "I should not have disturbed you at this hour. I—I'm a friend—of your—"

"Wife. My wife."

"Yes."

"We've been married for years."

Sebastien struggled to place his name. Bellisant? He was reedy, with fair, bedraggled hair, a thin face, the sensitive eyes and delicate hands of an artist or musician.

There was nothing intimidating about him on the

surface. Sebastien could knock him down with a flick of his wrist, which didn't make him any more inclined to invite him in for a cozy tête-à-tête.

In fact, it brought out an anger he hadn't known he could feel.

Arrogant upstart. Usurper. How dare you knock at my wife's door and—how often have you done so in the past?

Bellisant also appeared at a loss for words, a coy inconsistency in a man who had been banging to be let in a minute ago.

Sebastien wondered if he was simply embarrassed at finding himself face to face with Eleanor's long-absent husband. Or if he had been unaware that a husband existed. His expression suggested he might well be staring at a ghost.

I'm not dead. But he was bolted to the ground by all-too human instincts, possessiveness, and a fury, a shock that ran deep.

How stupid could he be? He should have realized that someone would have tried to take his place.

But that didn't mean he'd concede to a rival so early in his return. He wouldn't concede at all.

The rival seemed anxious to suddenly explain himself. "I assume you're Lord Boscastle. I'm—it's an honor to finally meet you. I wish I had made a better first impression."

Bellisant's unwieldly charm only worsened Sebastien's mood. One could not afford to fall under a competitor's spell, although it never hurt to analyze the enemy's appeal.

"You have the advantage of me, sir." Sebastien could turn the tables and play the same innocuous role. "You have been invited here for some purpose that has slipped my memory?"

Bellisant vigorously shook his head. "The fault is entirely mine. Creature of night impulse that I am, I happened to be driving home when I noticed the light in your drawing room. I have a book I borrowed from Lady Boscastle. I've been meaning to return it for some time."

Lady Boscastle. Sebastian would wager all his worth that Bellisant would not have used her title had she, and not her husband, opened the door.

He stared out into the street at a parked, single-horse-drawn phaeton. Not a grand vehicle.

But then neither was Bellisant dressed in particularly fashionable attire. His fox-trimmed cape and brown riding boots had seen better days, which meant he did not feel the need to impress on his appearance alone.

"You could have left it on the doorstep," he said bluntly.

"I should have thought of that."

Sebastien grunted.

Eleanor had always been more impressed by skill and character than by social standing. If Sebastian had not answered the door, would a servant have recognized Bellisant and discreetly admitted him into the house?

Why wasn't the bloody dog barking now? Sebastien's dog. Didn't it recognize a danger to his master at the door? His own instincts surely did.

"I shall give her the book," he said, one hand extended, the other already closing the door.

"Let me get it first." Bellisant ran back to the phaeton before Sebastien could accuse him of using the book as an excuse.

Obviously that's what it was. He scowled when Bellisant returned with the book moments later, his smile remorseful. He seemed to be an easy man to like, Sebastien thought, unless he happened to like your wife.

"Thank you, Lord Boscastle." Bellisant eased down the steps on his worn heels. "I do apologize again for intruding."

Intruding.

Sebastien realized in annoyance that his dog was trying to push around him to sniff at Bellisant's elegant hands. A man could not call another an intruder when it seemed he might have been invited to enter.

Perhaps *he* was the intruder tonight. He thought back to what he and Eleanor had done and wondered if he'd been so desperate for her that he'd taken the passion she'd meant to give another man.

"Little shit," he shouted as Bellisant jumped up onto his phaeton. Sebastien watched him drive away, knowing this was not the first time he had come to the house, wishing that he'd made certain it was Bellisant's last visit instead of benignly taking a book at the door.

Did his wife see something in this offhandedly attractive person? He tried to picture the two of them reading books together, sitting in the upstairs drawing room on a rainy night—how did Bellisant know the candlelight came from a private, second-floor retreat? How intimately did he know this house . . . Sebastien's wife?

He stopped at the bottom of the staircase, looking down. His dog wasn't growling at him or making any attempt whatsoever to prevent him from going back upstairs.

He stretched out his hand. "Have we come to an understanding?"

The dog licked his wrist, then proceeded to climb the stairs, nails clicking on the wood. Not a rejection, but not exactly acceptance, either. It was more an expression of sympathy.

Well, nothing was the way he'd left it.

Now that he'd proven himself to the Crown, he had to impress his wife.

He glanced up.

And his dog.

She listened to the subtle sounds of the night. Hoofbeats slowed in the street. Teg began to bark. She smiled reluctantly. Sebastien must have answered the door. It was probably Will coming back, wanting a brandy and praise for his pyrotechnic feat at the masquerade. He'd gotten in the habit of stopping by at the oddest hours.

A sudden hush came over the house. She wondered if Sebastien had gone out for the night. He'd left the wardrobe doors open, a sure invitation for moths if ever there was one.

She slipped out of bed. He hadn't closed the bottom drawer—that's why the cupboard wouldn't shut properly. And he'd been—oh, he *had* seen the christening gown.

She hadn't let herself look in this drawer for years. After her miscarriage, she had not been able to give the gown away, although she wouldn't use it even if she had another baby. It belonged to the child she would never have. She closed the drawer carefully, wondering if Sebastien had understood what he'd found.

An hour or two later she heard him moving about the room again, the splash of water from the washstand in the dressing closet. It was early morning. Was he only now coming to bed? Should she pretend to be asleep?

She could not deny how much she had missed the amorous delights that marriage allowed. In fact, she was fairly burning in anticipation of their next bout together. Judging by their recent encounter, he intended to make up for lost time. She kept her eyes closed, counting to one hundred.

The bedroom door opened and quietly closed. She waited, breathing unevenly until too many moments of silence went by. She sat up, searching the room for her husband's virile form.

"Sebastien?" she whispered, her gaze narrowing in vexation. "What are you doing?"

No answer, and she knew why.

The rogue was gone again. Desire and disappointment clashed inside her.

She flung back the covers and felt something hard against her hip. She looked down in the half-light at a book. Had he planned to read in bed while she was asleep?

Curious as to what literary work would engross him, she unwedged the slender volume from her backside, frowning in recognition. It was the book on the death of Apollo that she had lent to her friend Sir Nathan Bellisant. A folded scrap of vellum had been placed on the first page.

I hate the day because it lendeth light.
To see all things, and not my love to see.

It took her a moment to recognize the quote from Spenser, a writer whom she and Nathan both admired, copied in Nathan's flamboyant script. Nathan was a painter, an artist who lived in a world of his own fancy.

Gestures such as this were commonplace among his circle of acquaintances. It wasn't the first note of this nature that he had given her. She would have thought nothing of it had it not been passed to her from her husband.

Who clearly had read more into it than Eleanor herself would ever have acknowledged.

Chapter Eleven

❧ ❧

Sebastien had walked to the St. George Street residence of Mrs. Isabella Sampson and recovered the incriminating letter from her escritoire before the chambermaid stirred the first coals. He returned home as the sun rose.

The mission took the dangerous edge off his temper. The knowledge that he had pulled off another Masquer coup, a minor victory certain to vex his wife, gave him an admittedly petty sense of satisfaction.

He was home. They'd slept together. But nothing was the same. She had made love to him, yes, but she hadn't said that she still loved him.

He thought of her winsome smile, of her fire-dark hair that dropped like a curtain over her voluptuous curves.

He thought of the welcome she'd given him, of all the times he'd blithely disappeared from her life, and how he had never really noticed that on each return, she'd become less of a vulnerable wife and more of a force to be dealt with—on terms he had not expected.

Suspicions of infidelity. Letters from a would-be mistress who'd hoped to ally herself to a great man like Wellington. How the devil had he fallen into this female imbroglio? It was beyond male dignity. He was an officer, not a lady-in-intrigue.

And there was no question in his mind how it had happened.

He was so deeply in love with Eleanor that he would stand in the wings of her Drury Lane drama, awaiting his opportunity to play her hero again. Stealing gossipy letters from a sleeping woman was a far cry from jumping off a hill into a cart with a grenade in his teeth. He'd confronted true villains in the dirty missions he'd carried off, tracking criminals without conscience. The most ominous character the Masquer could expect to encounter was a frightened butler.

Or a sneaky spouse.

Take this precise moment, for example.

He was creeping back to his house through the back gate when he spotted Eleanor's cloaked figure in the shimmering mist. He considered hiding to observe her, but then she noticed him and came to a halt.

Who was catching whom?

He waved at her.

She folded her arms. Soft wisps of hair curled around her oval face. "There you are," she muttered.

He strolled toward her, remembering how much she had loved this garden when she had first seen it. He hadn't paid much attention to household matters, but she had taken pleasure in growing roses and medicinal herbs.

Now it was autumn.

The branches of the horse chestnut tree on which she had hoped to hang a swing for their children had gone bare. In fact, everything in the garden looked half-dead, forsaken. Hell, was he still paying the gardeners for this unmaintained mess?

"So," he said quietly. "Has the early rat caught the cat on her way out, or on her way in?"

She stared meaningfully at the black mask that dangled from his fingers. Her eyes locked with his. She gave a small smile of acknowledgment. She knew exactly where he had been. It was her whereabouts during his absence, the details of her life without him, that presented the mystery.

"I should ask you the same question," she said, lifting her cloak in one hand. "However, you needn't bother with an answer. It's my own fault for not realizing what you were up to."

"I mentioned it to you as I recall, darling. There's no need to trouble yourself with this assignment again."

"Yes, but I was distracted, darling. I won't be again. And—I've developed a liking for this assignment."

He gave a low whistle. "Things are going to be

different now that I'm back. You'll have many distractions."

She shook her head. "I shall have to be on constant guard against you."

He thought of the man who'd called at the house last night and his sickening love note. Sebastien would be on guard now, too.

She could have clobbered her devious husband. She had planned to present the treasures of her hunt to the Duchess of Wellington while Sebastien held out empty hands. The duchess was no more pleased with *her* husband's interference than was Eleanor with hers.

Upon finding the book in her bed, she had dressed and stolen downstairs into the kitchen for a tart green pippin and a wedge of cheese to sustain her. She'd intended to find Isabella Sampson's letter and go straight to the duchess's house on Harley Street.

"Is that apple for me?" Sebastien asked, holding out his hand. "What a thoughtful wife. I've worked up quite an appetite."

She dropped the apple into his gloved palm. "I assume you have the letter?"

He inclined his head, his blue-gray eyes gleaming. She had made a mistake. This was no rat. It was a wolf she had in her garden, hungry and cunning. She swallowed as his even white teeth crunched into the apple. She'd not let him outwit her again.

"We really should go inside." She motioned to the

house. "We can discuss this over a proper breakfast. You are rather lean."

"Breakfast? How civilized of us. By the way, you had a caller late last night."

"Yes." She half-turned to find him staring at her with an intensity that she felt to the bone. "I gather it was Sir Nathan Bellisant."

"Isn't that a charming name?"

"Were you rude to him?"

"Not at all." His vulpine smile stirred a shiver across her skin. "Although I didn't invite him in for tea, if that's what you meant."

"Sebastien—"

"And I didn't pummel him into a hundred pretty little pieces and throw his remains under a passing carriage."

She paled. "That sounds utterly barbaric," she said in a horrified voice.

"Doesn't it?"

"And you sound rather pleased that it does. He's under the duchess's protection, I'll have you know."

"It's a damn good thing. I thought I was quite polite, under the circumstances."

He offered her his arm. Numbly she took it and allowed him to lead her toward the house. "We'll sit down at the table and converse like a proper married couple," he said firmly.

"There's nothing proper about either of us anymore," she said under her breath.

His eyes twinkled down at her. "But we're still married. A couple."

"In a contest against each other," she added as he slipped his mask inside his coat.

He turned, capturing her hand in his. "We can call the contest off. I'll be happy to fulfill your obligation to her grace." He laced her fingers in his. "And you will be free to return to your wifely duties."

"I gave my word."

"To me first," he replied, his voice devilish.

Her lips curved in a cynical smile. "I thought you were hungry."

He drew her back into the heat of his body. His stubbled jaw brushed her cheek. "Lean and hungry," he said in a low voice. "But not for breakfast."

They met at the table two hours later, refreshed, Eleanor in a sky-blue merino dress, Sebastien in a white muslin shirt and tailored black broadcloth trousers, as if they were any other lord and lady in London who did not conduct secret lives.

Or who kept secrets from each other.

If Sebastien had wondered in bad conscience how many mornings Eleanor had eaten alone, missing his presence, he now had cause to question whether he had been missed at all.

Or whether his wife *had* been alone.

"Mary instructed Cook to make a chestnut pudding for you," she said without the slightest hint of wedded discord between them.

"Chestnut pudding?" He leaned back with a puzzled look.

"Coffee?" she asked, her hand resting on the

elegant silver pot. "Or have you taken to something stronger?"

"Coffee is fine," he said wryly. "And I don't care for chestnut pudding."

Or had he in the past? So many trivial associations still eluded him. It went beyond frustration to reach into one's mind for a memory and encounter a void.

"I thought pudding might appease that great appetite of yours." She poured steaming coffee into his cup. "Don't forget that we are going to the opera this evening."

He gave her a narrow look. How was he expected to remember an event as inconsequential as the opera when he was wondering whether anyone had shared his wife's bed?

"I don't care for the opera. I prefer to stay home."

There. He had taken another stand. They weren't attending the opera. Obviously if he'd been home to direct these little matters, she would not have wandered astray.

She regarded him with a provocative smile that made him think he had knotted his neckcloth too tightly, until he realized he had forgotten to put one on.

"I understand," she said, her voice pleasingly low. "But didn't we agree that we should appear together in public whenever possible to throw off anyone who might have caught the Masquer's scent?"

He shook his head. He refrained from expressing the unseemly thought that someone had already caught her scent, and that her posing as the Masquer had nothing to do with it at all. Or perhaps it did. Perhaps he wasn't in competition with anyone except this Mayfair scoundrel who, being his wife, presented an interesting opposition.

"Let us discuss the caller you had last night," he said bluntly. "I assume you found the book?"

She made a face, crumbling her biscuit onto her plate. "I did," she said with a sigh. "How considerate of you to place it where it couldn't be missed."

"I thought it might have some personal significance."

She looked up at him candidly. "It could have waited until later in the day."

"I thought the same thing about your"—he gestured with his fork—"whatever he is."

"A painter." She stared disapprovingly at the fork. He put it down. She was avoiding his gaze. This wasn't a good sign.

"Of portraits," she continued, suddenly glancing up at the wall. "The duchess has commissioned him to paint her sons as a Christmas surprise for the duke. And you can't let him know. . . ." She faltered. "It's meant to be a surprise."

"So you said." But it didn't explain why the brazen bugger had been knocking at *her* door. "Does he only paint these secret masterpieces in the middle of the night?"

Her mouth formed a faint moue. "I don't think so. Have you taken up an interest in art? Would you like to go to the museum next—"

"He writes you love notes," he said baldly.

She sighed again.

"Well?" he said. "I might not even have known if the corkbrain hadn't used me as a go-between."

She smiled vaguely. "Spenser wrote that passage, although Nathan has had a book of verse or two published."

"Did it have a special significance?"

"Not to me."

He frowned at her. "Is he in the habit of coming to the house so late at night?"

She shook her head, studying the arrangement of crumbs on her plate. "No. Well, he's dropped by on the odd occasion."

Now he was staring at the crumbs, too. "Does anyone else avail themselves of this open invitation?"

"I didn't invite him here last night," she answered calmly, glancing up without warning. "Nathan is one of those unfettered spirits who flies about as inspiration stirs him."

He made a face. "Nathan is invited to find his inspiration elsewhere. Or to fly off a steep cliff."

"I hope you don't tell him that if he calls again."

"I've a feeling he won't return."

"Well, we'll all be in trouble if he's too upset to finish painting the duke's sons."

"I assure you, the sentiments of some shabby young artist are the least of my concerns." He raised his voice. He watched her eyes widen as he emphasized his point. "And I believe I speak for the duke when I say that."

She was staring at his hand now. At the fork that he'd picked up again and stabbed emphatically into the air. Irritated, he laid it down.

A footman entered the room to clear the plates from the table, hazarding a cautious look at his master.

"My lord?"

"Yes, yes. I'm finished."

Yet he was still hungry.

And a hundred civilized breakfasts would not satisfy him until he regained the position of authority that he had unwillingly relinquished.

Chapter Twelve

❧ ⚬ ❧

She sat by herself at the fire for another hour, nursing a drop of sherry. She knew what he had wished to know. The same uncertainty haunted her thoughts.

Had she been faithful to him while he was gone? Was she to believe that during their separation he had not slept with another woman? A man of his deeply passionate nature? Was she to believe that no barmaid or ambassador's daughter had even once shared his bed?

And now he demanded to know if she had slept with another man. She had not. She had only become one. Had she ever been tempted, come close enough so that Sebastien would have cause to accuse her?

No. Although to this day Nathan Bellisant believed she would change her mind, and yes, she had enjoyed his attention at times.

An artist who followed his own code of morals, Nathan did not particularly care if Eleanor was married. He was a libertine without anchor, and while he was an amusing friend, she regretted agreeing to sit for the portrait of her he had painted.

When she'd refused to be his *belle amie,* he'd vowed he would wait for her to relent. She'd laughed and warned him he would wait forever.

The fact was that she had never been on fire for anyone but her husband, which might not be the same as loving him with the naïve hopes that he had extinguished on their wedding day.

But it was an element of her nature that had remained constant.

She was a woman who took a promise seriously, and if Sebastien did not realize that, then he, and not Eleanor, had married a complete stranger.

Sebastien had worked himself into a mood over a situation that appeared to unsettle him more than it did his wife. Her very calmness served the opposite effect upon his state of mind.

In truth, unmasking political malcontents had seemed easier than deciphering the person Eleanor had become under the duchess's sly guidance. The issue of her "friend" had not been resolved to his satisfaction.

He refused to drop the subject even as they dressed for the opera in their separate closets.

"The opera," he grumbled. "I *never* liked the opera. Didn't I say that I wouldn't go?"

"Are you talking to yourself?" she asked absently, sifting through her jewels.

He looked at his reflection in the cheval glass. "As a matter of fact, I am."

"Do you do this often?"

"Probably. Damnit, I only said that I dislike the opera."

She gave a deep sigh. "Then are we going or not?"

Suddenly he wondered what it was about the opera that she found so compelling. "We're going."

In fact, he thought it a good idea that henceforth he escort Eleanor on all her activities. He looked up from the glass at the bare oaken walls.

"Where is the portrait of you?" He stared in bemusement around their bedchamber.

"What did you say?" she asked from behind the door.

Every so often she would disappear into her closet in an interesting stage of dishabille, only to reemerge to pick up the dangling thread of their discussion. He suspected she was avoiding an honest confrontation. Well, he had no intention of being put off.

"The portrait that Bellflower did?"

She clasped an emerald pendant around her neck. For a moment he stared, his breathing suspended, certain *he* had not bought her that elegant necklace.

"That necklace—"

"What about it?" She touched the stone. "Is it too much? The green usually goes well with my hair, but this dress is so pale that—"

Before he could make a fool of himself with another accusation, he remembered that the pendant had belonged to her aunt.

He frowned to cover his embarrassment, as well as his relief. "It's fine. Pretty. I like it."

"Do you?" she asked with a skeptical lift of her brow. "Then why did you look so stricken when you saw it?"

"I—"

She lowered her hand in concern. "Dear Sebastien, are you all right?"

"I'm—" He took a breath, then another, wondering how she could be more beautiful than when he'd married her.

"We don't have to go," she said, looking uncertain, even a little afraid of him. "If you're not up to it, we will stay here."

He shook his head decisively. "We're going. I want to go. No, I don't."

She laughed, looking charmingly confused. "I'd like us to be together."

"So would I."

He felt a flare of heat assail him. She stood, temptation personified, in a lilac evening gown. Satin or silk. The hell if he cared. He was fascinated by the contrast of one sleeve fastened at her shoulder, the other listing to her elbow. Wife or wicked gentlewoman. He would take her either way.

"You're not even ready," he said, unable to keep the desire from his voice.

Her voice dropped even lower. His hopes rose. "Please, Sebastien. We'll arrive at the theater very late."

His eyes swept over her. "We'll arrive there very happy."

She shook her head in warning. But her eyes

glittered invitingly, and she stood unmoving when she could have retreated back into the closet.

"Are we meeting anyone there?" he asked, the air between them suddenly thick.

"No." Her voice was soft. Her gaze held his. Which of them wielded the strongest weapon?

He managed to shrug. "Well, if we're not meeting anyone, a few minutes won't matter."

"We can't arrive in the middle—"

"Why not? Lie with me again."

"I'm half-dressed," she protested.

"Half-undressed." He stared at her, smiling in anticipation. "It's a question of how one looks at it."

"One is looking at a rogue."

"A rogue who cannot resist his wife. Is that so wrong?"

"It takes getting used to. You've resisted me for a long time."

"What an idiot," he muttered.

"Excuse me?"

"I said I've been an idiot."

He took a decisive step, then another, bringing their conversation to a halt. She bowed her head, submissive or amused, perhaps both. But he recognized desire when he saw it. Steadily he slid his hands up her sides to her shoulders, untying the delicate net sleeve she had secured. Her eyes searched his, acknowledging his need. The unclasped pendant slithered down her throat into the creamy mounds of her cleavage.

She gasped.

"Let me get that," he said quickly.

"I can do it!"

"Allow me. I've missed these small moments."

"You've missed the large ones, too," she murmured.

"I realize that." His hooded gaze caressed her. "I won't again."

She parted her lips, but said nothing, an omission which Sebastien chose to believe signaled her consent. Staring at her in absorption, he stroked his fingers down her elegant throat and dipped into the cleft between her breasts. She exhaled quietly. She might well have moaned. He wasn't sure. He could not think properly for the quickening of blood, of his heartbeat, that pounded through his body.

"There it is," he murmured, wrapping the gold links around his finger. "I believe if this chain lingered here much longer, your warmth would melt even the metal."

"You are not fair," she said softly.

He bent his head, rubbing his face in the crook of her neck. "How so?" he whispered, smiling to himself.

"You're taking advantage."

He kissed the pulse that throbbed faintly in her throat. "Of—"

"—my neglected sinful nature."

He drew back, the blood in his veins surging. "Sinful is the state into which we are allegedly born. But neglected—we can't allow that."

Did that mean she had slept alone all this time?

He clasped the pendant in his palm and took her by the wrist.

"We'll have to remedy this problem immediately."

"How accommodating of you," she murmured, a shiver going through her.

"I have a lot to make up for you."

"I won't disagree."

His black gaze devoured her. "You were very agreeable last night."

She raised her other hand to her hair, fretting a little. "It took forever to arrange this just so."

"No one will notice."

"I have friends attending who certainly will. Some of them don't believe my husband even exists."

He pretended to understand, nodding in sympathy as she complained about the ruinous wrinkles he would put in her gown, about how long it would take to appear presentable again. Her hair lay in a braided knot upon her nape. Hypocrite that he was, he thought only of disarraying it, of how sensuous that heavy silk had felt against his groin.

Suddenly he needed air. No, no. He needed her, trusting again and uninhibited.

He needed not only to reassert his presence in her life, but to reassure her he would honor his vows.

He had always loved her.

He hadn't always acted as though he did.

And as a man he knew that sexual capitulation didn't necessarily mean commitment.

What a challenge this was.

"We are not going to the opera," he said firmly. He pulled her down, between his legs, onto the bed.

She rolled onto one side, barely within his reach. Her elbow pressed into his lower back, an old injury that still ached.

"Yes, we are. I want to," she added with a winsome smile clearly intended to persuade him. Which only strengthened his plans to amend the evening's entertainment.

"I can't go to the opera in this condition."

She glanced down at the bulge in his trousers. "My goodness, Sebastien. Absence has certainly made your male parts grow stronger."

He laughed.

"I don't want to be a stranger anymore. Just your husband again."

"Perhaps I want to go tonight to show you off," she whispered.

"And I want to stay home to keep you to myself." He pulled her back against him, lowering his head, and said, seconds before he kissed her, "I want *you*."

And what a Boscastle wanted, he always got. Eleanor had overheard a governess at a dance sharing that caution to another lady many years ago in London. The lady had not appeared to listen. Nor, unfortunately, had Eleanor.

She was a Boscastle now herself, if only in name. An equal in passion, she would have dearly loved to rip off his muslin drawers and bend him to her will. He deserved it. And so did she. She could draw out her terms a little later. For now she demanded pleasure and lost herself with unabashed enthusiasm in his delicious kisses.

"Eleanor," he said, and she heard the faint shearing of fabric through her dazed thoughts.

"My gown!" she cried as his warm hands forged upward beneath her silk overskirt.

"It's not your gown," he said soothingly. "It was my smalls."

His smalls. She felt laughter form deep inside her, like the bubbles of a hidden brook. "Oh, Sebastien. You are—"

"What am I?" he asked, grinning.

He was fire and darkness. Her soul's desire. "You're my estranged husband."

His breath chased a shiver down her neck. "Trust me?"

"Not really."

"Do you want me?"

"Unfortunately, yes."

He groaned and finished undressing her with one hand, himself with the other. When they landed on the floor he wasn't sure how it had happened, but as long as she seemed willing to continue, he did not care.

More than willing. She was eager. Ardent. His wife and yet someone else. What had she called him—her *estranged* husband? He didn't like that one bit.

He reached up to the bed for a pillow to thrust beneath her bottom. He leaned to suckle the tips of her breasts. She brought her hand down firmly on his shoulder and gave him a good push onto his back. He fell back, laughing. Her hair broke from its knot and tumbled against his belly. He was breathing so hard he thought he would black out.

"Isn't this better than the opera?" he whispered with a taunting smile. He lifted her by the waist and brought her down on his thick cock. The slick walls of her sheathe stretched to take him.

She sobbed, turning her head, bouncing gently on his curved shaft.

"My God," he groaned. He caught her by her buttocks, gripping her soft flesh. "That's good. Very nice. Do you want it harder?"

"Do you think it's possible?" she asked feverishly.

"I can't think at all."

"Then harder."

"Like this—"

He flexed, impaling her. Her back arched. She gave a low uninhibited moan. He groaned, lifting himself higher. She pushed down. He reared up, his eyes half-closed, his pulses quickening. Her knees dug into his hips. He increased the intensity of his strokes. She whimpered, her movements unbridled, her body meeting his thrust for thrust. Her cleft was soaking his groin. He would carry her delightful fragrance on his skin all night.

It took several minutes for both of them to recover. He felt like worshipping at her feet. Instead, he lay motionless on the floor, his mind drifting until she shook his arm. He jolted back into awareness.

"Don't fall asleep," she said.

"Asleep? I've never been more awake in my life."
He opened his eyes, studying her beautiful, unclad
body in the candlelight. "And aware. Now tell me
the truth, madam."

"Not again!"

"You never answered properly in the first place."

"Because there is nothing to say."

"Then placate me. Put my mind at ease."

She started to lean away. He sat up, his arm sliding
around her waist. "I want to know," he said fiercely.
"I *have* to know. What is this Bellisant to you?"

She settled back against his arm. His body heated
involuntarily and sought her closeness. He stroked
his knuckles across her dusky nipples. "He is champagne," she said after a silence that seemed to last
forever.

"Champagne?" he said with an insulting laugh.
"Isn't that lovely?"

She turned her head and scattered kisses across
his bare chest. "Champagne," she whispered.
"Pleasant enough at first, but its lightness is deceptive, an acquired taste."

"Spare me," he said, his anger rising as he sifted
his hands through her heavy hair.

"You," she went on, her voice completely even,
"are water."

"Water?" he said in disgust. "So I am
ordinary—"

"—essential," she corrected him. "One can survive without champagne. But not without water."

She rose before he could stop her. "Water," he

said, his gaze cynical as he followed her movements across the room.

She looked back over her shoulder with a wistful smile that stole his breath. He gazed down at her arse before staring back up at her face. "Oh, all right. Water mixed with raw Scottish whiskey. That's a little better, but not quite what I wanted to hear."

She shook her head. "Why do I have a feeling that you're going to get what you want?"

He smiled before rousing himself from the floor. "Why do I have the feeling the day will come when you can't tell your wants from mine?"

"The day when the gates of hell are frozen shut?" she asked laughingly before disappearing into the closet again.

"Or when the flames of passion set them ablaze?" he retorted with a grin right before the door slammed.

Chapter Thirteen

❧ ❧

Was her husband an accomplished schemer or sincere in his promise to make amends? She sat beside him in their opera box, contemplating his character. It was a challenge to feign absorption in the concert when his presence engrossed her every thought. She felt rather plain in his presence, dressed in her sweet lilac taffeta dress.

He wore black.

Undeniably he was the finest-looking lord in London, if an utter enigma to Eleanor.

No sooner had they set foot from the carriage than several old acquaintances rushed forth to welcome him into the shallows of the beau monde. One gentleman rather rudely inquired whether his return meant that offspring could be expected. Eleanor lifted her nose and pretended she had not heard the question.

The subject of heirs seemed to be in the air.

She had headed toward the stairs, although not quickly enough to escape hearing Sebastien reply, "Soon. It is my primary objective. Eleanor, wait for me, darling. Don't wander off in the dark alone."

"Your primary objective?" she whispered on the stairs when he caught up with her. "You might have shown restraint instead of announcing your breeding intentions to a virtual stranger."

He shrugged, his amused eyes searching her face. "What else could I say?"

"You should have just smiled in a lordly manner, and said nothing."

And so he said nothing, in what he judged to be a lordly manner, until the opening aria ended. Then he slid his hand up her back, to her nape, a fleeting caress that left her trembling inside.

"You were right," he said in an undertone. "I should have discussed my intentions with you first."

"You really don't like the opera, do you?"

He smiled, tugging a little curl at her nape. "I'd rather play than watch."

She flashed him a look. He grinned back at her, tracing his fingers down her throat to where her pendant lay.

Her lips parted. She moistened the corners of her mouth with her pink tongue. He leaned forward, apparently keen to prove what a player he was, when someone called her name from another box.

They both ignored it.

"I don't think the gentleman in the lobby meant to be vulgar," he said reflectively. "Nor did I. I grew up in a large, boisterous family. It isn't wrong to hope we will start one of our own. Didn't we discuss this? We've been married for years."

She snapped open her rose-scented fan, her face suddenly hot, and stared at the stage. "I'm glad you've noticed."

"I've noticed nothing but you since I came home."

She lowered her fan to her lap.

Another voice, young and male, shouted from an opposite box.

Sebastien came to his feet, scowling in the sap-skull's direction. "This is very distracting. What kind of friends have you made while I was gone?"

"Impetuous ones, obviously. Sit down, Sebastien. They'll stop if you act as if you can't hear them."

He settled back into his seat. "If this persists, I shall have him, them, thrown out of the theater."

"No, you won't." She eyed his strong figure in se-cret delight. "We must appear to be a well-behaved man and wife. It doesn't help our other cause to at-tract notice."

"Our cause? Well, all right."

Her words appeared to calm him. After a moment he laid his hand upon hers, a gesture of warm pos-session that she wished were not so pleasant. Clearly he had no idea that she was still grieving the child she'd lost. Did he even remember? She thought of how alone she had felt, of how angry that he hadn't been there to comfort her, and tried unsuccessfully to pull her hand from his. He wouldn't let go.

Her fan slid from her lap to the floor. They

reached for it at the same moment, his clean-shaven cheek touching hers. The accidental intimacy, the scent of his mossy eau de cologne, disarmed her.

But not nearly as much as when he asked, softly, "Don't you want a child, Elle? I thought you did once."

"May I have my fan?" she asked instead of answering.

"I saw the christening gown in the drawer."

"Oh," she whispered, biting the inside of her cheek. "Then you do remember?"

He nodded. When he handed her the fan, she gave him a tremulous smile that went straight through his heart like an iron shard. The pain turned him inside out. But whether it would prove to be a necessary pain of healing or an irreparable break, he could not predict. Perhaps he should not have mentioned the baby. Until he'd seen that gown, he had not truly understood . . .

. . . how small a baby was.

He fidgeted. She gave him another look. Surreptitiously he lifted his opera glasses and scanned the other boxes for signs of her smitten admirers. At last he saw several pair of gloved hands waving in his direction.

He frowned, lowering the glasses, then raised them again.

"For goodness' sake, what are you doing?" she whispered, trying to peer over his arm.

"There are three elderly women waving at us."

"Well, wave back."

He handed her the glasses. "I don't know them—do I?"

"No, but I do. They're agents for the duchess," she confided, studying the enthusiastic trio who formed part of an elite spying network, comprised mostly of gentlewomen and street girls, that the duchess operated in London. On any given day one of them might be employed to spy on an unfaithful husband and report back to his wife. Another might sneak into a milliner's shop and scrutinize the hats in progress so that the duchess would always appear in an original creation. Sometimes her grace wanted to know the inside odds on a racehorse. Her underground ladies took pride in their assignments. As did she.

"They must be in their seventies," he said in disbelief. "And you say that they're—"

"Lady Savile is ninety-three," she murmured. "And still going strong."

"Agents?" he said, blinking. "You don't expect me to believe that an association of old ladies—"

"I'm hardly ancient."

"—are agents?"

She glanced at Sebastien, restraining a smile at his astonishment. How naughty of her to enjoy unsettling his manly assumptions. "Underestimate us at your own peril."

"I'm learning that." His voice was resigned, but droll. "Do they know that you're the Masquer?"

"They will if you announce it to the whole theater.

Dear heavens, I thought I was bad enough. Can't you sit still?"

"I can if there's nothing better to do." He looked perplexed. "I sat for hours in cellars, in caves, in kegs, in coffins even. I didn't move a muscle."

"Men do have all the adventures," she said with a sigh of envy.

"You haven't done so badly yourself."

A compliment. Why did his approval move her so deeply?

"Thank you."

She stared at him.

He stared at her.

Then she stretched upward and kissed his cheek.

He blinked again, his nostrils tightening. "That was nice. I'd like more, please."

"Wait until we get home," she whispered against his chin.

"Why?" His heart was thundering. He placed his arm around her shoulders and drew her toward him. "I asked politely."

"Sebastien," she said, more breathless than reproachful.

"Isn't this a private box?" He pressed hard, hot kisses down her neck. His finger circled the pendant, slipped inside her gown to twirl the tips of her breasts. "And you're my wife."

She gasped, then slowly lifted her hands to his chest. "People can see."

He glanced up. From the corner of his eye, he

spotted a footman hastening from his post to close the curtains on this *acte d'amour*. For this favor Sebastien would tip him excessively at the end of the performance—and make arrangements to attend the opera with Eleanor again soon.

"I can't see anything," he murmured. "Except you."

She smiled, arching her neck as he kissed a particularly sensitive spot behind her ear. "You'd see the stage if you used the opera glasses properly," she whispered rather weakly.

"No," he said, his voice stubborn. "I'd still only see you."

And there wasn't any doubt in his mind that his powers of persuasion had taken effect and that presently she, seeing reason, would put aside her masquerade and concentrate on him.

She awoke two hours before daybreak and dressed in the dark. When she'd finished, she crept back to the bed to make certain Sebastien hadn't roused. She studied his broad forehead, the strong cheekbones and spell-caster blue Boscastle eyes that, if opened, would shatter her concentration for several hours. Even though he was interfering in her duty, not to mention his scandalous behavior at the opera last night, she had to admit she liked awakening beside the handsome devil.

And a good thing she had awakened first. She spied his boots and a small case of housebreaking utensils by the door. Subtle, wasn't he? Or did he assume that all his delicious lovemaking had left her witless? Or . . . was it possible that *she* had exhausted him?

She sat down at her desk and scribbled a message to remind him that she would be breakfasting with the duchess. If he thought for a moment that he had diverted her from her duty, he had a surprise coming. He was still sleeping as she propped the note on her pillow and sneaked outside.

Even when she stopped to stare up at their window from the street, she did not see a figure behind the curtains.

What a relief. She still had a wit or two left that he hadn't stolen.

She hadn't thought it would be that easy to escape. He might not have stopped her, but it had been damned hard to leave his bed.

Shadows shifted in the street, some endearingly pathetic, some to be avoided. Scavengers scoured the gutters for treasures to sell at market. Bone-pickers poked sticks into mounds of pungent horse ordure, their bags already bulging. An errand boy rushed past her, breathless, his spectacles gleaming in the mist. She almost collided with an apprentice who was chasing a dog who'd stolen his master's cane.

London. Dirty. Teeming. Lovely city.

She wiggled her fingers inside her black kidskin gloves. Will had parked in his customary place on the corner, her disguise hidden within the carriage. The Masquer would not be his dashing self this morning, but a mere servant girl instead, whom no one would look at twice. She hurried forward without looking back at her house again.

Not that she wasn't tempted.

In fact, it was the first time since beginning her masquerade that the life of Lady Boscastle seemed more enticing than that of her other identity.

Chapter Fourteen

꧁ ꧂

Tess Elliot had fallen upon hard times to judge by her current dwellings. Her lodging house occupied an unfashionable corner off Covent Garden near a pawnbroker's establishment.

The only person Sebastien spotted in the vicinity was a buxom laundress in a frilly cap who, upon sighting him, froze and then began haphazardly yanking half-damp sheets and shifts from a communal clothesline that stretched between the houses. That she seemed unnerved by his appearance did not offend him in the least.

What sensible woman would wish to attract the attention of a big man skulking about the back alleys of London at this hour? At any hour, if the truth be told. He only wished his own wife would observe such cautions.

He watched the rotund laundress scurry off with her wicker basket. Sorrowful. Did every woman in London have to make him think of Eleanor?

Miss Elliot's bedchamber overlooked a stygian back alley that bore the scent of chamber pot slops and stagnant rain. Sebastien jimmied the servants' entry door and proceeded inside while his manservant Mick acted as crow in the alleyway.

From the partially opened door of a bedroom emerged a duet of snores. He glanced inside.

Tess sprawled, bare arse rising, across her corpulent partner, who was also naked, but for a grimy cloak fastened about his flabby neck. A flintlock musket stood propped against the bedpost.

His mouth flattened in distaste. Hardly a challenge here. He'd be halfway across Town before this pair could disentangle themselves to give chase, let alone possess the wits to find their clothes.

He was glad Eleanor had not accompanied him. He disliked the notion of bringing her to a low neighborhood even if she had ventured to such dives with Will serving as her dubious protector.

She believed herself invulnerable, a lady of adventure. He could teach her a trick or two about the art of furtive ingress and infiltration.

He moved silently around the bed to a dressing table thumbnail-thick with dust. As he lit his pocket taper, he thought of his wife, of her soft red mouth swallowing him, inch by inch, their bodies bathed afterward in the fragrance of sex and intimate secrets. His head swam with a black desire.

A blob of wax slid onto his glove.

Damn.

She distracted him even when they were apart.

If he didn't concentrate, he'd set this heap on fire, himself included.

He frowned, searching the wardrobe and dressing case of Mistress Elliot. Sad, really, that a beauty had come to this. Baubles—a comb, a broken watch, some cheap paste jewelry, two letters from a cousin in Surrey demanding payment on a loan, a golden sovereign.

Nothing. Nothing of interest.

In his mind he could hear Eleanor laughing, teasing that she would beat him at his own game. He smiled and imagined how he would tease her back. She would probably still be with the duchess when he got home. He would try to be modest about besting her. She'd forgive him and admit to his superior skill once they were alone again.

The colossus on the bed behind him emitted a gurgling snort.

He knelt at the low chest of drawers. More trinkets. No signs of intrigue. Bloody waste of time. Humiliating.

Ah, a . . . chastity belt? Apparently never worn. Eleanor had been chaste on their wedding night. Was it all that long ago?

She wasn't innocent now, God help him. Why hadn't she taken up another pastime like writing poetry or painting—

No. Not painting.

Probably not reading poems, either.

The last drawer.

Concentrate.

His lower back ached, an unwelcome reminder of the past.

He found a folded paper buried under a fan of broken peacock feathers.

He unfolded it and scrutinized the message in the faint light.

Darling Rival,
I forgot to mention last night that I would lo-
cate the next letter. Do be careful of the dog on
your way out. He's even more unfriendly than
Teg.

A reluctant smile tightened his mouth. How had she gotten here first? Why? To remind him again not to underestimate her?

He'd never do that again.

A short blow on a whistle came from the alley.

Mick's warning.

He closed the drawer, straightened, and escaped the house with only seconds to spare before a mastiff bounded from the drawing room with a deep-throated growl.

She felt wickedly victorious as she reached her room, dropping the wicker basket of damp laundry at her feet. She'd find a way to return the stolen laundry later. For now she would have to hide it. She suspected that her lady's maid had witnessed her clandestine return to the house. Eleanor was certain she'd seen a shadow at the bottom of the stairs when she had been running up.

But then Mary had witnessed many peculiarities

in the course of her service, and had never uttered more than a sigh of censure.

She untied her frilly cap and withdrew the bulky breast padding from beneath her cloak. Sighing with the pleasure of another letter recovered, she leaned her head back against the door. Her heart had finally slowed enough that she could breathe.

How she would have loved to be in Miss Elliot's room when Sebastien discovered her hidden note. Had he laughed? Sworn to get even? Was he this moment tromping back home in defeat?

Not that she meant to gloat, but she had to admit that her changed husband had brought out a competitive energy she hadn't felt since she'd been a girl vying for her father's attention between patients. The odds were that the male would win, but if he didn't—

For a moment, anything seemed possible.

She could be Robin Hood stealing from the rich and not Maid Marian moping about praying he hadn't gotten caught.

A king who ordered beheadings and not Anne Boleyn.

She could be a man's wife *and* the Mayfair Masquer.

When she came back to herself, she realized how empty the room seemed. The cheval glass reflected an unremarkable woman with bedraggled hair and someone else's laundry.

A woman who slept alone.

She did not look adventurous at all.

"Sebastien?" she called out tentatively in the direction of the dressing closet, just in case he had beaten her back home.

At the answering silence she saw that the wardrobe door had been left open and that he'd hung his nightshirt neatly on a peg. She laughed, throwing herself across the bed.

He said he'd stay this time. For better or worse, it would seem, she was not a woman who slept alone anymore.

Chapter Fifteen

❧ ❧

Sebastien could not bring himself to go straight home after conceding her little victory. In fact, sitting in the carriage that Mick drove through the bustling London streets, he realized how brazenly Eleanor had tricked him.

The laundress, of course. He pictured that plump figure with her basket of sodden bedding and started to laugh. No wonder she'd been so anxious to get away from him. And why she'd reminded him of his wife.

Well, let her enjoy her moment of triumph, short-lived as he intended it to be.

He examined the peacock feather he held in his hand.

She had given him no choice but to retaliate, and with her own weapon, as it were.

It was only fair that the punishment fit the crime.

He doubted she would complain about his form of revenge.

From now on, however, he would deal with the

Mayfair Masquer man to man—and take advantage of the wily fellow in every way he could.

Yet for the second time that day, as he perhaps should have anticipated, it was his wife who delivered the surprise.

When he returned to his Belgrave Square house, he discovered her in the drawing room, another man holding her hand. He could have been knocked down with the Masquer's feather. How many secrets had she been keeping from him? Had he not been forceful enough in explaining that he desired a conventional English marriage?

Indeed, neither she nor her stoop-shouldered visitor, long, graying hair streaming over his bony shoulders, paid much attention to his arrival.

The pair of them sat on the sofa in clandestine absorption. He waited, dumbfounded, the feather he held seeming to wilt a little in commiseration.

The unattractive stranger had grasped her delicate hand in his gnarled fingers, as if he were—was he studying her palm? What utter nonsense was this now?

The curtains had been closed on this conspiracy. The woodsy odor of burning herbs arose from the grate.

"Pardon me," he said, tossing his coat, hat, and gloves onto an unoccupied chair. "Does my presence bother either of you?"

"I would appreciate it if you would not stand in the light," the odd man murmured.

"What light?" Sebastien asked, tempted to raise his arms like bat wings into the air.

Eleanor glanced up at him. Her eyes glinted in the false gloom, and her white shoulders shone as if inviting kisses. "I see you've made it home for an early supper. How nice. Did you get the message I left you this morning?"

He slipped the feather into his waistcoat pocket. He noticed a bottle of Scots whiskey on the sideboard. "I did. It was awfully good of you to warn me about the dog."

Her appraising glance slid over him. "I'm glad that you escaped none the worse for wear."

He'd make her glad, all right. Giddy. Quite out of her head.

He poured a splash of whiskey into a glass, then offered it to her.

She shook her head.

He took a sip. Undiluted. Not watered down at all. A man's drink, this.

"Is he your glovemaker?" he asked as the whiskey settled in his stomach.

"Four, madam," the presumptuous man said, rudely ignoring Sebastien. "Four, including the one lost. This concurs with your astrological chart."

"Sir Perceval is my fortune-teller." Eleanor peered down at her outstretched palm. "The duchess consults him on every important decision."

"Madam and her grace are too generous," Sir Perceval said with an ingratiating smile.

Sebastien fixed her with a disbelieving stare.

She stared back briefly, a sultry scold, then looked back down. He studied her lowered head, the wisps of hair upon her nape, that pearly skin.

Four what? he wondered. Four lovers? Letters? Four husbands?

Including the one lost.

He wanted to see what this humbug saw in her future.

The soothsayer mumbled some incantation. The flames in the fire danced.

Eleanor glanced up again, her mirthful eyes meeting his.

"What rot," Sebastien said under his breath. "How long does this go on?"

"Sir Perceval," she said with a gentle smile, "perhaps we should continue at another time?"

"As you wish, madam. One cannot ignore the influence of either devils or angels."

Sebastien waited to address her until after the wiry figure had collected his cape, then charts, and taken his leave. "You caught me unaware today," he began. "I admit it."

Eleanor remained on the sofa, barely restraining a grin. If she hadn't been so pleased with herself, she would have sensed he was up to something. Well, they would both live and learn.

"Then you aren't upset that I found the letter first?" she asked gleefully.

He unbuttoned his waistcoat. He always felt warm in her company. He would presently return the favor.

"Of course I am." He frowned at her. "More so that you visited such a dangerous part of town. You have not been there before today, I hope."

She stared for a moment at his unbuttoned waistcoat, then warily shook her head. He was afraid she had probably been to worse. Why had Will gone along with her schemes?

"I—we—employ a servant with family in that neighborhood," she said in a careful voice. "I have passed through once or twice."

He glanced away. The strain in her tone suggested she had begun to question the direction of their conversation.

"That doesn't speak well of this servant's character," he said, looking at her again.

"After four years in service to my father, then six to me, I daresay Mary's character is not in question. Furthermore, one cannot choose one's relations."

"The same does not go for one's friends. Eleanor, really. Who are these people you bring home? Fortune-tellers, portrait painters—who will I find in the library next? A troupe of traveling mountebanks?"

"I don't think there's room. You've obviously forgotten you ordered that monstrous desk when you last visited. It occupies all the space."

"I did not visit," he said with a flare of annoyance, reaching for his glass again. "A man does not *visit* his home."

"Oh." Her mouth glistened like a sugar plum. He felt his body heat in anticipation. "Of course you're right. It was a regrettable observation on my part."

"Come here, Eleanor." He motioned to the armchair upon which he'd placed his coat, hat, and gloves. The whiskey had given him confidence to implement his lesson. The darkened windows heightened his wicked mood. "Sit down a minute."

"I am sitting," she said, flicking him a curious look.

"Near me," he said lightly.

"Why?"

"You'll see in a minute. Come."

She rose, glancing over her shoulder. "What mischief are you about now?"

"Afraid I'll one up you?" he asked with an innocuous smile.

She laughed. "No."

"I have a surprise for you."

Her gaze followed his movements as he gestured with his black silk hat. "What sort of surprise?"

"If I told you, it would take all the pleasure out of it, don't you think?"

She walked slowly from the sofa, approaching him cautiously as one would an untamed animal. "That depends on which of us is meant to have this . . . pleasure."

He smiled as guilelessly as he could. "I hope what I have in store is mutually pleasurable."

She crossed her arms. "I don't trust you for a moment."

"I trusted *you* to trust my judgment."

"I've locked away the letter if that's what you're after."

She reached the chair.

He reached behind to push the door shut. The lock failed to catch.

"I'm not going to apologize," she said with a thin smile. "I warned you what I would do. You shouldn't have interfered."

"We'll address that matter afterward. Now sit."

"Why should I?"

"Please, darling. Humor me."

"I suppose you'll keep on until I do."

"That's right."

She sat stiffly, and he deliberately kept her waiting, returning to the sideboard to finish the whiskey he'd poured. "You make a beautiful prisoner, by the way."

She laughed uneasily. "Is this an interrogation?"

He shook his dark head in mock dismay. "That doesn't sound pleasurable."

Her eyes widened in realization as he drew two strips of black silk from his coat. "You would not dare," she said with a breathless laugh. "In the middle of the day, in our drawing room. *On a chair.* Baron, you are a wicked one."

"I don't suppose you would prefer the table?" he asked with a hopeful smile.

"Between the teacups?" she said in shocked amusement as he advanced on her. "As if I were—"

"A dessert?" He bent, his hands braced on the back of the chair, his arms entrapping her.

Her heart thudded as she stared up from his throat into his sardonic face.

His mouth quirked into a dangerous smile. Her pulses soared. This was trouble.

She made a belated attempt to rise; he knelt, one scarf between his even white teeth, the other brought forth to quickly bind her wrists to the chair.

"Sebastien, this is so preposterous," she said, then subsided, curious, despite herself, to see what he planned to do. And to what she would submit. "I have never been put in such a position."

"Ssh."

"It's embarrassing," she whispered, the crimson heat in her cheeks stealing down her neck.

"Not from my standpoint. Embarrassing is being chased through an alley with a mastiff at your heels."

"Have you done this to people before?" she asked, half-rising again in a spurt of indignation. "Oh, you *have*."

"Not for the same purpose I intend," he said with a droll smile.

"Did you torture—?" She gave a small huff of panic, testing the strength of the silk bindings. "Don't answer."

He shook his head, his face dark with desire. "I won't."

"You haven't closed the door all the way," she exclaimed. "Someone could walk by and see us. You would be hard-pressed to explain tying me to a chair."

He nodded gravely. "Which is why I advise you to be very quiet. To save us the trouble of an awkward explanation. After all, we have appearances to maintain."

She gazed down into his merciless eyes. "Do you plan on leaving me in this humiliating position?"

"That would be a most ungentlemanly act." He swept his hands over her skirts and placed them around her ankles. "You have beautiful legs," he murmured. "Good muscles."

"All the better to give you a kick in the—"

"But you won't." He stroked her calves through her pale stockings.

She quivered. Her back arched in such desperation that he felt the briefest moment of shame. "You've made your point, Sebastien."

"Not quite," he said, his voice soothing.

"Yes, you have," she insisted. "You resent that I checked you, and this is your retaliation."

His slow grin lit a fire in her belly. "One person's retaliation might be another's redress."

His hands glided up her calves, raising her skirt in tantalizing stages. She strained her wrists, crossing one leg over his forearm to discourage him. At this admittedly belated effort he merely captured her ankles again and lifted his head in warning.

"Be still, baroness," he said, and rose up briefly to give her a kiss more potent than the whiskey she tasted on his lips.

"That was a very dangerous neighborhood you visited today," he said against her mouth.

"I seem to be in more danger now," she whispered.

"You need me," he said with infuriating certainty.

"Not to tie me to a chair."

"And I need you."

His capable hands climbed higher, beneath her knees, infiltrating the hollow of her inner thighs. A scandalous heat infused her body, welled up, washed through her veins in stinging awareness. Anticipation of her husband's seduction, not flimsy silk, bound her to the chair.

"You could at least"—she broke off, gasping, as he lowered his head, leaving her with little choice but to address his broad shoulders—"close that door properly."

"I'm preoccupied."

"*Sebastien,* really."

It was clear he intended to continue, privacy be damned. Excitement and frustration interwove into sensations too tangled to separate. Her feet could not find purchase with the floor until she accidentally stepped on his hat.

In desperation, she worked the toes of her pointed pump beneath the brim and kicked it across the room.

The hat shot through the half-opened door and landed in the hall.

His shoulders shook with laughter. "Well, if that doesn't give us away, I don't know what will."

"I shall scream," she said, looking as if she meant it.

"Please, don't," he replied, and before she could make good that threat, he rose, locked the door, and returned to the chair—this time twirling a peacock feather between his fingers.

"I'm not the least bit ticklish," she said quickly, her breasts lifting with an indrawn breath.

"We'll see."

She stared down into his darkly mocking face, her body twisting. "The next time I won't even leave you a feather. I should have let the mastiff get you."

He brushed the feather across her mouth, then her chin, sketching it in sensual drifts to her throat. "That Mayfair Masquer is an undisciplined young man. He won't get the better of me again."

"Do you know that this is polishing day and it's only a matter of time before the maids will want to come in?"

"It was my fault for underestimating you," he continued, brushing the feather across the tops of her breasts. Her body quivered, a reaction she could not hide from him.

"Are you comfortable, darling?" he inquired softly.

She turned her wrists to and fro against the bindings. "How do I look?"

"Enticing." He flicked the feather against the cleft in her chin. "Vulnerable."

She moistened her lips. "This isn't going to stop me."

"It certainly slows you down a bit." His gaze

moved over her in appreciation. "Does the duchess know we are reconciled?"

"She knows we are working together."

"And that we are again man and wife?"

She refused to acknowledge the question. Her body ached for relief even as she kept her gaze fastened on the door. The wretch had raised her gown again, this time uncovering her thighs. She dared not look down. The feather traced the vulnerable flesh below her corset, slipping, teasing, below to the wispy hair below her belly. What sinful delight he was inflicting on her. How dreadful of her to enjoy it.

"Open your legs wider." His voice sounded stern, not to be disobeyed. "I'll stop if you don't."

And as she followed his earthy directions, he dropped the feather on the floor and buried his face between her thighs. Wet. Swollen. He plunged his tongue into the delta of her sex. Almost immediately she died a little death. He had trained her to crave him, to anticipate relief the moment he entered a room. What hope was there for dignity?

He refused to stop. He drew her taut pearl between his teeth. Her pulses leaped. A flush suffused her. She bucked her hips. His hands clamped down firmly on her knees. She bit her cheek to keep from crying out. "Undo me," she ground out, quite desperate.

"I am," he replied, his voice muffled in pleasure, his tongue delving inside her secret place.

One of the maidservants working upstairs

dropped something, a broom, a poker, a picture. Eleanor started in alarm only to feel Sebastien's mouth distract her from this domestic crisis.

The sensations he provoked demanded immediate attention. Her cleft wept. She made a token effort at resistance. A waste of effort. She felt his hands nudge her thighs further apart. Let the brooms fall or take flight. She could not pretend to care.

She strained, then slid deeper into his power. His devilish voice soothed her. His silken tongue aroused. What did it matter that she desired him and enjoyed his bold nature?

The Mayfair Masquer might have pledged her loyalty to the Duchess of Wellington, and loyal Eleanor would prove to the end.

But she also understood that a wife's first duty came to her husband.

And if the staff happened upon a black hat in the hallway, which raised a brow or two, there must be no interruption of duty, or of their lord and lady's pleasure.

Chapter Sixteen

❧ ❧

Sebastien congratulated himself on taking home affairs under control.

The tide had turned in his favor, and he resolved to grasp every chance afforded him. Soon he and Eleanor would put the duchess's business, their estrangement, behind them—and it *was* time to start a family.

He felt like a man finally able enough to accept his own weaknesses, and possibly one who could even offer wisdom to his potential offspring. Satisfied, he wandered through his house until he found Eleanor reading in their private drawing room. She glanced up once, her eyes shadowed with pleasure.

"Off to bed?"

"Coming up soon?" He bent and gave her a quick goodnight kiss. "I don't feel tired. I should. And you?"

"I think I'll read for a while."

"And you're *not* going out?"

"No, Sebastien. Not at this hour."

He grunted good-naturedly. "We aren't expecting any visitors tonight?"

She drew her lap robe over her knees.

"You offended Sir Perceval, I think. He happens to be a skilled phrenologist as well as a fortune-teller. Do you know that he has personally examined the duchess's skull?"

"I won't ask what he found, or didn't, rather. I don't believe in fortune-tellers."

"Neither do I," she said, half-smiling. She laid aside the newspaper she had been reading. "Do you want to talk to me?"

He wished suddenly to sit down beside her. He could remember his father reading with his mother on peaceful country evenings. "Anything interesting in the news?"

"There's always a mention of the Boscastle family."

He nodded, revealing little emotion. "The London branch."

She bit her lip. She seemed to have forgiven him for tying her to that chair. "You do come from a large family."

"Some would call us ignominious."

"I'm not sure of that. One of your cousins has just announced that she will admit wayward young girls into her elite academy. Just think. I could have had a spot."

He smiled. "Our family never did follow the rules."

"That doesn't surprise me. I fear the Prescotts are not much better."

"Pity our children."

"The thirteen?" she asked, glancing up quickly before he had a chance to conceal his reaction.

"Thirteen." He laughed. "I remember *that* conversation."

"So do I," she said with grim humor.

He stared down at her. Sometimes a truce was a win. "Sleep well," he said in a low voice.

"And you, Sebastien."

He left the room, resisting the urge to return to her.

If a husband and wife could outwit each other and laugh about it afterward, the future offered no end to its blessings.

No matter that his wife had still not agreed to abandon her questionable obligations to another, her unrestrained enthusiasm in the bedchamber gave him great hope that he would presently sway her to his sensible point of view. And now they were becoming friends.

Only fleetingly did it occur to him that hers would be the stronger influence.

He had her in his bed, at his side, under his protection. As far as his other duties went, Sebastien maintained contact with the Home Office and Wellington's agents, confident that when the duke returned to England, he would ask Sebastien to serve in some useful capacity.

And that his wife would have her hands otherwise occupied and cease her unseemly pursuits.

Thirteen. An improbable but pleasant number. Unlikely or not, he relished the prospect of raising sons and daughters, having come from a big family himself. And even though he, the other Boscastles, and his three brothers had parted ways long ago, he recalled their earliest years with deep affection.

He had loved the beasts, especially his older brother Colin, who'd taught Sebastien everything a seventeen-year-old boy thought he needed to know.

At least the lessons they had learned together had mattered then. They had run away from home when their father died.

Sebastien hadn't realized at the time that both of them had been running away from what really mattered and that sooner or later, if a boy ran far enough, he would come back as a man to what he had hoped to escape.

His father's death had broken his family apart.

Joshua Boscastle, Viscount Norwood, had filled his house with energy until the very day he'd been found dead on his own doorstep. The doctor said his heart had failed.

But Sebastien's older brother Colin claimed that their father had dined the evening before with an old friend who held a grudge against Joshua for a business venture that had gone bad.

Colin swore that their father had been poisoned. He said the doctor was a drunk who couldn't piss in a straight line, let alone see the evidence of arsenic when it stared him in the face. Colin's mother refused to believe him. No one did except Sebastien.

The two brothers made a blood pact.

They would leave home and not return until they'd hunted down Joshua Boscastle's murderer. They could earn enough money cleaning stables and clearing stones from fields across the world if they needed to. They'd felt strong, invincible, fueled by righteous anger.

Of course Colin and Sebastien's grand scheme had ended in utter failure.

One night, after almost two years of chasing justice, they'd woken up in a barn and realized they had no money, no more leads to follow, and that Colin's good shirt was hanging from his brawny back in tatters.

Worse than being penniless was being beaten down in spirit.

When Colin shook Sebastien awake that night after he'd just fallen asleep, he acted and sounded ten years older.

Sebastien only had to look at his brother's terse, grimy face to acknowledge what they'd both realized but couldn't admit—they'd gone on a wild goose chase after a man too clever to get himself caught.

Sebastien, his skinny arse freezing, had been on the verge of tears until Colin kicked him in the knee. "It's time to grow up," Colin said.

"You mean give up," Sebastien replied bitterly.

"Look, for all we know, it might have been his heart that killed him."

"That's a lie." Sebastien's voice rose into the rafters of the barn.

"Maybe it was a lie before." Colin was already putting on his boots. "I don't know the damned truth, Sebastien. I'm not even sure I care after all this time wasted tilting at windmills and dragging you along like a lost puppy."

"Are we going home?"

"I'm joining the army."

"Then so am I."

Colin shook his head and swore. "I don't want you at my side for the rest of my life. Find your own way."

And so he had.

Family. His wife. Did anything matter more?

He had begun to move what little personal belongings he possessed from his boat into the wardrobe that he and Eleanor now shared.

He carefully avoided the drawer that held the unused christening gown.

He hung his ornamented regimental jacket beside her grandest evening gown, the one he'd noticed bore a wine stain.

Still puzzled by this apparent aberration, he drew it toward him by the delicate, pearl-buttoned sleeve.

She ought to have new frocks. He could well afford them.

His unspeakable deeds in France had not gone without compensation.

The thought of spoiling her, of surprising her with generous gestures, appealed to him.

But the light revealed a truth that the other evening had been kind enough to conceal.

With a frown, he saw clearly it was not a wine stain that marked the low-edged bodice, but a blotch of oil paint.

Chapter Seventeen

❧ ❧

Eleanor felt quite confident that she could keep her husband under control, or at least divert him so that he did not interfere with her work. She intended to play two roles, one as the duchess's agent, the other the dutiful wife. Admittedly acting as a woman who loved her masterful lord required little sacrifice on her part. As it did not benefit her to protest Sebastien's authority in certain private matters, she submitted when he pursued her.

And vice versa.

And while she might not have succeeded in tying him to a chair and seducing him insensible with a feather, she did manage to implement certain of her own feminine instincts when the mood arose.

He appeared to be in the mood every waking hour.

She was also aware, however, that regarding her other obligations, Sebastien was not to be trusted even while he slept. She could not thump her pillow during the night without him rolling up against her, his large body impeding any attempt to escape from their bed.

"Bad dreams?" he'd ask. And she would stare into his slumberous blue eyes, resisting the urge to smooth his rumpled hair.

"There are dangerous things outside in the dark," he whispered once, his arms enfolding her.

"Not to mention the one lying in this bed."

He chuckled. "Haven't I behaved myself?"

She gave a tiny shrug of assent.

"At least acknowledge that I'm trying."

She shrugged again.

"It's better this way, you and I together on a cold night instead of . . . those other activities."

She smiled. "Perhaps."

And then, just as she felt a wave of tenderness for the scoundrel, he added, "I knew you'd come around sooner or later. I'm only surprised it took this long."

He would indeed have been surprised had he realized that when she wandered each afternoon to the back gate to purchase wares from the curd-and-whey seller, she was in fact receiving her current instructions from the duchess.

Employing the glib street girl as her courier, the Duchess suggested that Eleanor would be wise to delay any covert activities until further advised.

Her grace cautioned that the Bow Street Runners had stationed seasoned detectives throughout the West End, in the hope of catching London's elusive celebrity.

"Seasoned detectives," Eleanor said with a scornful smile, and hid the message in her shoe.

It only proved how far afield the runners were in capturing the Masquer.

She turned, frowning thoughtfully, and walked straight into her husband. "Not more curds and whey," he said, raising his brow at her.

She stared down at her bowl. "Yes, I—I've taken a powerful fancy to them."

"Any particular reason?"

"I—"

"Let me carry the bowl for you."

"It isn't heavy," she said quickly.

"Don't worry, Miss Muffett. I'm not going to eat your snack." He glanced past her to the gate. "That girl isn't selling her wares to any other house. Are you sure she's not planning to rob us?"

She grasped his arm and propelled him toward the house. "I thought you were meeting with the architect in the library."

He looked down again. The contents of the bowl were sloshing dangerously over the sides. "Yes. We're discussing the renovation of the Sussex house."

Their country estate, if one could call the small manor that.

He pulled a handkerchief from his pocket and wiped off his knuckles. "That's actually why I came to fetch you."

"To seek *my* opinion?"

"Naturally."

"That's very sweet of you, Sebastien."

But when she followed him into the library, the

architect immediately showed her the blueprint for the nursery addition that Lord Boscastle had planned for the country house.

A very large nursery. One that even the architect's apprentice slyly remarked took up the whole upper West Wing, and was his lordship hoping to raise a cricket team?

When she went upstairs to dress for supper, she discovered that he'd gone through her wardrobe again. The evening gown with the stain hung in plain view, as if he were letting her know he'd noticed it. And wasn't pleased. Her husband was anything but subtle.

She bit her lip and would have felt guilty had she not realized a few minutes later that the rascal had also been nosing through the drawer of the writing desk. He might have been devious enough to pick the lock of the small escritoire, but he had left evidence of his illicit entry. The imperceptible coating of rice powder she routinely sprinkled before closing the drawer had been unsettled.

Nothing appeared to be missing, not any of her personal correspondences, nor the last two letters yet to be delivered to the duchess.

But the peacock feathers she had left crossed at a certain angle had been cleverly rearranged, although not in their previous formation.

Did Sebastien assume she would never notice? True, he had flummoxed her with his silk scarves and chair seduction. Was it possible she had not followed her cautious routine as well as she should have?

She closed the drawer carefully. Despite their precarious marriage, she'd always felt she could trust his integrity. He had convinced her he didn't give a farthing about the contents of the duchess's letters. Only about her. He didn't even read the gossip papers.

It was one thing for him to accompany her on her assignments, but quite another for him to snoop in this manner.

There was a bite in the air when Sebastien sat down to supper with his wife three hours later. He noticed that although fresh coals had been laid in the grate, burning fitfully, Eleanor had not bothered with her shawl. Her gleaming white shoulders rivaled the water pearls at her throat for simple beauty.

She dug her fork into a heaping portion of potatoes lathered in parsley butter. "You're late," she remarked pleasantly. "Were you still making designs for the house?"

"Yes."

"And that family of thirteen?" she asked with a chuckle.

He steepled his fingers under his chin. "I've been thinking. Perhaps we should have a portrait painted of you."

"Of me?"

"Yes. For the house."

"Well. I gathered that." She sliced unmercifully at her slice of minted lamb. "But before we plan our wall coverings, I feel it's only fair to warn you that I can't leave London until my obligation to the duchess is met."

"That's very high-minded of you," he said in obvious amusement.

She put down her knife. "I know it is within your rights to go through our wardrobe, husband dearest, but really, I must insist you respect the privacy of my only locked drawer."

"What are you talking about?"

"The last letters that we found were not in the same position that I left them," she said, suddenly doubting herself at his affronted tone.

He sat back in his chair. "And you think that *I* unlocked your drawer to read some inane confessions of thwarted love?"

"You didn't?"

He reached for his wine goblet. "Absolutely not." His eyes glinted with arrogance. "And had I done so, you would never have known it."

"I shall bear that in mind." She hesitated. "There must be something in these letters that the duke does not wish anyone to know."

He glanced down at the table, stung by an unexpected moment of guilt. The duke probably didn't even remember that the letters existed.

"Is something wrong?" she asked.

He glanced at the fire and then at her.

"Actually, there is. It's the matter of that stain upon your gown."

Her lips parted. "My gown? The one that you—"

He gave her a steely frown.

"There is an explanation," she said softly.

"One that I'm dying to hear."

"It's oil paint. From Bellisant's brush—"

He stood abruptly.

She blinked as their wine goblets trembled on the table. He ran his hands through his hair in agitation. "Answer me," he said, his voice rising.

"Answer what?"

"Did this Bellflower person paint a portrait of you?"

She nodded mutely.

"Then where is it?" he demanded, leaning over her.

"I think he has it," she said in a small voice.

"Ah. Of course." He closed his eyes briefly. "And just one more question—which I know is absurd, but do bear with me—are you wearing your gown in this painting?"

She sprang up from her chair, practically bumping her head on his chin. His hand shot out to steady her. She pushed it off. "How could you even ask?"

"You were clothed?" he queried, bracing for another outburst of indignation.

"I shall not answer such a demeaning question!"

Two footmen knocked at that dangerous moment, asking whether his lordship required more coals on the fire, and another bottle of German wine.

"No. And yes," he snapped as he and Eleanor returned to their respective places at the table.

One must keep up appearances.

Even when appearances deceived.

"One would think," he said, steering to another subject, "that the women who received Viola Hutchinson's letters would value the integrity of England above their petty correspondences."

"Or that they would value themselves," she said absently, spearing her lamb again. "I cannot fathom how any man or woman could take pleasure in exposing an adulterous affair. It seems a mortification to admit one indulged in the first place, let alone to expose that fact with others."

He studied her face. "Assuming there was an affair to begin with," he said guardedly.

Their eyes met across the table.

The light from the silver candelabra glittered darkly between them. "Do *you* think the duke was unfaithful to his wife?" she asked in a thoughtful voice.

He drank his wine. "No." He shook his head for emphasis.

"Why not?"

"Well, he's a moral person for one thing, and I can't picture him wasting his spare moments when the peace of the world is at stake."

"But opportunity—"

"Of course." He could not deny that. "They have been apart—for longer than us, even."

"I suppose," she said in a reflective voice, "that one could even argue to justify an affair in such a case."

He hoped he wasn't about to learn of such justification.

He frowned. "Do *you* think he was disloyal?"

"It seems naïve to believe otherwise," Eleanor said.

Two of the candles had gone out. He thought he heard the patter of rain, perhaps even hail at the windows. He'd have to see about hiring a glazier. He'd ignored the basics of maintaining a fine house. One could not take anything of worth for granted.

Neither windows. Nor wives.

"I think the duchess doubts him," Eleanor mused, dabbing her finger at the drop of wine that had spilled on the tablecloth. "He's been gone such a long time, and princesses and parlormaids all over the world adore him. Would it not be normal for him to fall prey to temptation when no one is looking?"

"Not if his heart has been captured as mine has."

She smiled cryptically. "How lovely of you to—" She broke off as he rose from the table, his food untouched. "Where are *you* going? Did I say something wrong?"

"I have a little matter that must be dealt with," he said amicably. "Don't worry if I'm late. And no masquerades tonight."

Her mouth opened. She started to object, but then he came to her side, bending to kiss her as if they were any other husband and wife parting for a few hours. Her lips tingling, she heard him summon the footman Burton for his coat. And then he walked out of the house into the wet night. She sat at the table for a few moments longer, recalling all the other times she had dined by herself. He didn't really think *she* had been unfaithful? She pushed back her chair and rose, running out into the hall. As she flung open the front door, she spotted Sebastien striding down the street, his greatcoat over his arm.

"I don't believe he betrayed her!" she called after him. "He's above such behavior! He's as trustworthy as . . . as you," she finished quietly.

She glanced up as a sudden downpour hit the street.

The rain swallowed up Sebastien's receding figure. She huddled back into the doorway.

"Madam!"

She turned as the trim figure of her maid emerged from the dark hallway behind her. After years of dedicated service, Mary always sensed when something was wrong. "Is there anything I can do to help?" she asked, hurrying to the door.

She had no idea how much Mary had heard, or what she thought. Not an aristocrat by birth, her upbringing rather unconventional, Eleanor oftentimes neglected to observe the distance a lady must put between herself and those she employed. Still, it was Mary who had supervised the preparation of the special supper dishes that Sebastien barely tasted and who orchestrated the undercurrents of domestic life. Eleanor would be lost without her.

"There's no need to worry," she said gamely, backing into the hall, her hair already damp. "I'm meeting his lordship later. Would you please lay out my evening wear? And have the carriage brought around. My husband appears to have walked to his destination."

"But, madam, this damp—"

She went straight to the stairs; if she paused to consider her position from her maidservant's perspective, she might lose her nerve. "I'm accustomed to taking care of myself."

She barely caught Mary's response. "And here I thought that the situation had changed."

Chapter Eighteen

❧ ❧

By the time Sebastien reached Sir Nathan Bellisant's rooms in St. Martin's Lane, the rain had lightened to a drizzling fog. The walk in the damp failed to extinguish the doubts that simmered inside him. This time he would be the one to pay the surprise call. He knew of no better way to judge a man's character than to visit him unannounced at his home. It seemed only fair. Bellisant felt comfortable calling on Eleanor at all hours.

He ought not to complain when the insult was reversed.

By Eleanor's husband.

He knocked hard at the door and heard shuffling, a woman's voice from within. He had just left his wife at home. It was irrational to think she'd read his intentions and had rushed to warn Bellisant before him. What *would* he do if the impossible presented itself and he found her here? Would he even have the heart to fight them?

Yes. He decided he would.

Dear God, he wasn't thinking straight.

Eleanor wasn't here.

But an intimate portrait of her was.

An elderly housekeeper opened the door, her expression harried as if she'd been turning away unwelcome callers all night, and didn't care for any of them. Sebastien did not bother to introduce himself.

A macaw screeched from a perch in the corner. He thought he heard men conversing in muted voices from the back of the house. A door closed.

He saw Bellisant standing at the bottom of the staircase, his white shirt splotched, his fair hair tied back in tangled negligence at the nape.

"Lord Boscastle," he said, his astonishment genuine. "It's all right, Mrs. French. You may leave us alone. Please, come in, my lord, but mind where you walk."

Sebastien nodded, following Bellisant's slender figure up the stairs to a drawing room studio. The air bore the mingled scent of linseed oil, spirits of turpentine, and—his nostrils flared—of absinthe. He felt Bellisant's dark eyes regard him as he looked around the room.

Sketching easels stood before the tall sash windows. There were candles burning in at least a dozen girandoles upon the walls where paintings did not hang. Jars of paint sat upon several tables of mismatched veneers. Well-worn books tottered in piles upon the unlit hearth. What a bloody mess. He reassured himself that there was no evidence of his wife.

And then he saw her.

His gaze lifted to the painting that occupied the place of honor above the mantelpiece. Shock fired his nerves. It felt like a violation and privilege at once, to view a painting of Eleanor in such an unguarded pose. She reclined on a royal-blue couch, a black velvet band upon her tousled hair, a black silk half-mask in her hand. Her smile struck him as hauntingly sad. He recognized the gown.

But who was the lady who both tempted and held herself aloof from the beholder?

He was not an artist. Even so he could not deny Bellisant's genius of delicacy and perception. The texture intrigued the eye. The balance of dark and light brought Eleanor so alive she might have stood between the two men who flanked the fireplace.

"She refused to take her portrait," Bellisant mused.

"I'll take it," Sebastien said without thinking, and his voice warned that it would not be in exchange for his wife.

"I shall have it sent to you in the morning."

Sebastien turned. Bellisant was still studying the portrait, mesmerized by either his work or the woman who had inspired it—Sebastien did not give a damn.

"Do you love my wife?" he asked before he could stop himself.

"I would not have kept her portrait where I could see it if I didn't."

Anger swelled in Sebastien's throat. "But she doesn't love you."

Nathan edged around a sketching easel as if he thought it would protect him. "I wouldn't be letting this painting go if she did," he said cautiously.

"Bloody hell. You do realize that nothing is going to stand between me and my wife?" He glanced down. "Not even an easel."

"I do not believe it is me you have to convince." Bellisant swallowed. "If you challenge me to a duel, I shall grant you the first shot. I'm—I'm frightened of guns."

"For God's sake," he said in disgust.

"It's true," Bellisant said quietly. "I saw my father shot to death. I grow faint at the sight of a pistol."

Sebastien grunted.

"Are you still angry at me?"

"Angry? Oh—what's the point?"

Sebastien strode from the room without another word. Had he gotten what he'd come for? How poetic to think that in claiming possession of the portrait he could reclaim what he might have lost. Was it too late? Something about the smile of that Eleanor in the painting conveyed a message he should have noticed a dozen times before. How had he missed the sadness in her eyes?

Even worse, had he been the cause?

He walked through a labyrinth of small streets toward the Thames. He wasn't sure what he would say to Eleanor, or whether he'd say anything at all. Should he apologize and let the matter mend itself as many issues between a man and wife were wont to do? He wasn't sorry he'd confronted Bellisant, only that he had doubted her.

And perhaps that he hadn't clipped her amorous painter in the jaw for good measure.

The evening fog seemed to thicken by the moment.

Easy for a man to lose himself in the maze of London at this hour.

He knew he was being followed shortly after he hailed a hackney to take him to the waterfront where he docked his boat.

So did the ruthlessly cheerful driver, who warned him to " 'Ang on fer dear life. We'll lead the blighter right into the river, eh, my lord?"

"As long as we don't end up there ourselves," he said dryly.

The driver broke into hearty laughter. "Running away from a wronged husband? I see we've got company."

Sebastien glanced around instinctively. A small carriage rattled behind with neither links nor running footmen. The fog rendered identifying it impossible.

"I know London," the driver chatted on, oblivious to the fact that his passenger was more concerned about getting his throat cut than with conversation. "You won't be the first gent I've helped escape a cuckold's wrath. Tisn't 'ard to elude a person in this soup."

"True enough."

In this fog, practically anyone could materialize or disappear. Sebastien glimpsed a gypsy girl in a doorway, calling at him to have his fortune read. His lip curled.

What had Eleanor been hoping to see in her palm? *Four. Including the one lost.* What had she lost? Their child? *Four* children. *Not four lovers, you nitwit.* The start of their cricket team. God, how thick he was. Thicker than London fog.

Almost at the river's edge.

"Slow down," he said.

A pair of oars creaked in the mist. The muddy water in the unseen craft's wake bubbled up like a witch's cauldron. By day the ribald cries of the watermen, the flapping sails of East Indian merchant ships, enlivened the wharves. Late at night, the penny wherries and cockle boats, the soap boilers and potteries, lay at rest. He thought of the mudlarks who slept in the tents below the tunnels, dreaming of a decent meal. Sooner or later every broken heart in London came to the river's edge.

Here and there a voice from the ale houses drifted through the shadowed arches of the river. Sebastien heard a whore singing a drunken ballad to her audience of sailors. Further down the shore stood the secluded estates of the aristocracy. If he listened hard enough, he would probably overhear a husband asking his wife for another chance.

"Stop here," he said to the driver without warning.

" 'Ere? This ain't the fanciest part of town—"

"Well, I'm not the fanciest gentleman, either."

"It's your funeral. I 'ope she was worth the trouble."

Sebastien smiled darkly and paid him thrice the fare. "She's worth more than I ever realized."

"Good luck then, my lord."

Eleanor had attempted several suggestive poses with which to surprise her husband. In the end, given the limited space afforded by the small vessel, she had settled for a half-recumbent position on the red-satin couch that occupied most of the cabin's space. Unless he had already come and gone, Sebastien ought to have been here by now. She didn't fancy waiting here alone until her coachman returned to collect her.

She was starting to wish she hadn't sent him away at all.

She had unashamedly checked for signs of another woman's presence. Thankfully her search proved fruitless. But if the cabin revealed no incriminating evidence, the black oaken panelwork, lavishly carved with ample-breasted mermaids being chased by lustful seamen, certainly did not match the Sebastien she knew.

Nor did the delicate tulipwood desk that was embellished with ormolu scrollwork and gilt marquetry seem compatible with his masculinity. The contents of its drawers appeared innocent enough—a pen, a few charts, an almanac of the tides, and a sketch she had once given him of a ruined Spanish castle.

She realized that in the course of secret service he might have been forced to assume various identities. It was challenging, however, to picture him at a desk more suited to Marie Antoinette than to that of an English baron. She tapped her forefinger on a gold flower and a hidden compartment slowly opened. Her heart quickened.

Nothing in it, either . . . except one of her old hair ribbons.

Which meant that either Sebastien really did love her or he'd been dressing up as a lady to mislead his enemies.

What a thought.

She closed the compartment and returned to the couch, startled to realize that she couldn't see a thing through the cabin window. A bank of pearlescent fog engulfed the shallop. It seemed unlikely she'd be able to implement her ambush on the boat's absent master, or to even make her way back onto the wharf.

Suddenly all the newspaper reports she'd read of dismembered bodies discovered in floating tobacco hogsheads took on a personal significance.

Her Masquer deeds seemed tame in comparison to what went on at the water's edge. The fog amplified every creak and squeak . . .

A squeak—

Surely that was only the water lapping at the shore, and not a large rodent.

Where had her river rat gone? What manner of people did he meet here, anyway?

What if he'd changed his mind and returned home?

What if he was waiting for her by a warm fire, wondering where she'd gone?

Did he require solitude? He couldn't have picked a lonelier spot in all of London.

She nestled deeper into the cushions. The unveiled desire in his eyes when he'd stared at her across the table haunted her. Why hadn't she realized right away that his indirect questions about the duke's fidelity had been his way of questioning *her*?

She glanced up at a muffled sound from the shore. She waited and heard nothing more. The shallop rocked lightly. The rhythm of her heart escalated wildly as a broad-shouldered silhouette appeared in the portal. A pistol gleamed in the dark. She caught her breath, her heart thumping in more than desire.

Sebastien laughed in surprised recognition.

"Madam," he said as he laid his gun on the desk and drew off his coat, "you have taken the advantage."

"I doubt that very much, Sebastien," she murmured, her blood running in warm eddies through her body.

"You would not doubt it if you could feel how my heart is pounding."

"As is mine."

"Is it, indeed?" His gaze moved over her deceptively relaxed figure. "I wish you had warned me to expect you."

"I would have," she said with conviction, "had I expected you to enter with a big gun in hand. For a moment I thought I was breathing my last."

He smiled grimly. "I have more experience than to shoot at anything that awaits me in the dark."

"Thank goodness for that." She refrained from asking what manner of things, or persons, he *had* shot at. One day she'd insist he tell her. Until then he would remain a delicious enigma for her to decipher.

"I believe I might have been followed to the river," he said. "You'll forgive me if I was prepared for an ambush."

She shivered lightly. "Perhaps you should leave that gun where you can reach it."

"Perhaps you should have listened when I said this was no place for you. However, now that you're here, you might as well make yourself comfortable."

She cast a skeptical glance around the cabin. "Speaking of comfort, I did wonder about your choice of décor. I never dreamt your taste ran to bosomy mermaids and red satin."

"The boat used to be a floating brothel," he said after a brief hesitation.

"A—" She stared at him in dismay. "Not one that you patronized, I hope."

"Certainly not. I stole it in the line of duty."

"Good gracious."

"And you are never to come here alone again."

"I had our coachman walk me to the dock."

"It isn't a safe place," he added.

"I can imagine, considering its history." She

caught the smile that crossed his face. "You aren't still upset about the portrait?"

He swore softly.

"I called after you."

"I heard."

"And you ignored me?"

His eyes glinted. "I'm not ignoring you now." He leaned his hip back against the desk.

"We don't really know each other, do we?" she asked softly.

"I know enough to realize that I'll never want anyone else except you."

"Then why, may I ask, are you standing over there?"

He laughed richly.

She sat up. Her hair fell down, twining in the damp. She made no attempt to tame it. Her current mood played into her wilder instincts. She may as well look the part—unexpected how exciting it was to plan the seduction of one's own husband, to catch him in his lair. She felt a little dangerous. He looked completely so, his black hair glistening with droplets of mist, his lean body moving silently in the darkness.

She watched impatiently as he opened a cupboard bolted to the wall, and made a cursory examination of its contents. How had she missed those shelves? Ah. There were no knobs.

"What else are you hiding from me?" she asked in curiosity.

He reached her side in one languid stride. His

heavily lidded eyes swept over her. "Nothing. I'm an open book. Read me."

She gave a sigh of pleasure as he sat down beside her. "Very well." She walked her fingers up his arm to the back of his neck. His crisp linen shirt bore the scent of damp air and starch.

"Page one," she whispered as she pulled off his coat. "Where did you go when you left the house tonight?"

"To see your painter friend."

She glanced up in dismay. "That isn't why you had that gun with you?"

He leaned over her. "A husband is justified in confronting a man who has pursued his wife."

"Am I justified in shooting the women who pursued you while you were away?"

"What women?"

"Honestly, Sebastien. You can't expect me to believe that no other lady has ever tried to coax you to her bed?"

"I didn't say that." His smile was heartless. "I can promise you, though, that in all of Europe there doesn't exist a portrait of me painted by a lovesick admirer."

"Did you actually *see* the portrait?"

"I could hardly have missed it."

"Was it that unflattering?"

"No. It was that obvious. And not unflattering at all. Haven't *you* seen it?"

"Not the finished work. Bellisant only showed me the early sketch. He's rather shy about such things."

"The poor dear," he said in a disgruntled voice. "He's actually proud of the painting."

Several moments went by.

"I'm rather afraid to ask what you did to it, and to him," she said.

His mouth tightened. "He's still alive, and the portrait, as well as its subject, belong to me."

"You're very masterful."

He kissed her lightly on the mouth. "So are you."

She giggled. "And you don't mind?"

"No."

She sighed, easing him back against the cushions. Before she could take off his neckcloth, he reached up and unbuttoned her bodice. Not to be outdone, she teased her hand down his shirt and unfastened his fly.

"Now tell me that I am the first woman you've brought here," she whispered.

He slipped her gown off her shoulders and smiled. "No."

"You—"

He lowered his body over hers.

"You're the only one. To admit you're the first implies that others will follow."

"Oh," she said softly. "That was a good answer."

"Elle." He rained burning kisses down her throat, her shoulders, then the tops of her pale breasts. "I left the table still hungry tonight."

"You were offered dessert."

His chiseled lips curved. He stroked his fingers

across her swollen nipples. "May I return with apologies?"

She swallowed, completely seduced by his touch. "I came here to make peace."

"I like the sound of that."

He drew her skirts up to her waist, then pulled down his trousers and settled his muscular body between her thighs. She laid her head back on the couch, anchoring her legs around his buttocks. She lifted herself, inviting. He accepted greedily, spreading her open with the fingers of one hand, the other pinching her bud until she bucked against him.

"I'm so glad that you waited for me," he whispered.

"Do you mean here tonight, or in general?"

"Both," he answered, guiding his thick shaft to her passage.

She whimpered as he removed his fingers. He pushed her knees farther apart and thrust, forcing a gasp of shocked pleasure from her. Her body clenched him. He withdrew several inches, leaving her panting in need, until she drummed her heels against his back.

"Very masterful, indeed," she breathed as he ground his hips and pumped deeply into her pulsing warmth.

"Dear God," he said moments later, both of them subsiding in a breathless exhaustion upon the couch. "To think I was about to give up this boat."

She wriggled upward from the warm pocket

between the cushions and his muscular torso. "I suppose this is what is called a pleasure barge."

He grinned. "It is now."

"We should get dressed," she said idly, and made no attempt to move.

"No more pleasure?"

"I asked Tilden to come back at midnight in case you didn't show up."

She eased out of his arms, dressing surreptitiously in the dark. As he buttoned his shirt, she picked up the gun on the desk, then quickly put it down. Through the cabin window she glimpsed a scull that carried two lovers; it slipped like a dark swan in the mist. She heard Sebastien come up behind her.

When he locked his arm around her waist, his face buried in her loosened hair, she tried not to think of the prior lewd acts that had taken place on this boat.

"You're coming home with me, I assume," she said, leaning her head back.

"Of—"

He broke off, his body tensing. A board creaked ominously in the night. They listened for a moment longer. Then he seized her by the shoulders and steered her toward the back of the cabin.

"There's a secret compartment behind the mariner's map," he whispered, reaching for his gun. "Get inside now."

In view of his shady associations, she hastened to obey. The furtive footsteps on the deck were unmistakable now. She headed straight for the oilskin map, lifted it and squeezed into a musty crevice that had a peephole carved into its central section.

Barely able to breathe, she watched her husband wait with enviable calm as the door slowly opened. She flinched as she heard the pistol cock. To her relief, instead of shooting the intruder on the spot, he swore at him.

"You bloody bonehead! You hen-brained, half-arsed son of—"

"Don't shoot me!"

"What on earth are you doing here?"

"Will?" she said unthinkingly, pressing against the thin panel.

Her cousin stood in the doorway with his hands crossed in front of his face. She edged around her husband, who had slipped his gun into his waistband. She gave Will an irate look and plucked a dangling cobweb from her hair.

"What are you doing here?" she demanded, more shaken than she'd realized.

"I came here to protect you," he said indignantly. "Mary was worried that you'd be alone at the river. And now that I've visited this wharf at night, I understand her concern. A rat the size of a small dog just ran over my foot."

Sebastien sighed.

Will lowered his hands. "Well, I thought I was supposed to accompany her on her adventures." He hazarded a hopeful look at Sebastien. "Wasn't I?"

"Yes," Sebastien agreed quietly. "You were. And

I appreciate your vigilance. Was it *you* who followed me here in that carriage?"

"Yes."

"Then why the hell didn't you announce yourself?"

"I got lost on the wharves," he said sheepishly.

"Honestly, Will," Eleanor said, frowning at him. "I would have asked you if I thought you should come here tonight."

Silence ensued. Will glanced from Eleanor's tousled hair to Sebastien's half-buttoned shirt and loosened cravat. She blushed as she felt her husband's hand slip surreptitiously up her back to secure the hooks and eyelets she had been unable to reach. There was little point in explaining that Will had arrived at the end of a heated tryst with her husband. Their disarrayed state spoke for itself.

Chapter Nineteen

❧ ❧

In keeping with appearances, Lord and Lady Boscastle returned that night from the river to Belgrave Square, went straight to bed, and arose early the next day. Upon completing their morning toilette, they dressed, then sat cordially together for a leisurely breakfast. Sebastien scanned the newspaper for any mention of unusual political activity, a gentleman who gave every impression of settling into domesticity. Eleanor, in a most demure dove-gray muslin dress, her dark-red hair arranged in soft curls, made appropriately distressed comments as her husband began relating the latest news on the Mayfair Masquer.

"I have an appointment later today," she murmured, refraining from snatching the newspaper from his hands.

He sat back in his chair. "I think he should retire altogether. Do you know that one editorial proposes he be placed in the Tower?"

"I don't pay attention to that nonsense. He hasn't done any harm, anyway."

"What if he is harmed?" He laid aside the paper, confronting her, and yet concerned.

"Unlikely," she said, shaking her head. It was difficult to decide how deeply his concern went. Or what part his male pride played in controlling her.

"I shall be glad when we leave London for the country," he said in an undertone.

"So you have told me." She sipped her tea with an innocent smile. "I shall be glad when you have severed all ties to your line of work, too."

He frowned, but made no reply, neither a denial nor an agreement. She felt a stab of regret, in fact, for even suggesting he do so. In all honesty, she doubted he would ever retire from service. He wasn't a man to find contentment in the conventional pursuits of a gentleman.

Had it been so, it seemed doubtful he would have chosen to marry her.

Three hours later, however, she discovered something about her husband that swept all her guilty feelings away. She was collected at the corner by the duchess's driver and taken for a coach ride around the park with Her grace's personal secretary, Mr. Herbert Loveridge. Without a word she handed him the letters she had recovered. She'd be proud to answer that she hadn't read a single word of them, if interrogated.

"Her grace wishes to inform you that she is unable to meet you herself today," he announced in his stentorian voice.

Eleanor studied the trim, nondescript young gentleman who frequently served as intermediary between the duchess and her agents. If Loveridge resented carrying secret messages from his employer to sausage vendors or curd-and-whey girls, he concealed it behind a grave demeanor.

Eleanor had witnessed him accepting coded notes from filthy female pickpockets with the same respect one would accord a princess.

She guessed Mr. Loveridge was well paid for his services. She also sensed that his devotion to the duchess went beyond monetary compensation. The Duchess of Wellington was herself a devoted friend to those who served her. Her uncommon kindness to the poor and lonely touched hearts throughout London.

"Lord Charles has a loose tooth," Loveridge explained, referring to the duchess's youngest boy. "Her grace was awake all night."

"Oh, dear," Eleanor said. "I hope the situation has resolved itself."

Loveridge's thin lips twitched. "What nature does not resolve, the dozen or so dentists summoned to attend the young lord will surely do so."

"I understand." As a surgeon's daughter, with considerable practical experience in medical emergencies, Eleanor had been called to a few command performances herself at the duchess's house. The duchess requested her every time one of her sons had a rash or upset stomach. "Did her grace have the presence of mind to issue me any new instructions?"

A shadow crossed Loveridge's usually neutral countenance. "She has, my lady. I am to forewarn you, however, that she must preface her orders with unwelcome news."

Eleanor's heart sank. The Masquer was to be retired. Of course she'd known that one way or another, either at the duchess's behest or at her husband's, his demise was inevitable. She had only hoped for the opportunity to fulfill his destiny. After delivering the two remaining letters, she would have happily abdicated his reign. But it bothered her to live with unfinished business.

"Well, out with it, Mr. Loveridge," she said more brusquely than he deserved. "Please deliver her grace's message verbatim."

He shook his head in regret. "It concerns Lancelot."

"Who—? Oh." Eleanor restrained a sigh. Lancelot was the Duchess of Wellington's code name for Sebastien. King Arthur was, of course, the duke. Her grace wanted to be known as Guinevere, and Eleanor's operative name on the streets was Merlin. "What has Lancelot to do with . . . Camelot?" she asked, managing to keep a straight face.

"Lancelot is a knight errant in this matter. The queen has learned that he approached King Arthur and begged permission to joust in the tournament."

"What the deuce—" She wished that he would stop speaking in this ridiculous code and explain outright what he meant. But suddenly she knew. Sebastien hadn't been ordered to interfere in her business.

"Let me understand this," she said, her gloved

hand curling into a fist. "My hus—Lancelot—is *not* acting under Arthur's orders?"

He nodded somberly. "That is the queen's understanding."

"That sneaky bugger."

"I beg your pardon."

"It is I who should beg yours. I am beside myself, Loveridge."

"Yes, my lady."

"I want to murder him."

"Dear heaven."

She thought for several moments. "Does Guinevere have any advice as to what she wishes her sorcerer to do?"

He smiled faintly, confirming Eleanor's suspicion that he enjoyed these intrigues as much as she and the duchess did. "She hopes that this will not discourage Merlin from what he has promised."

Eleanor sat in silence. She should have been more upset or even surprised at this revelation, and yet she was not. Sebastien had fibbed to her, which didn't necessarily mean his declarations of love were false as much as it meant he had a devious mind. Or an ambitious one. Perhaps he even hoped to emerge as the duke's hero in the end. Steal her thunder, would he?

The carriage slowed at the corner. Loveridge handed her the customary pile of parcels from the duchess should Eleanor require proof of an afternoon's shopping when she returned to the house.

"Tell the queen that Lancelot will be put under a spell."

His eyes lit up. "Indeed. And the tournament—"

"—will proceed full tilt as planned."

Eleanor was relieved when she entered the house and found a note from Sebastien explaining that he had gone to his club for an early supper. He promised he would return at a reasonable hour, and would she wait up for him?

Good heavens, this marriage had waited years for his return. What possible difference could a few hours make?

"Will I wait up for him?" she muttered, marching into the drawing room to drop his note into the fire. "No. I will not."

The Masquer had work to do. Only two more letters. "Love will wait," she said. "But duty—"

She spun from the fireplace in embarrassment, noticing Mary at the door with a worried look.

"It wasn't bad news was it, madam?"

Eleanor gazed at the leaping flames. "I haven't decided."

Mary slipped into the room. "You shouldn't breathe that smoke. It'll damage your lungs."

"You are good to me, Mary."

The maid stared at the smoldering letter in consternation. "I do wish, madam, that you were more good to yourself."

Eleanor looked up slowly. "What do you mean?"

Mary shook her head, her eyes averted. She knew. Of course she knew. She mended Eleanor's costumes, observed her comings and goings. She had never uttered a word. When the other servants stood whispering at the door about the Masquer's latest scandal, Mary had not participated, except to remind the staff that there was work to be done.

"Draw me a light bath," Eleanor said in a soft voice. "And lay out my costume."

"Another masquerade?" Mary asked in unhidden disapproval. "I thought the season for these events was over."

Eleanor felt both annoyance and affection for this concern. "There won't be many more parties." She turned decisively from the fire.

Mary followed her halfway to the door. "His lordship will need his costume, too?"

"No." She hesitated. "But make sure the fire is still burning when he comes home. In fact, have the footmen heap on every last coal in the cellar. I want him to have a warm welcome."

Chapter Twenty

❧ ☙

Filching a letter from London's most exclusive brothel on Bruton Street presented the riskiest challenge she had attempted so far. Audrey Watson maintained an elegant house, so well guarded that even if Eleanor managed to gain entrance, she might not as easily escape. She had been studying the original architectural plan of the house for a month. One of the duchess's contacts had provided her with a skeletal description of the interior design.

This information provided limited help. There were said to be secret traps laid throughout the house to catch intruders—journalists who hoped to expose an MP as well as other young aspiring sinners who'd risk life and limb to brag they'd spent an evening at Mrs. Watson's.

Only a select few gentlemen were invited into the celebrated rooms. Others paid a fortune for the privilege. The privacy of the guests was as legendary as the pleasures—culinary, intellectual, and carnal—that Audrey and her trained staff offered.

Eleanor had never taken a risk so weighted

against her before. If she failed, the game would be over.

If she succeeded, she and the duchess would crow together in delight for the rest of their days. What lady in London wasn't a little curious as to what went on inside Mrs. Watson's house?

She had not discussed infiltrating the seraglio with Sebastien. It seemed he was too familiar with brothel designs as it was. She could only be grateful he did not seem to be familiar with the ladies of such an establishment. Deceptive she and her husband might be. Drawn to danger, yes. But not unfaithful.

In hindsight, Eleanor would realize it had been far too easy to break into the House of Venus.

Mrs. Watson's bodyguards, virile young men in expensive evening wear, were known to casually patrol the establishment and its environs while blending in with the beautiful guests whose personal tastes they were paid to protect.

She had been warned to find a sentry at every point of entry or exit. On the balconies, at the stairs, and outside the private chambers in which a guest could enjoy any manner of unmentionable acts. But no one intercepted her in the private garden behind the house. No guard dogs came bounding forth from the neatly trimmed bushes.

And when she used her cutter to unhook the iron clasp of the drawing room window, she encountered only an unnatural darkness.

She wasn't sure what she had expected. Perhaps

some sort of orgy in which one shy guest wouldn't be noticed.

She climbed gingerly over the sill and stood, listening to the muted drifts of laughter, the clink of glasses, and the occasional footstep from the upper floors.

The room appeared empty. Nor did anyone seem to protect the stairwell hidden behind the false bookcase that rose to the plasterwork ceiling. She closed the curtains to conceal the open window, in the event she could escape as easily as she had entered.

With one last look around the room, she proceeded to climb the steep staircase.

She had prepared a story in case she was caught. What young fellow did not wish a peek inside this infamous establishment? She was but a curious lad.

She'd never slept with a woman—one had only to look at her unimpressive frame to understand why the ladies shunned her. She would be the envy of all the boys if she could claim she'd broken into the house and retrieved some small evidence of her visit.

A tassel from a pillow. A comb threaded with a courtesan's hair. *A letter. Find the letter. Escape. Do it. Don't think. Act.*

Her heart thumped in her throat. She reached the top of the stairs and opened the narrow door onto a torchlit hall. Where were the infamous guards?

Her skin prickled in foreboding. She glanced over her shoulder. Quiet as a mausoleum. The walls must have been designed to muffle sound.

Her intuition cautioned her she was walking into trouble. She ignored it. The thrill of danger pulsed in her blood. This could well be the Masquer's last appearance. Let him at least go out with a tale to tell.

Sebastien studied the distorted shadows that moved in the fog. He could barely make out the bulky shape of Will's carriage down the street. He knew that Mrs. Watson's guards had noted its appearance. For all he knew they had also spotted him.

Still, if he had been Will, he would have parked in front of the half-timbered inn at the corner and acted as if he were a patron.

But then he wouldn't have brought Eleanor here at all. He stepped forward involuntarily as a figure emerged from Mrs. Watson's house, striding in the other direction.

Not Eleanor. She was taking too long. Should he intervene?

His family name alone would allow him entrée into this house. A Boscastle carried carte blanche in the half-world, or so Sebastien had heard. He couldn't bloody well knock at the door asking for his adventurous wife. And if he interrupted her, or ended up thwarting her escape, she would never forgive him.

Then again he would not forgive himself if she came to any harm.

Ten minutes crawled by. Then twenty. Too long.

Why had he pretended not to know what she was about? She was obviously in trouble. She might even have been accosted by a guest who thought a lady in male clothing was one of the house's offerings.

Eleanor had half-expected her adventure to come to a sudden end. She had found not one, but two letters from Lady Viola Hutchinson in Mrs. Watson's room. She had not expected Mrs. Watson to find her, though.

She turned, assessing the reflection that wavered in the myriad Venetian glass mirrors on the wall. An attractive, auburn-haired woman in wine silk had entered the room from a side passageway. Two husky young bodyguards waited in rigid attention at the double doors.

She considered her options. None. No possible flight back down the too-quiet hallway, nor through the iron-barred windows, artfully concealed behind vermillion damask curtains. She would have to wait for Mrs. Watson to make her move.

"Are you armed?" asked the woman whose elegant demeanor more bespoke a society matron than it did the most popular courtesan in the city.

"Yes."

"Then be a good boy and give the guards your weapons."

Again there was no choice. Eleanor withdrew her pearl-inlaid pistol and surrendered it before she could be searched.

"Now then," the other woman said, raising her

delicate shoulders in question. "What are you doing inside my house?"

Could she bluff her way through this? Probably not, but she'd give it a damned good try. "I was curious."

"Curiosity killed the cat. What did you hope to find in my room?"

"You, perhaps. Is there any better attraction in London for a country boy?"

Mrs. Watson's eyes darkened in dangerous amusement. "Your first time?" She began to untie the bows of her elbow-length sleeves. "Leave us alone, please," she said to her guards without glancing around.

The men disappeared. A key turned in an outer lock, a loud sound in the silence. Eleanor felt a peculiar sense of detachment. Of all the fates that could have befallen the Masquer, being invited into a courtesan's bed was the last she had anticipated. *Talk yourself out of* this *one, clever Elle.*

"Disrobe," Mrs. Watson said, lifting her hand to unknot her heavy coil of hair. "You've caught me in an amorous mood."

Of all the sodding luck.

Eleanor glanced up at the mirror. "I'd prefer to keep my clothes on, if it's all the same to you," she replied in the gruffest voice she could manage.

"We can't make love properly if we're dressed. Come, boy, don't tell me you're shy. Not when you break in here armed."

"Your guards just confiscated my pistol, madam."

Mrs. Watson stared down meaningfully at Eleanor's belt. "A young man has other weapons."

God help her. The Masquer had London's most notorious whore on his hands, in a mood to be lewd, no less. "I guarantee that you would be disappointed in my—"

"What do you know of oral stimulation?"

Fire rushed to Eleanor's face. "I think conversation is a lost art."

Mrs. Watson laughed. "You're either the bravest young man who has ever broken into my house, or the most foolish."

"May I not be both?" Eleanor asked, blinking in horror as Audrey backed her into the sideboard.

"In this house you can be or do anything you desire—"

"I desire my freedom."

"—at a price." She gestured with a white perfumed hand, suddenly a woman of business. "However, I find you intriguing. Take off your mask."

"No," Eleanor said.

"Take—"

Audrey reached out without warning and wrenched Eleanor's gloved wrist back against her arm. The two letters that she had folded in the cuff of her glove slipped to the carpet. Audrey stared down in a silence that seemed to last for hours, and when she finally looked up, the glitter of understanding in her eyes dashed Eleanor's hopes to death.

"You," the woman breathed in amazement, studying Eleanor up and down. "*You're* the Mayfair Masquer—and it's letters you're after. Not jewels. Not forbidden pleasure. Why?"

Another nail in the coffin. Mrs. Watson would have to be an intelligent whore. A perceptive one. "I do this for the hell of it."

"Then you've come to the right place. I'll give you hell—"

Eleanor shrugged. "Do it."

"Every woman in London wants you."

Eleanor laughed at the irony.

"But you are mine," Audrey said in a thoughtful undertone. She shook her head. "It has to be blackmail," she mused. "Which in my case, at least, is an utter waste of effort. I have more skeletons in my closet than there are in the Cross Bones Graveyard."

"It isn't blackmail." She untied her mask, sighing in self-disgust. "And I'm not anything *you* want, I assure you."

She stared into Audrey's eyes, defiant, defeated, it made little difference. She was in no position to resist, and Mrs. Watson was too experienced to believe her pretense.

Wait. That was all she would do. One never knew what could happen by waiting. The walls could cave in. London could catch fire again.

Audrey stared at her in disbelief. "A woman," she whispered, lifting her fingers to her throat. "And if your motive is not blackmail, then—"

"Just a . . . a lark. A means to enliven an otherwise empty life. Don't read anything into it. I'm a fraud—"

"Who do you work for?" Audrey asked, lowering her hand to cut her off.

"King Midas of Phrygia."

Audrey laughed. "Don't we all?" She bent to pick up the letters on the carpet. Her face pensive, she ran a manicured thumbnail across the crackled wax seals. "I don't know who you really are, or what you want, but I can find out. Let us not underestimate each other." She looked up levelly into Eleanor's face. "I can be your dearest friend or worst enemy."

Eleanor knelt impulsively, her voice low with urgency. "I work for the good of England."

"As I also do," Audrey said in acid tones.

"But that is all I can say."

"The good of England—do you expect me to believe that the Masquer's mischief is a screen for heroics?"

"I'm no one's hero."

"In fact, my dear, you are. And with heroism comes responsibility."

Eleanor swallowed. How would Sebastien escape if he were caught in an establishment of this nature? No mystery there. He would remove his mask, perhaps even his clothes, revealing the beauty of a Greek god, and Audrey would move heaven and earth to support his cause because he wielded that power over women.

All Eleanor had now as a weapon was a peacock feather, a bent one at that.

A quiet knock came at the door. A man asked in hesitation, "Madam, do you need us?"

Eleanor felt the tendons in her back tighten another notch. Was it only last night that she'd pitied the unfortunates who had been stuffed in rock-weighted sacks or hogsheads and dropped to the bottom of the Thames? The disappearance of Lady Boscastle would make the morning papers. She thought of Sebastien's reaction when the tide washed her body to shore.

"Have I met you before?" Audrey asked unexpectedly.

"No." Not a lie exactly. They *had* attended the same exhibition last year but had not been introduced.

"What am I to do with you?"

Eleanor ground her teeth. "I don't give a damn at this moment. Call the police for all I care."

"The police? Oh, please. How uncouth."

They stared at each other again, enemies, allies, women who shared an unconventional streak. "I had you watched from the minute you approached my house. But I confess I did not guess your identity. I would have invited you inside had I known."

Eleanor grasped Audrey's hands on impulse. No going back now. "Then I beg you—if you have any sympathy at all for the Masquer, let him leave."

Audrey smiled slowly.

"I think I might be persuaded."

"And the letters?"

"No." Audrey's mouth firmed. "You're fortunate that I have a weakness for rogues. Do not test my tolerance further."

"Madam," the voice at the door said, more forcefully now. "Do you require our intervention or not?"

Audrey broke free and quickly hid the letters inside a gold urn on the mantelpiece. "I have never betrayed a secret in my life," she said as she turned. "If you trust me, you will not have cause to regret it."

"Sadly, I am past the age of trust."

"Madam," the voice said at the door, as tough as an ogre's now, "do you—"

"Yes," Audrey said impatiently. "I require your help, but only from one of you. I wish you to escort our special guest outside in the most discreet manner possible."

Chapter Twenty-one

❦ ❦

She was blindfolded and escorted by a guard down another staircase that led to a back courtyard. From there he took her through a stuffy tunnel that she guessed lay beneath several of the neighboring houses. The solicitous hand at her back guided her up a short flight of stairs and onto the pavement. She drew several deep breaths.

Then she was free, her blindfold removed, her face bathed in cooling fog—no, her mistake. She was trapped again, surrounded by flames. His Satanic Majesty Sebastien Boscastle awaited her, his features dark and unforgiving. She steeled herself for what was to come.

"If you ever do this again," he said, grasping her by the shoulders, "I will personally shackle you to—"

She pushed around him, not having the heart to fight. He cursed loudly, using the most shocking words she'd ever heard. How he'd known to wait for her here she did not care.

"Where is the carriage?" she muttered, walking several steps before he stopped her.

"In the other direction."

"No, it—"

"For the bloody love of God, Eleanor."

"Are you praying or cursing me? Where *is* the carriage?"

He brought his hand down on hers in a vise that sent a shock through her torpor. "I moved it."

"Where is Will?" she asked in bewilderment.

"I moved him, too."

"You—"

"Never mind Will. What happened to *you*?"

She shivered as his gaze impaled her. She felt his fury, his concern, and then suddenly she allowed herself to feel her own vulnerability again. His arms closed around her. She let him hold her, knowing that she deserved his anger but that even more she needed his strength.

"Are you all right?" he whispered roughly as she laid her head on his chest, biting her lip when his large hand stroked her nape.

She nodded, wishing there were a way to avoid telling him she had failed.

"How did you manage to escape?"

"I'm not certain that I did," she said slowly. "It might be only a reprieve."

"Didn't you get the letter?"

"No." She broke away, shaking her head in bitterness. "There were two of them. I was caught."

"By the guards?" he asked, glancing back down the street.

"No, by—"

The murmur of male voices carried from some unseen doorway. He gripped her hand again and propelled her down the street. Her boot heel caught on a cobble. He steadied her, swearing to himself, or at her. She only knew she could breathe again and that his hand felt warm and reassuring.

Will was pacing beside the carriage, a fashionable figure in his camel wool cape and high beaver hat. His blond-red hair appeared disheveled, however, and Eleanor detected the scent of brandy on his breath as she approached him.

"Your husband," he said, with a fearful glance in Sebastien's direction, "is a veritable monster. I thought he—he was going to—"

Sebastien stepped between them. "Chatter like a chambermaid at home. Your job is to drive."

Will nodded meekly and scrambled up onto the driver's box. A moment later Eleanor found herself all but stuffed into the carriage opposite her brooding husband, who sat back slowly as the pair of grays took off at a racing pace.

For an eternity he regarded her, then said, "Do you wish to explain what happened?"

"Audrey Watson caught me red-handed, and let me go."

He frowned, absently rubbing his face. "Why?"

"I think—I believe she might have some understanding of why I am doing this."

"Pray that she will enlighten me," he bit out. "Why, Eleanor? Why did you start this?"

She turned from his forbidding scowl.

"I asked you a question, madam."

"Do you really want to know?"

"Yes."

"I enjoy it."

"You enjoy stealing in and out of bedchambers, risking disgrace?"

"It was a way to pass the time."

"Does Mrs. Watson know who you are?" he inquired after a pause.

"Not yet."

"You've met her before?" he asked in surprise.

"We both attended a royal academy auction last summer to view Bellisant's watercolor exhibition."

He threw up his hands. "Of course."

Eleanor shrank down against the squabs. Sebastien's well-deserved disapproval stung. It would only be a matter of time before Audrey Watson placed her. The duchess would suffer a double humiliation, not only by having her husband's alleged indiscretions exposed, but by the most popular half-world hostess in society.

"I lost my favorite pistol," she muttered.

"A small price to pay for your freedom. I was ready to storm the house to bring you out."

"That would have caused a scene," she said with a reluctant smile.

He grunted. "It would have been nothing compared to what I'd have done had anything happened to you."

She sighed. It wasn't fair that all the blue in the world should be concentrated in one man's eyes.

Or that the concern in his voice dissipated every cold and resentful feeling she'd hidden behind to protect herself from falling in love with him again.

And it *wasn't* fair that for years she would have sworn he avoided looking at her when now his stare cut straight to her core.

"Why take these risks?"

He moved onto the seat beside her.

He was breaking her down with his concern.

She wanted to cry. "For the reward, of course."

"Which is?" He frowned. "Is it monetary? Did the duchess offer you wealth?"

"Not exactly. You do realize that the duke will return to England one day and become an important political figure?"

"It is assumed."

"There are benefits to being attached to those in power," she said slowly. "Benefits promised to one's family."

He shook his head. "Then this is not just make-believe over tea? The duchess *has* promised to reward you?"

"Yes. And *you*, as well as any children we might conceive. Is that the answer you wanted?"

"I'm not sure, but at least it is one I can understand." His hard chin brushed her cheek. "Promise me that you will not put yourself in danger again. I know you to be a woman of her word."

And yet he still had not been honest with her. Would he ever admit that he was not acting under the duke's orders?

She twirled her fingers into the crisp hair at his nape. "I do keep my word," she said softly.

He reached up to grasp her hand. "Are you done with this dangerous affair?"

She looked up into his piercing gaze. After her close call on Bruton Street, she had to admit that danger had lost some of its appeal. Or perhaps she had all the danger she could ever crave sitting right beside her.

"Well?" he said, his mouth close to hers.

"Not tonight. I have to think."

"Then think of this." He laced his fingers in hers. "There will be children for us," he said.

"But not the one we lost."

"I'm sorry for that, Eleanor."

"I know."

"Our children cannot have the Mayfair Masquer for their mother."

"Probably not," she murmured.

He looked down, shaking his head.

This, he thought in frustration, had been the threat to their marriage all along. Not Bellisant or any other young buck, but a monster of her own making. One larger than life. One who did not even exist but against whose fictional acclaim he must compete.

"Please," he said. "Don't let me lose you, too."

Chapter Twenty-two

Sebastien brought tea and the morning paper to his wife's bed the following morning. Her maid, Mary, shook her head in mute reproach when she intercepted him on his way back up the stairs.

Her gaze lowered to the paper tucked under his arm. "The mistress usually likes the tray set by her door after an evening abroad."

Which he supposed was Mary's way of reminding him that she knew more of Eleanor's habits than her husband did. "I'll manage," he said, winking at her.

She smiled back without enthusiasm. Sebastien had to grin. She really hadn't warmed to him. "Would you like me to have a tray sent up for you, my lord?"

Probably one that offered mercury-laden biscuits and hemlock tea.

"No, but thank you."

"Lord Boscastle—"

"Yes, Mary?"

"Forgive my impertinence, but her ladyship does not care to be awakened this early in the day."

"That I remember," he said wryly. "Leave her temper to me."

Indeed, when he carried the tray into the room and gently touched his wife on the shoulder, she sat up with a disoriented shout that caused him to reconsider the maid's warning. Eleanor had never been a sunny morning girl. He knew that from the start. Pity he hadn't known what a late-night firecracker she would become.

He sat the tray down on the bedside table, whistling cheerfully. He couldn't pretend he was not delighted that she would finally be all his again.

"I need to talk with you," he said before her drowsy beauty could distract him.

She stared blankly at the window as if she'd just risen from the dead.

"Later. Tomorrow. Next month. My thoughts are afog."

"Have a cup of tea first, darling. This cannot wait."

He stood at the window, fiddling with the curtains while giving her time to rouse. An entire pot of tea later, he heard the paper he had laid upon the bed rustle, a sharp gasp, and then silence.

He wondered what another man would do in his place. He did not know what it said for his character, but he'd rather be the husband of a woman who held London in thrall than one who had been cuckolded.

"Oh, Sebastien. This is awful."

He made a soothing sound in his throat. She was

staring aghast at the print that depicted the latest of the Masquer's exploits.

"You brought me this to gloat," she accused him, wide awake now.

"Untrue," he said.

"Did you read it?"

" 'What does he seek?' " he quoted, moving out of the late-morning light.

" 'A few crumbs of love and the attention of the most beautiful ladies in London,' " Eleanor read on. " 'Two Bow Street Runners were summoned to a notorious Bruton Street brothel at two o'clock in the morning. The proprietress gave evidence that she had caught and confronted the man whose appearances in numerous bedchambers has caused an uproar around the city these past three months.' " Eleanor groaned, quoting Mrs. Watson's report. " 'I convinced the Mayfair Masquer to unmask.' "

Sebastien sat down on the bed.

" 'And when he did—' "

" '—he revealed himself to be one of the most hideously scarred gentlemen it has ever been my misfortune to behold.' " He read over her shoulder, savoring the intimate contact. " 'Upon gently questioning his motives, he confessed that he was a Cornishman who had been disfigured in a mining accident. His only pleasure, this pitiful creature confided, is to pay secret visits to beautiful women who would shun him were his disfigurement revealed. His crime is a love of beauty and lonely desire.' "

"What a fable," Eleanor said with a little frown. "I've never set foot in Cornwall."

He was enticed by the scent of her tousled hair. "Would you like to spend a week in Penzance? We can walk along the beach together. I'd enjoy that."

She turned slightly at the shoulder, still for several heartbeats. "Did you *see* this picture of the Masquer?"

He laughed. "One could hardly miss it."

And they both stared down in grave contemplation at the caricature of a short, hawk-nosed gentleman who had not only removed his mask but also pulled down his trousers to bare his buttocks in a celestially rude gesture.

"He's got a bit of a cheek," Sebastien said unhelpfully.

"Did she have to make him out to be so unattractive?" she asked, biting her lip.

"Those of us who truly know him would tend to appreciate the diversionary tactic."

"I can't very well insist she revise her evidence."

He said, after another pensive silence, "At least it lays all his romantic pretensions to rest."

She sighed. "To be honest, I find his past more compelling than I did when—it didn't exist."

He wouldn't win. Surely he should ignore the devil on his shoulder that urged him to argue the point.

"But his element of intrigue is gone," he said. "He's more an object of sympathy now than a dashing figure."

"Poor Masquer," Eleanor murmured, smoothing her hand over the cartoon of her fallen self. "I had no idea he was so tragically scarred. I'm quite moved by his story."

"Perhaps," Sebastien said, wresting the paper from her hands, "we should place our attention on giving him a happy ending."

"I haven't failed, after all," she said, her spirits apparently rallying.

He gave her a look meant to quelch her resurging confidence. "You cannot do this again."

"I agree."

He lifted the tray from the bed and put it on the floor. "Ah. Shall we inform the duchess together?"

"If she sees this, which she will, I'm not certain I shall be able to show my face to her again."

"Not after this picture shows—"

He laid his head back onto the pillow; she leaned back against his chest. He knew she had evaded a commitment. And that he'd have to resort to more persuasive means to secure her word.

He waited a few moments to make his move, only to realize she had beaten him to the start line.

"I do have to disagree on your previous remark," she said, her fingers straying down his thigh.

She might be playing him, but still he savored the moment, the closeness that he was learning led to indescribable sex. His body heated. He smiled inwardly, wondering which of them would prove the more persuasive.

"The Masquer's romantic pretensions have *not*

been laid to rest," she ventured at his lack of response.

"To hell with it," he said, and pulled her between his thighs.

A knock at the door resounded through the chamber. Mary's frantic voice brought husband and wife off the bed and onto their feet.

"Lord Boscastle! My lady! I would never disturb you under other circumstances, but the duchess has sent her page to the door. It seems she is in high dudgeon. She demands to see both of you at four o'clock."

And then, as if she hadn't made the urgency of this request perfectly clear, she added, "In formal afternoon attire."

Eleanor did not need the mystical insight of Sir Perceval to understand what Sebastien had left unsaid about last night's fiasco. He knew she had blundered. But it was what he didn't know that worried her. She would shrivel up in shame if he found out that Mrs. Watson had been on the verge of seducing her. And even though the woman had apparently done her a good turn, she remembered that Audrey had mentioned a price. One did not become a demimonde hostess without an instinct for marketing.

Instinct.

When had Eleanor ever done anything *except* on instinct? Look where it had landed her. She was so upset that she practically vaulted over Sebastien like a steeplechaser to drive their curricle to their interview with the duchess.

He was clenching his teeth as she guided the horses past a crowd of urchins who stood watching a fight on the corner. It was that sort of day in London, the air unbreathable with soot and pent-up passions. If she slowed down, she knew she would see housewives and tradesmen studying the posters of the Mayfair Masquer that had been pasted up overnight.

Anonymous No Longer!

From the corner of her eye she saw Sebastien studying a large copy of the cartoon that showed the Masquer exposing his bum.

She could elude the entire city of London, she could trick the police, but not the man sitting beside her. "You needn't look so pleased about this."

"I'm not." He shook his head. "I'm just trying to hang on to my molars. It's not as if I enjoy seeing my wife's posterior on every corner and tavern window in town."

"That's not my—well, mine."

He glanced down. "There isn't any resemblance."

"Mrs. Watson must be having a good laugh at my expense."

"Possibly. But at least her description won't lead anyone to your door." He folded his arms. "I heard the footmen telling each other that the Prince of Wales has challenged the Masquer to give himself up and seek political sanctuary."

"At the Royal Pavilion in Brighton?" she asked. "With Carême doing the cooking?"

"His offer was not meant to be a private holiday," he said. "But it does indicate he understands the threat the Masquer faces from his admirers as well as the threat his existence poses to the rest of London."

Eleanor narrowed her eyes at him. "What do you mean?"

"It appears that his unmasking has sparked a wicked trend in Town."

"Breaking into ladies' bedchambers?" she asked in consternation.

"No. Pulling down a stranger's pantaloons and making a run for it."

She drove a little faster, a little more recklessly. "I hope the duchess doesn't hear that disturbing piece of news."

"She'd have to be walled in the family vault for it not to reach her," he said with infuriating certainty. "We can only hope she understands it was a bit of exaggeration."

"It was ever so much more than a bit of exaggeration!" She veered toward a group of pedestrians, who made a run for the pavement. "I did not take anything off except my mask."

"Did Audrey take anything off?" he asked casually.

"What a mind you have," she muttered.

He studied her from the side of his eye. "Well, she is a courtesan. And—"

She raised her brow. He stopped. She said, "Oh, do go on, he who owns a floating brothel, but has never frequented one."

He brushed a stray lock of hair from her cheek. "Darling, it's only that I have a curious mind. And the Masquer did take off his clothes, or so the story goes—"

"The story is an utter fabrication—"

"—according to the newspapers," he amended. "Good heavens, you do not think me a total dolt to believe everything I read."

"I—What are you doing?"

She drew back sharply on the reins as a pair of street beggars in plaid coats dove for the handful of shillings he had tossed into the street. She bumped down hard on the seat.

"You seem flustered," he said in a concerned voice.

"You are an oracle of perception."

He smiled. "Why don't you allow me to take the reins?"

She glanced up as a dark shape appeared in the sky. An enormous raven flew overhead, then settled spread-winged on a church spire. A messenger of impending evil, Sir Perceval and Mary would say, although Eleanor's father would only laugh in scorn at such a superstition.

How could a bird predict the future? he would ask her in his grumbly voice. Doesn't a predator have to eat? She recalled Sir Perceval's last prediction, of a large family and a happy marriage. Naturally she wished to see these hopes realized. Still, one could not believe in signs of good fortune without acknowledging the bad omens, too.

Sebastien swore, startling her. He placed his hand firmly upon her wrist. "Eleanor, I must insist." He did look rather white, now that she took a moment to examine him. "You are quite inattentive. Allow me to drive."

"As you like. I didn't realize that city driving unnerved you."

"It doesn't," he said through his teeth, as if she hadn't nearly bowled over a snake charmer at the curb and prompted a hackney driver to hurl curses back in their direction. "In fact, I could use some practice myself. An apple cart led by a lone donkey on a Norman lane isn't quite the same as navigating the streets of London."

She sighed and pulled over so that they could exchange positions. "You wrote me a letter once, from an apple cart," she reflected. "I always wondered how you managed to drive and write at the same time. And why that was the only letter you ever sent me."

"I wasn't driving at the time. I was hiding. And I was afraid it might be my last letter to you." He reached across her lap for the reins she had taken back without thinking. Their eyes met.

"Have I become that difficult to live with?" he asked.

She pursed her lips in admiration as he expertly merged back into the street between a coal-seller's cart and a lumbering carriage. "Perhaps *I've* become too accustomed to living alone." She didn't mean to provoke him, only to be honest, and he appeared to understand.

He nodded. "Then whatever I must do to remedy that ailment, be assured that I will."

"That seems more like a gauntlet thrown than a reaffirmation of our vows."

He laughed richly, as sure of himself as the day they'd met. "It might be, depending on you."

Chapter Twenty-three

❧ ❧

The former Kitty Packenham, now known as Catherine Wellesley, the Duchess of Wellington and wife of the most important man in the world, received Lord and Lady Boscastle in an aggrieved mood. Foreign and local newspapers lay scattered about the Aubusson carpet of her brother-in-law's drawing room in Apsley House. The duchess's usual empathy for Eleanor was displaced by a stab of envy as she surveyed the strikingly handsome man who accompanied her.

So, the officer-saboteur had finally come home. How he'd persuaded the duke to let him meddle in Kitty's private affairs she didn't know. It was only evident that the demon threatened to spoil all the fun. And if he wronged her dear friend and favorite agent, Eleanor, the duchess would make certain he'd pay. Still, he was pleasant on the eye in his black top hat, gray frock coat, and pleated black pantaloons.

She kicked one of the scurrilous papers describing her own husband's activities under a chair. The duke might have his hands full as the world's foremost arbitrator, but his family had paid a price. He might have died at war for all his children knew him.

"Lord Boscastle," she said as the elegant figure led his wife into Kitty's presence. "How delightful to see you home."

And how she wished it were Arthur standing in his place instead of this unfairly magnificent example of English manhood. It wasn't that long ago that her own beloved had been an impoverished captain of dragoons. Now, as Kitty sat on her duff collecting dust, the crowned heads of the Continent fêted her husband. And their empty-headed female counterparts pursued him between church sermons and state banquets.

Kitty prided herself on how she had endured both his neglect and the criticism of society with dignity and ducal grace. Let the morally bankrupt assign her the insulting sobriquet of ugly ambassadress—a dull sparrow unfit to soar into her conquering husband's lofty sphere.

His wife she was indeed, the mother of his two fine young sons. As holder of this privilege, Kitty had surmounted countless scandals. She viewed her obligation from the heights of unclouded maternal instinct. She understood her influence as one capable of charting a course that even the duke could not imagine. For her children she would sacrifice so that posterity might benefit from her absent husband's brilliance.

Arthur could defend himself against the physical

dangers of assassination plots and would-be abductions. Kitty's duty was to shield her family from the slings and arrows of outrageous scandal.

Even if she had indirectly unleashed the latest one herself.

Who could blame her if she took pleasure in the little intrigue that she and Eleanor had invented? Their game had given both neglected wives a small measure of revenge, although last evening's incident could have ended badly.

Of course the newspaper accounts could be wrong. The man caught in the seraglio could have been an impostor.

Kitty restrained a smile. How unseemly of her to have caused this stir while her husband was placating the world's powers. She ought to feel ashamed of herself.

She didn't. She lived vicariously through the adventures of her spying ring.

"Your grace," Sebastien said with aplomb as he bowed before her chair. "Time has not touched you, except to enhance the power of your beauty."

"It has also enhanced the power of your silver tongue, Boscastle," she replied with a faint sigh. "No wonder Eleanor has not visited me of late. I have missed her company."

Eleanor curtsied. "The young lords are now well, your grace?"

The duchess's eyes darkened in worry. "Lord Arthur has not been himself since his last cold. He eats nothing and brandishes a new bruise on his shins every day. I fear a blood ailment. I have written to your father in France. He is the only physician I trust."

This announcement was followed by a loud whoop of laughter from the adjoining room. The nursemaid shouted in warning to the boys to beware of the falling screen. A crash followed. A man's voice, familiar to Eleanor, shouted in exasperation that he could not work with the nursemaid bellowing out a caution at every moment, and could she not allow the boys to be boys.

The voice belonged to Bellisant, Eleanor realized, and when she turned her head she caught Sebastien regarding her in an appraising but self-assured manner.

"Sir Nathan has promised to complete his portrait of the boys before my husband comes home for Christmas," the duchess said, wincing as a door slammed in the anteroom. "Although how he can work when Ares and his little general refuse to sit for a single moment is past my understanding."

Neither Eleanor nor Sebastien replied.

Eleanor was imagining what it would be like to have her own children. Of course she would have their portraits painted. Of course, being Boscastles, they would be rambunctious, brimming with charm. When she looked up, she saw Sebastien studying her again in that same self-assured manner.

But this time he was smiling. And she thought they might be thinking the same thing.

The duchess sighed.

Eleanor blinked, remembering why she had been summoned here. Certainly not for tea and cream cakes. One did not celebrate a monumental disgrace.

As if attuned to the underlying tension, the duchess gestured to the newspapers that lay upon the ottoman in front of her.

"Please sit." She picked up the closest paper. "I assume you have both read the morning news? May I quote? 'Masquer Bares All for Abbess.'"

Eleanor looked up from the array of morning editions that revealed the Masquer in his indignious glory. "Your grace," she said as she met the duchess's gaze, "I am mortified—"

"I should imagine so," Kitty said with an acerbic smile. "In Mrs. Watson's house, of all places, and by London's finest ladybird. It must have been a shocking affair."

Sebastien nodded in agreement. "To all parties involved."

The duchess narrowed her eyes in speculation. "Which one of you was caught?"

Eleanor wished suddenly for a cloak of invisibility. From Audrey's deliberate misaccounting of the Masquer's description, to Fleet Street's detailed if deceptive caricature, the culprit could be said to resemble Sebastien as much as it did her.

Until Kitty had posed the question as to which of them was caught, however, she had not considered that *he* could be suspected of the previous evening's embarrassment.

But it made sense. He and Eleanor were now working together.

"Your grace," she began again, "I can say in complete honesty that it was—"

"—me," Sebastien cut in smoothly. "I should have known better than to enter an establishment of such disrepute during its busiest hours. I'd have been wiser to employ a more subtle means of infiltration. My competitive nature overcame my better judgment."

Eleanor lifted her brow. She doubted the duchess would believe this bald deception, but his chivalry moved her, nonetheless. Sebastien, gallant and strong, lying through his teeth to defend his wife's impossible aspirations.

Oh, how she resented his cleverness. She was indebted to him more now than on their wedding day. He had saved her bacon and would never let her forget it. She wondered briefly whether he had planned this sacrifice all along, or had merely submitted to impulse.

"Your grace," she said, for the third time, "my husband is too valiant."

"As is mine," the duchess said in a rueful voice. She stared at the papers on the floor. "Military reviews, operas, plays, and suppers. There is not a woman in Paris, on the entire Continent, who does not worship at the Duke of Wellington's boots."

Sebastien drew his breath. "When one is as great as—"

"Who is La Grassini?" the duchess lamented, her voice rising, her toe poking at one of the papers. "Who are these women without shame and self-respect that they interfere with his duties? These harlots, these—"

"I have never heard of La Grassini," Eleanor broke in tactfully. "She cannot be anyone of international acclaim."

"She's a nothing," Sebastien said, with a dismissive shrug. "A little nobody. An overrated squeaky-voiced coquette."

"Do you know her?" Eleanor inquired after a long pause.

"Well, not personally, but one draws certain conclusions."

"Perhaps you have not read the newspapers," the duchess said in a tone that could have been criticism or praise. "She is a famous opera singer."

"Not as famous as *you*," Sebastien said.

Eleanor rolled her eyes. Lord, but the man knew how to lay on the charm.

The duchess heaved a sigh. "I don't suppose you were able to get the letters."

"No," Sebastien and Eleanor answered at the same time.

Eleanor frowned at him.

He smiled at her, then looked at the duchess and said, "Another time. Rest assured. I have my ways."

"He certainly does," Eleanor said with a tight smile.

The duchess fingered the pearls at her throat.

"All charm aside, Boscastle, it does occur to me that Eleanor never got caught on any of her previous missions."

His brow furrowed. "Well, neither did I."

"Until last night," Eleanor whispered, suddenly not feeling guilty at all for letting him take the blame. After all, he had deceived her about working for the duke. And, even worse, he'd made her want him desperately. Let the rat gnaw his way out of this.

"What I meant," the duchess hastened to add, "is that perhaps this is a mission of too much delicacy for a man."

"It's damned dangerous," he said with a scowl.

The duchess gave him a soothing smile. "You must have been frightened to death when they caught you last night."

"No, I was only frightened for—your reaction."

The duchess turned pink.

Sebastien glanced at Eleanor with a grin of triumph that made her want to slap him with one of the duchess's newspapers.

And then she glanced down at a cartoon of the Masquer's plump behind.

"People know better than to trust anonymous journalists," Eleanor said, nudging the paper under her chair.

"Who can the people trust?" the duchess snapped back. "Not our poor mad sovereign in Windsor. Prinny is a proper mess. Even Lord Byron is tainted by some type of unspeakable scandal."

"Incest," Sebastien murmured.

"I said *unspeakable*." A sigh fluttered from her lips. "To whom, I beg you—to whom can an honest Englishman turn to in these troublesome times?"

Sebastien flashed her a smile. "To *you*, your grace."

Her mouth trembled in wry pleasure. "I am hardly a political force, flatterer. I suppose you charmed your way out of last night's situation."

Sebastien hesitated, his blue eyes twinkling.

The duchess raised her hand. "Say nothing. It never happened. The letters will be found. I trust you. That said, I prefer you give me any impressions you have received from Paris of late."

The request signaled a change of direction.

The duchess rang for refreshments. Soon a battalion of servants sallied back and forth bearing pots of tea, coffee, and her grace's preferred afternoon ratafia, a liqueur of steeped fruit and almonds.

The conversation stayed on safer topics until the clamor of voices from the exterior hallway brought the appointment to an end. "That is young Ares with his army of one and their Amazonian nursemaid again," the duchess said. "I must go." She gave Sebastien a fond smile. "Young boys can be terribly naughty at times, can't they?"

He bowed. "Young girls can be worse. Or so I've heard," he added with a sidelong glance at Eleanor.

"You will be careful, both of you?" the duchess said in hesitation.

He straightened. "My wife has agreed to let me

handle this matter entirely. She realizes that I possess certain skills in subterfuge."

"If not in subtlety," Eleanor said in a wry voice.

Sebastien followed Eleanor through the vast hallway. He let her lead the way, noting that she walked
straight past the open door of the gallery in which
Bellisant worked, his slender white-shirted form
wreathed in light.

Even if she were tempted to look back, the impulse was thwarted by the two red-jacketed little
soldiers who jumped out at her from behind a Gre-
cian statue.

Her shriek echoed to the ceiling, intertwined with
gusts of boyish laughter.

"Help me!" she cried. "I'm under attack!"

"Where do you think you're going?" The eldest
boy, the duke's nine-year-old heir Arthur, advanced
on Sebastien while his brother took Eleanor prisoner. "We're at war, you know."

"War is all very well and good." Sebastien watched
young Charles wrap a rope around Eleanor's arms as
she pretended to plead for mercy. "But—"

"War is very good," the boy stated. "My father is
the best general in the world."

"True, but—may I untie my wife?"

"No."

"Why not?"

"Because she's the enemy. She'll get shot dead in
a minute. You can collect her body then. That is,
whatever's left of it after we torture her."

"She won't crack," Sebastien confided. "She's one tough prisoner, and I ought to know."

Sebastien watched Eleanor wriggling her shoulders like a moth trapped in a cobweb. She made a fetching captive. And he couldn't help noticing that the boys were fond of her.

"I prefer to take my prisoners alive, thank you. Especially when one of them is my wife."

Charles jabbed his wooden sword into his brother's armpit. "That's stupid. Lady B isn't your wife. She's Sir Nathan's."

"No," Sebastien said, forcing a smile. "She's mine. *I* married her some time ago when I was a soldier."

The two boys shared a look, shrugged, and resumed their swordplay, lurching and retreating into the room from which they'd escaped.

Even after Eleanor threw off her rope, she did not make any attempt to acknowledge Bellisant. And Sebastien would have noticed because he was watching her like a hawk. Nor did the artist betray that he was aware of her presence, although Sebastien saw through the half-opened door that he'd drifted to the windows and appeared to be deep in thought.

"I don't want to be captured again, Sebastien," Eleanor whispered over his shoulder. "Let's escape before the boys decide we're both from the enemy camp."

She took his hand. He closed his fingers over hers, a protective instinct he could not explain. Something more menacing than swordfights or even jealousy overshadowed the moment. He wanted to take her home and keep her safe, to himself. He angled his head.

"Do you intend to thank me for defending you to the duchess?"

She laughed slyly. "Can you at least wait for a private moment to demand your due?"

He slid his other hand beneath her arm. His head lowered to hers. "Surely in a house this spacious, no one would notice if I kissed you."

"Behave yourself in front of those boys," she breathed. "And do not stand so close to me with that look in your eye."

"What look would that be, Lady Boscastle?"

"The one that is lighting a fire inside me."

"Then let us go home and stoke it."

As he escorted her toward the two servants in gold-braided livery who awaited their exit, the murmur of Bellisant's voice and a chorus of youthful complaints drifted into the hall.

A wistful smile crossed Eleanor's face. "Listen."

"To the shouting?" He winced. "Painful, isn't it?"

"It's a pleasant noise, that of children," she said. "I had no brothers or sisters when I was growing up. I only had Will."

He glanced around.

The duke's heir stood at the end of the stairs, one foot planted on his younger brother's chest, his toy sword raised to deliver the coup de grâce.

"I have three brothers," he said when Eleanor

stared back to question why he hadn't followed. "And I never appreciated them until it was too late."

"It isn't too late, Sebastien."

He nodded. "Perhaps. I don't know how they feel, though."

"If they are anything like you, I imagine they miss those days, too."

Only one person in London knew that Audrey Watson, tutor to courtesans and young noblemen alike, was as much a fictional invention as was the Mayfair Masquer. Unlike the notorious person Audrey had confronted last night, however, she had no intention of being caught, blackmailed, or exposed to the same ruthless society that paid her bills. She'd worked her way up in the half-world, sometimes on her back, mostly with her wits.

Her former life did not exist.

Married once to a tyrant, imprisoned by a brother who had betrayed his country, she had nothing but painful memories of her past. The present, at least, was of her own design. She was safe, if scandalous, a woman who controlled her own destiny.

Lord Heath Boscastle was the man who had saved her years ago when she had given up all hope. From him she had learned there was no trait more compelling than honor.

There wasn't a wile in her book of naughty secrets that would seduce him. She wouldn't have insulted him by trying, even though she teased all the Boscastle men when she met them at a party.

Audrey might envy the women these beautiful men had married. Nevertheless, she would not give up her freedom for anyone.

Loyalty, however, needed to be repaid with interest.

She kissed Heath's cheek as he entered her private suite. He had come within an hour of her message.

His black hair was swept back from his strong face. His intelligent blue eyes took in every detail. Lean and impeccably dressed, he was a masterpiece.

He unbuttoned the three lower buttons of his dark-gray greatcoat and sat in the chair by the door.

A Boscastle always sent invisible sparks through a room.

Some of them set fires by merely smiling.

Heath had a habit of looking into one's eyes during his conversations. He had perfected the art of the unnerving silence.

Audrey suspected that he could interpret what wasn't said as fluently as he could what was spoken. Only after they parted did she realize that while she had shared secrets she'd vowed to take to the grave, he had not revealed anything about himself. Or about anyone else, to his credit.

"How may I help you, Audrey?"

She shook her head. The house was quiet this early in the afternoon, and she preferred loud noises, disruptions, to the stillness. She had wrestled with her decision for hours after she realized whom exactly she had unmasked last night.

It went against her instincts to betray a woman in

trouble, but she trusted Heath's judgment better than her own.

She wasn't certain that in abetting Eleanor Boscastle she had done her a service.

He waited.

If she changed her mind and asked him to leave, he would go without another question. The quiet had become too unsettling. She glanced down at the newspaper covered beneath her yellow riding gloves, then looked up.

Not quick enough.

His gaze followed.

He'd seen the headline. He needed little else to put everything together.

"You've read about my exciting confrontation?"

He smiled thinly. "You were brave to beard such an infamous miscreant and turn his description over to the police."

"You think that it was brave of me?"

"I thought that it was . . . interesting."

"And?"

"I'm certain that your reason for doing it was interesting as well." He exhaled, glancing down at the paper. "And that however it involves me shall soon be revealed."

He paused, allowing her time to respond. She didn't say anything. He gestured with his hand. ". . . shall soon be revealed."

She stared at him.

"Soon," he said. "This afternoon would be nice."

"A member of the Boscastle family is in trouble," she said finally.

He laughed. "Did the sun rise this morning? One of us is *always* in trouble. But surely you didn't ask me here to—"

They both stared down at the cartoon of the bare-buttocked poseur who had made more than one dowager call for a vinaigrette in her drawing room that same morning. Heath had endured a similar embarrassment himself three years ago, only then it had been a sketch of his privates that had taken London by storm. A man never lived that down. Especially when those parts were involved.

"I can't say I recognize anyone in my family having that big a behind," he said. "Well, possibly an aunt or two. And there was a time when my cousin Gabriel was suspected. But he's not—"

"It isn't your aunt. Nor Gabriel. It's your cousin-in-law."

Once Audrey started to confess, of course, she couldn't stop.

Nor did he interrupt again. She felt relieved to have unburdened herself, for now Eleanor's fate was no longer in her hands. God knew Audrey despised those who passed judgment on others.

Heath, naturally, did not offer any opinions on the behavior of Eleanor Boscastle.

He thanked Audrey for her trust in him and took the letters Eleanor had sought. He was as cool as always when he left.

In fact, he was so cool that she wondered whether she had enlightened him, or whether he had known the Masquer's identity all along.

If so, then Eleanor Boscastle did indeed work for the good of England. And Audrey was glad she had followed her instincts and let the Masquer escape.

Chapter Twenty-four

❧ ❧

Eleanor looked up from her writing desk to see Sebastien emerge from his dressing closet in a walking cape and black woolen evening wear. She was still in her Chinese silk robe, comfortable from a hot bath and a cup of chocolate.

"Have I forgotten an entertainment?" she asked, studying his elegant figure.

"*I* have an appointment."

He didn't elaborate.

She put down her pen. "It's almost dark. And it's misting."

"It's still early." He paused behind her chair. "I'll take Teg along for the walk. You'll have an hour to catch up on your neglected correspondences."

She lowered her gaze. "We have not discussed how to find the last of the letters in Castle Eaton." She glanced up. "On the coast."

"I know where the castle is."

She sifted through her tray of letters, waiting for an argument. After a moment passed she swiveled around and said, "The earl is an eccentric. His current wife has ruled his life for the last five years and is said to have tricked him into marriage. One would assume the countess would not dispose of any incriminating letters when she could use them for future insurance. If I were her, I'd hide them under lock and key."

He straightened. "Well, you're not her, and you're not that other fellow anymore, either. And I have my own way of finding what is hidden, even what is under lock and key."

"Oh, yes. Those ways you have."

She lowered the letter she was holding to her lap. "Have *you* already made a plan to infiltrate the castle?"

He sat in the chair across from her.

"Perhaps," he said cautiously.

She drew in a breath. "Without me?"

"Without you? No. The Masquer, however, has retired." His demeanor grew pensive. "It's time for a new strategy. A plausible one with references of character."

She cast him a cynical smile. "So you're planning to assume a new identity?"

"I can grow a mustache."

"How superior of you."

"And a beard. I speak passable Italian."

She studied the cards on her lap, unable to resist teasing him. "I can just picture you at the castle revels. Scaramouche with his sweeping cloak and melodramatic prose. Very subtle. Quite the dashing scoundrel. Perhaps you could do a sword fight up and down the stairs."

He looked undeterred. "We agreed that I would run the risk from now on."

"What if you are recognized?"

"*I* won't be caught." He stretched back in the chair. "Better yet, *you* won't be placed in jeopardy."

She rose, tossing her letters back onto the desk. "I suppose you're right. Loveridge's plan would never have worked."

"What was his plan?" he inquired curiously.

"I was to appear during the party as a new chambermaid, a position that affords access—"

"—to gentlemen who wish their beds warmed by more than a hot brick," he said sourly. "I do not like the idea of my wife attending a party at which debauched acts are a possibility."

"A possibility?" She picked up his gloves from the dressing table. "The guests attend for no other reason. But that is neither here nor there."

He took his gloves from her and reached across the bed for his hat. "Not that I'm rubbing your whiskers in it, Cat, but after last night's capture, you have no choice but to let me assume command."

"Perhaps I overreacted last night."

"No, darling," he said quietly, and drew on his gloves. "We can discuss my plan when I come back."

He ran down the stairs, still early for his meeting with his London contact. The dog was howling in the garden, locked out by the servants who had gathered in the street to watch an Italian puppet show. As he let Teg into the house, he noticed a boy sitting on a bench by the back door. He clutched a small pouch in one hand, and a stone in the other, which Sebastien guessed would serve as a weapon in case the howling Teg attacked.

"What are you doing here?" Sebastien asked.

"I've medicine for her ladyship. I knocked, but no one's 'ome."

"Medicine?" Sebastien confiscated the pouch and stone. He peered inside at a green phial of a substance that looked disgusting.

"It's a blood tonic," the boy said, grimacing. "Don't drop it. It stinks to 'ell. She's gotta drink up fast."

"A blood tonic?" Sebastien said in concern.

He fished in his pocket for a coin. A guinea. Too much, or not enough? He had never seen Eleanor take a drop of medicine since he'd known her.

He stared dubiously at the phial. He didn't want to think of Eleanor sick. She never fussed about such things. But he remembered that her mother had died young, of a mysterious ailment that had stopped her heart. There was an odd astrological marking on one side of the bottle, and tiny seeds floating about in amber oil. He squinted to read the inscription: Agnus Castus.

"What are you doing here, Alex?" a crisp voice of authority demanded over Sebastien's shoulder.

He lowered the bottle, the seeds sinking to the murky red-amber dregs.

The boy backed away from the bench.

Mary, Eleanor's maid, marched out onto the step in a mist-sprinkled shawl. She nodded at Sebastien. "I'll take that, my lord. It makes a hideous mess if it isn't tightly stopped."

"It's for my wife?"

She nodded. "You wouldn't want to take it, trust me."

"Why would I want her to drink it, then?"

"It's a help to females for babies and things I don't wanna know about," the boy muttered, glaring back at Mary's tight, indignant face. "Well, sorry," he said defensively. "No telling how it'd influence his manhood if he drank it."

"I shall report your impertinence," Mary cried as he scampered off with a grin. "You aren't paid to blether or to dispense medical advice."

Sebastien handed Mary the bottle. "I'm late. Will you give this to my wife—assuming it is safe for her to take?"

"I'll be happy to, my lord."

"I—thank you, then."

"It tastes worse every time," Eleanor said a few minutes later, handing Mary the silver spoon with a grimace. "Should I take another? No. Listen to me, the surgeon's daughter. More is not better."

"Dr. Went's is the best apothecary in town." Mary

put the elixir in the closet cupboard. "It's behind the other bottles, my lady."

"Do you think it will work?" Eleanor asked.

The maid hesitated at the door, allowing herself a smile. "It worked for me. But I—"

"You haven't spoken of Harold in two months. I know you're worried, but perhaps he's turned himself in." Mary's only son had written last spring to ask for cash, claiming he was buying a small shop. Another letter arrived a few weeks later from Mary's brother, warning her that the boy had stolen a carriage and that the shop had never existed. "How old is he now?"

"Twenty-two."

"Give him time. Perhaps it was just a prank to impress his friends."

"He has no friends," Mary said. "None that are decent."

Time might heal some wounds, but it made others fester. "Perhaps he could come here to visit you. Or we could find him a position in the house."

Mary shook her head. "He's better off in the country. The city is too full of temptation for a boy like him."

"I'm sure there's more good than bad in him, if he's anything like you."

"I hoped that once, too. But he's got his father's ways. Running off after one scheme or another."

Eleanor nodded, trying to look as if she understood. Was it possible to lose hope in your own child?

"I don't know how it happened," Mary said quickly, turning her head before Eleanor could see her crying. "One day his father turned into a man I've never met, and then his son grew up in his image. If I'd known before I never would have—"

Married him? Not conceived the child who now caused her so much heartbreak? Would every woman go back if she could and make another choice? Eleanor remembered stolen kisses on a sultry summer night in Spain. Would she give up Sebastien to have made a safer marriage?

"There's still time for your son to change," she said.

Mary glanced back. "True. But he's done things that nothing can change."

"It can't be that bad."

Mary's silence said it was. Her son had committed other crimes.

Mary gave her a watery smile. "Don't forget your cordial, Lady Boscastle."

She nodded. Some instincts were stronger than death or destiny. If a woman listened to every warning about the woes of loving men and having children, she'd run before that first kiss and refuse to hold an infant niece or nephew in her lap at a dinner party. She would never, ever breathe in the scent of a newborn baby's skin. If she chained up her heart the first time she heard that love could change frogs into princes and forest huts into enchanted castles, she would become a well-respected witch in her own right. She wouldn't be tempted to buy slippers that hurt her feet or prick her own finger in her father's tent and wait for the one man to walk in and make her believe in magic.

He pondered his last conversation with Eleanor on his way to the wharf to meet his London contact. A chambermaid, indeed. It was enough to addle his brains. Fortunately the sight of Lord Heath Boscastle seated in the shallop's cabin brought his mind back into focus.

So this was to be his home contact. They had been boys when they'd last met.

Since then, Heath had become a respected officer, a spymaster and code-breaker whose sense of honor had inspired commissioned and irregular soldiers alike.

For a very brief moment, as Heath rose to grip his hand, they were merely cousins again.

"It's been a hell of a long time," Sebastien said, laughing.

Heath shook his head. "I can't quite believe it."

"Nor can I."

Sebastien and his brothers had raced against the other Boscastle cousins at picnics and birthdays. On the rare occasion Sebastien had gone over to the London side, but not for long. The respective brothers always ended up back together before they went home.

By the time they'd piled into their carriages, calling out threats and insults to one another, the bond of family relations had become rather frayed. But it

had never been completely severed. It was only after the death of Sebastien's father that his branch of
the family had broken off from the London Boscastles. It was a shame, really.

"It's good to see you again, Heath."

"And you."

Heath sat again, facing the door, in exactly the
same spot Sebastien always occupied. He even
wedged his left shoulder against the wood shelf of
a mermaid's bosom, which to anyone else might
have appeared as if he were simply making himself
comfortable. But Sebastien recognized a man who
never let down his guard when he met another man.

He waited, curious, as Heath reached into his
waist pocket to withdraw two letters tied with a
crimson ribbon.

"These are yours," Heath said with a fleeting
smile. "Courtesy of a well-wisher who advises me
she is glad someone has use of them."

Mrs. Watson's letters. So it was true that she had
a weakness for the Boscastles. He couldn't wait to
see Eleanor's reaction. Would she be indignant? Relieved?

He hoped she would be impressed. How many
wives in England would treasure forgotten letters
over diamonds and social status?

Only his.

"Have you read them?" he asked.

"No. It's your game. However, if you require my
advice, I'm not hard to persuade. I enjoy solving
puzzles, if that is what this is."

A modest admission.

"I may indeed ask for your help."

Sebastien put the letters down on his desk. His hand still trembled at unpredictable intervals. Most men didn't notice. Others assumed he was prone to drink. But when Heath looked up, there was understanding in his eyes.

"I know you have only recently come home," Heath said. "Because of your past experience, I deemed it necessary to tell you we have reason to believe an assassination attempt will be made against Wellington."

Plot. Purpose. The tide always came in. "By whom?"

"We have our eye on a group of home-bred radicals. We thought them to be harmless at first, but current information suggests otherwise."

Sebastien stared past Heath as a barge drifted along the river. A British prime minister had been assassinated in the House of Commons only four years ago. "The duke isn't home until Christmas."

"This is what he told the duchess," Heath said. "But you and I know that he is determined to set both the world and his country to rights and will sacrifice to do so."

"Between Paris and London any number of political causes might divert him. An ambush, perhaps. What do you wish me to do?"

"Be alert. As you know, these plots usually blow over before they come to anything."

"Perhaps I should not go to this masquerade at

Castle Eaton that my wife is set on. You wouldn't believe what she is planning. Or perhaps you would. You know about Mrs. Watson." He laughed. "Chasing after frivolous letters when a plot is in progress makes little sense."

"But a marriage is a priority, is it not?"

"I shouldn't be surprised that you understand."

Heath stood. "I shall be in touch. And if your wife wishes to go to that party it can be arranged. Sometimes one gleans useful information from gossip."

For some time after Heath left, Sebastien sat and listened to the water lapping against the boat. At first his mind raced. He would give the letters to his wife immediately, and she would not read them. Should he?

An assassination plot.

Why here? It didn't make sense. But that only indicated he had missed something. One had to be more vigilant. It would help to know against whom.

Would Eleanor complain if he crept off to frequent clubs and public houses? A smile settled on his lips. Not his wife. She would only fret if he kept his work a secret from her again.

Chapter Twenty-five

❧ ❧

Eleanor wore an off-the-shoulder figured silk gown at supper and a strand of pearls. She had allowed Mary to arrange her hair in a knot with a few curls that fell in studied negligence at her nape.

"That's better," Mary said in satisfaction.

Eleanor had even dusted herself with a beautifying powder that promised to plump up her cheeks and décolletage.

She decided she had delayed the inevitable long enough. It was time to act like a wife and permit her handsome husband to be the only man of the house, as it were. Unfortunately he was so lost in thought that she might have been wearing a tablecloth and dusted in soot for all he seemed to notice. He had been in the most absentminded mood since returning home from his walk with Teg.

He looked . . . not himself.

He kept glancing at the clock on the fireplace mantel, and not at her. She tapped her spoon lightly against the salt cellar. He didn't notice.

She dropped the spoon. He glanced at the table, then looked at the door. "How was your meeting with whomever you met?" she asked quietly.

He shook his head. "Fine."

"Was it really?"

"Yes."

"It sounds interesting," she said, leaning forward on her elbows to prompt him.

He shrugged vaguely. "Oh, you know how these things are."

"No. I don't. Would you like to tell me?"

"Tell you what?"

"About your meeting, dearest."

"I already told you. It was fine."

"For heaven's sake," she said. "Any other wife would suspect you were up to no good."

His eyes flashed with humor. "Speaking as a wife *who* is usually up to no good herself."

"I am reforming," she said in an offended voice.

He lifted his brow. "Oh?"

"Can't you see?"

"What am I supposed to see?"

She rose from the table and approached his seat. He sat back and waited, slowly lifting his gaze to hers. Her heart hammered in her chest.

His eyes gleamed in the candlelight with an emotion she had not seen in a long time. Neither doubt nor fear, but something that stirred her nerves.

Passion of a design other than amorous. Purpose. That was it.

And whatever had sparked this energy made him

irresistible. She stopped behind his chair, twining her arms around his neck.

"You have ignored me all evening," she whispered in his ear. "If I am being forced into retirement, I insist I am at least informed of your adventures. What happened?"

He turned his head. "I wouldn't call it an adventure."

"It had to be more exciting than having Mary take hot tongs to your hair and—"

"It hasn't even been a whole day," he said with a dark smile. "You haven't retired with grace."

"—and you didn't even notice."

"Notice?"

"My hair. The curls that fall just so to captivate a husband's attention."

He studied her for several moments. "You look very lovely, but then you always do."

"What happened when you went out?" she demanded. "Please, Sebastien. I know something is going on."

"I met my cousin at the wharf. Heath Boscastle."

"I take it this wasn't a family reunion."

"He works with a man named Colonel Hartwell of the—"

"I know who Hartwell is." She sank down into the empty chair beside his, staring at him in dread. "He didn't ask you to take another assignment? He did. And it's dangerous, which is why you're bristling with excitement, you selfish thing. How could you keep this from me?"

He blinked. "I'm not bristling. And I'm not keeping anything from you yet. This is a different sort of assignment."

"Are you allowed to tell me?"

"Yes. As long as you don't—"

Some sort of commotion arose from the street. People cheering and banging what sounded like pots and pans. Raised voices resounded from the entrance hall as a footman hurried to the door to investigate. Eleanor and Sebastien glanced toward the window simultaneously at the clatter of coach wheels that rattled past the house.

"What is that row, Burton?" Sebastien called in annoyance.

The footman appeared at the door. "I'm not sure, my lord," he replied in bewilderment. "There seems to be a mob gathering at the square."

Sebastien made to rise. Eleanor grasped hold of his hand. "Never mind the mob. What did your cousin want from you?"

"Vigilance. Someone in the city is plotting to kill Wellington."

"My lady, the duchess?" she asked, her voice low with worry.

He frowned. "The Duke of Wellington."

"But he isn't here."

"He will be at Christmas."

She felt a chill. "What a ghastly notion. The children would be with him. They could be harmed."

"It might come to nothing," he said quietly.

"What are we supposed to do in the meantime?"

"*I* am merely to keep my ears and eyes open. You, well, I'll ask you to do the same, but from a distance."

"Would you like to wall me in the West Wing?"

"I wouldn't mind. Now that you mention it, it's not a bad idea. Impractical though. Perhaps you could simply be attentive during your daily activities. Listen to gossip. You know, mine the resources of those street girls who like to play spy."

She put her hand to her throat. "You're right. I *did* hear something about a plot at the market last week."

"Oh?"

"Yes. The butcher's wife planned to do in a pullet for one of her customer's dinners."

"Excellent work," he said dryly. His gaze flickered over her. She had the sense that it was the first time all evening that he'd truly seen her. "Have you done something different to your hair?"

For a moment she could have cheerfully murdered him.

"I—" He faltered. "And that dress—the pearls— were you—"

"Trying to seduce you?"

His eyes glittered in sudden understanding. "Is it too late to take you up on that offer?" he asked with a decadent smile.

Her heart thumped in anticipation. She decided she'd ask Mary to buy more beautifying powder. And tomorrow she would agree to go shopping with her old boarding-school friend, Lady Phoebe

Haywood, whose invitations to tea, balloon ascensions, and other meaningless pastimes she had rudely ignored.

Tomorrow she truly meant to become a wife in every sense of the word.

Even if tonight she wasn't a lady at all.

Chapter Twenty-six

❧ ❧

They rose from the table at the same moment. Sebastien could not have testified in a court of law whether she reached for him first or he pulled her against him. He'd been preoccupied for hours, but now that he realized she had been angling for his attention, he was entirely hers.

"You can leave the pearls on," he said, kissing her on the mouth, then the throat, and her prettily dusted décolletage. "But everything else—"

Another chorus of cheers and light explosions erupted from the street. Sebastien let go of her and rushed into the hall. His entire household stood in the doorway staring at the swell of people marching toward the pub. Firecrackers shot up into the sky from the square garden.

"What is it?" Eleanor whispered over his shoulder, vying for a view.

"I don't know. Some sort of celebration. Stay here a minute while I find out."

"But I'm—good gracious. I think that's Will stuck

behind those carts. I hope he hasn't been injured."

He turned and gave her a distracted kiss on the cheek. "Give Will my regards and ask him to come back tomorrow."

"Ask him yourself. He's almost here."

He glanced down the street and saw Will running toward them. A line of carriage lights burned in the mist like the eyes of a dozen banshees. The waiting horses whickered uneasily.

"Get inside the house!" Will shouted. "They're going insane!"

"There must be some sort of important person passing through," Eleanor observed. "I wonder who it is."

"I'll find out," Sebastien said.

"But we—"

"And I'll be right back. I need to know what is going on."

More flickering lights shifted in the fog. He ran past Will on the pavement and muttered, "Both of you, go inside. And behave yourselves."

"You don't need to ask me twice," Will retorted.

Sebastien hurried toward the square to investigate whatever mischief was afoot. If he hadn't promised Heath Boscastle that he would stay on the alert, he would have thought twice about leaving the house again.

He might even have thought long enough to realize that his dearly beloved was the cause of the uproar raging across Town.

*   *   *

Will handed his coat to the maid and a crumpled edition of the evening news to Eleanor. "Do you think that I should go with him?" he asked, turning back to the door.

She cast a concerned look into the street. "No. He'll be fine. And you aren't supposed to come here at all hours anymore. I'm making an effort to reform."

They looked at each other for several moments. Suddenly her conscience stung her. She knew her cousin had thought Sebastien would never come home to stay, and now he had not only returned but had displaced Will. She blamed herself for encouraging him to visit at all hours.

"I'm sorry," she said, smiling wistfully. "Reforming isn't easy on me, either."

He grinned back at her. "You might have no choice. Read the news."

Her frown deepening, she walked toward the wall sconce for better light and scanned the paper, skimming over the usual heartening rumors of riots, sedition, and Prinny's excesses, to a subject closer to home. A little too close, it seemed.

So many people have volunteered to patrol Mayfair after midnight that the police have resorted to drawing names at the station from a high-crowned hat for the honour. Several gentlemen have turned themselves in, professing guilt. The lock-up rooms are overflowing with impostors.

The Bow Street Office has stated it might be-
come necessary to conduct a door-to-door search
for the Masquer's own protection.

She lowered the paper. "Well, at least the police can't start searching tonight with whatever celebration is in progress."

Will paused. "Don't you understand?"

The blood drained from her face. "You mean that the mob—"

"Yes. They are celebrating the Masquer. And staging their own hunt for him."

Chapter Twenty-seven

❦ ❦

Eleanor practically dragged Sebastien through the doorway into the hall when he returned an hour later. He was relieved to find her as he'd left her. And also that her cousin had gone home. He wasn't in a mood for Will's hysterics.

He glanced into the darkened corridors, then back at the door. Everything appeared to be in order—except for the small arsenal of brickbats, walking sticks, and parasols stacked against the hallstand.

His brows rose.

"Are we preparing to walk in bad weather or build a nursery?" he asked, unfastening his cloak.

"You didn't see the swarm of people?"

"Of course I did."

"They were hunting for the Masquer, Sebastien."

"Yes," he agreed. "We have a problem on our hands."

"What are you going to do?" she asked, following at his heels. "I cannot leave the house alone."

"Yes, you can." He hesitated. "But the Masquer can't."

She gave him a baleful look. "Nor can he handle an impassioned mob should his identity be discovered."

"Isn't it a good thing I'm here to take care of you?"

"I'm not convinced that even you could hold back that crowd." She waved a newspaper under his nose. "Read this. The police are—"

"Yes. I've heard. It's all the people in the street can talk about." He drew her against him, enfolding her in his arms. "You have caused quite a scandal, my love."

"It wasn't supposed to be like this."

"Secrets have a way of entangling us."

"Yes," she said. "Don't they?"

He felt potent, protective, capable of solving all her problems. "I have got everything under control," he said consolingly. "I also have a plan." He smiled, glancing past her. "And fortunately I don't think it involves parasols."

"What is it?"

"We're leaving London."

She escaped his embrace, looking subdued. "What about the masquerade at Castle Eaton?"

"We attend, under my supervision. And then we shall retire to the country like any other well-bred couple. No one will question our sudden departure at this time of year. In fact, it would seem odd if we stayed here."

She stared down at the newspaper she was still holding.

"What do you say, Eleanor?"

"You're right."

Five minutes later they were upstairs packing their belongings for a winter sojourn in Sussex.

Trousers, his and hers, were heaped upon the chairs, the stool, and even the escritoire. He walked into the dressing closet and spotted the bottle that the apothecary's boy had delivered that day. With his earlier focus on a possible assassination plot, he had forgotten. Dear God. Was she sick?

"What is this bottle of foul-looking stuff that came for you today?" he called to her from the depths of the closet.

"My elixir, you mean?"

He returned to their room. "I wasn't prying. But if anything is wrong, I think I ought to know." He looked at her. "But if there isn't—I, well, what I'm trying to say is that I don't want anything to be wrong with you." Plots and mobs he could handle.

She had already undressed and slipped into a lawn nightrail. Before she'd tightened the drawstrings, he removed his outer garments and put on his black dressing robe. For all their uninhibited behavior in bed, he and Eleanor were too essentially English to engage in naked conversation during a crisis.

"When I lost our baby," she said, with a directness that seemed unmerciful at first, "I could not imagine that I should want another. And, of course, conception seemed unlikely without you home. But now— well, I'm taking a tonic." There was no plea for his pity in her voice; nor did he detect any blame.

"A tonic? For . . . ?" he inquired after an awkward pause.

"Do not be thick, Sebastien. It is to enhance my fertility."

"Is it safe?"

"It seems to be." She bit her bottom lip. "Half the time I only pretend to take it to please Mary. But there should be no reason why we cannot have another child."

"I care more that I have you."

She nodded, and he thought that she finally believed him. Now if he could convince her to trust him in other ways, everything would be fine.

She settled into one of the two wing chairs at the window, glancing amusedly around the room. "Where did we bury the evening post that Mary brought up?"

She looked well, he reassured himself. She had the energy of ten soldiers. And he desired her enough for a dozen men. Did either of them need a tonic when they had each other?

"There it is," she said in relief. "On the desk. Let's have a gander."

He sat opposite her, leafing with feigned enthusiasm through the letters that had been hidden under his shirts. "Shall I read them to you?"

"I'm not an invalid all of a sudden," she said with a chuckle, curling into her chair.

"Perhaps the country will do you good."

"Bore me silly, you should say."

"There will be other entertainments," he said meaningfully.

She blushed.

"You're as bad as the duchess's boys."

"Perhaps *I* should take you captive."

"You already have."

"No. It's the other way around."

He cleared his throat, breaking an elaborate seal. "Here we go. An invitation to a Christmas ball in Kent."

"From?"

"My cousin the Marquess of Sedgecroft and his wife." He shook his head ruefully. "My mother was afraid of my father's family, I think."

"Perhaps it's time to mend the family divide."

"I don't need anybody else," he said. "Only you and . . ."

"Our dog?"

"I wasn't thinking of Teg."

"Well, he is family."

He laughed. "At least he's my friend again."

"Yes." She sighed in resignation. "You've won us all back over."

"Except for Mary. And Will is scared of me."

"Open the other letter," she urged him. "A Christmas ball has possibilities. Plum pudding and pantomimes."

He did, his brow lifting slightly. "It appears to be another invitation. Aren't we the sought-after couple?"

She leaned forward. The scent of her hair enticed him. He stopped, everything, but her, suddenly forgotten. "Come closer," he invited in a dangerous voice. "I won't bite hard."

"But you do bite," she whispered, her dark eyes amused.

"So do you," he retorted.

Her smile tightened his heart. "Continue reading."

He shook himself, trying to look surprised as he read on. "What a coincidence. This is a *legitimate* invitation to the masquerade at Castle Eaton. We won't have to pose as chambermaids after all. Fancy that."

"You cheat," she said slowly. "You underhanded, beguiling *rat*. You planned this—you listened to me babble on about Loveridge's damned stupid—"

He laughed helplessly. "It was Heath. He told me he could wangle an invitation. I had no idea how fast."

"Conniving clearly runs in your family."

"Then our children will be doomed." He traced his thumb across her tender lower lip. "It's not such a bad plan, is it, for us to masquerade as man and wife?"

"No," she agreed after a deep silence. "Who knows? We might just start a fashion in society for devotion in marriage again."

"I hope so." He leaned over her, his gaze intent. "I have never looked forward to a winter as much as this one."

"I shall need a new wardrobe," she said thoughtfully.

"One without trousers, I hope."

"Actually I had this costume designed—"

"Elle," he interrupted firmly. "It is a good time for us to go. I don't want to share you with all of London."

She lifted the letters from his hand and dropped them one by one on the desk. "You do know how to get your way, don't you?"

He lifted her into his arms and carried her to the bed, undressing her in fervent need. Their clothing fell willy-nilly to the floor. She pulled the bed curtains closed and wrapped her arms around his naked body. He kissed every inch of her bare skin. She made threats. He made vows. She groaned. He whispered her name between kisses so bittersweet that she quivered, and though the past might still matter, it wasn't enough to keep them from each other.

He broke before her, and her body drank, overflowed, following him into bliss moments after. Heated pleasure expanded her veins. She floated. He soothed the taut skin of her ribs with his fingers and listened to the slowing of his heart and breath until he drifted off.

When the church bells woke him hours later, he realized he and Eleanor still lay entangled. A floorboard creaked somewhere in the house. He eased out from her arms and half-sat, pushing the bed curtains apart.

Not a blade of light penetrated the curtained

windows. Something other than the bells had awakened him. He stared at the door. Had he seen candlelight?

She stirred. "It's early. Is anything wrong?"

He shook his head. "Have you ever read any of the letters that you've recovered for the duchess?"

"Of course not." She snuggled deeper into the covers. "They're private. If they contained secrets that would embarrass her or the duke, I should not wish to know."

A cart rumbled over the cobbles below the window.

"Why did you ask?"

"Just curious."

"I thought you were above our petty affairs."

He laughed.

She rose on her elbow, studying her silent husband, the masculine angles of his body, his shoulders, his narrow hips. His hard features lent his profile a forbidding look.

When would he tell her the truth? Should she confront him, or let him play his hand? If he didn't work for the duke, could he be working for someone else? A double agent? Impossible. What would a spy want with love letters?

He glanced around suddenly, his gaze so penetrating that she shivered. In the dark he looked a little fierce, harder than the man she had married.

Overwhelming, to want someone this desperately.

The cart in the street slowed. A back door in the house creaked open.

"What is that?" he asked, rising to stare out the window.

"The coal man, I imagine."

"I thought he came earlier this week."

"Pray don't say they're coming for me," she whispered in alarm. "I haven't even got my new wardrobe. And you—You aren't wearing a stitch."

He laughed, a warm sound in the shadows that dispelled her fears. "Nobody will take you away when I'm here."

Chapter Twenty-eight

❧ ❧

After a subdued breakfast, the topic of the Masquer not discussed, Sebastien dropped off Eleanor and her long-ignored friend Lady Phoebe Haywood at the shopping district of Bond Street.

He cautioned Burton, the footman, to keep the two ladies in view and said he would return after a quick coffee in St. Giles with some old friends.

Eleanor muttered that she wished she could send the footman to watch over her husband. St. Giles and its overcrowded rookeries bore a nasty reputation, she reminded him.

"And furthermore," she added. "I know why you're going. This is part of your agreement to put your ear to the ground."

"Well, let us tell the world," he replied, glancing at her clueless-looking companion.

Dutifully he waited in his carriage until she and Phoebe entered the glovemaker's shop. Aside from a poster or two blowing in the gutter, he saw no evidence of last night's impassioned mob.

A lady ought to be safe enough buying a pair of gloves, he reasoned as he rapped on the carriage roof to alert his driver, Tilden.

The ladies stood at the counter for over an hour. Not because they were selecting pretty gloves. Eleanor might have enjoyed that. What she did not enjoy was Phoebe chatting her head off to every customer and assistant about how terrified she was of the Masquer while moved to tears at the same time, and what would happen should the mob find him before the police?

Would he be torn to bits or be given sanctuary by an aging prostitute?

Eleanor could have gagged her friend with the expensive onyx-buttoned gloves she'd finally purchased. She suspected that even then Phoebe would not remain silent. She had been a chatterbox in school who'd fainted at least once a week.

"You haven't bought a thing," Phoebe exclaimed as she followed Eleanor outside. "I don't know why you didn't take those pink leather gloves with the pearl buttons. They'd look ever so nice on you."

Eleanor breathed a sigh of relief. She had most of her gowns, and a few Masquer costumes, made by a French modiste who lived on the outskirts of Town and did not care for Society in general. Efficient, discreet, selective about her clients, she served Eleanor only because Eleanor had once saved her cat from choking on a fish bone. Perhaps Eleanor could persuade her to come to the country to make her a few heavy dresses and a woolen mantle or two for walking.

She and Sebastien had not walked together since Spain. She sighed happily at the thought.

She glanced down as Phoebe laid her hand gently upon hers. "May I make an honest remark between friends?"

Eleanor doubted that she could stop her.

"It's that you're so different," Phoebe blurted out indelicately. "You're not anything like the girl I remember from boarding school."

"One grows."

Phoebe pursed her small mouth. "Yes, but does one have to grow so dull?"

Eleanor noticed a group of well-heeled gentlewomen spill from a carriage across the street. They were a rather determined-looking lot, presumably intent on a day of shopping. In fact, they seemed to be marching her way in a military formation. She decided that she had developed an aversion to daylight activity.

"I'm dull?" she asked, suddenly realizing the insult she had just been dealt.

Phoebe gave her a sheepish grin. "Well, you used to be enormously fun. Climbing out of windows, putting leeches down Mrs. Paulton's dress—"

"Did I do that? What a waste of leeches. And what a horrible person I was."

"But you were *Eleanor,* she who entertained us

and dared to act out all the wicked deeds we lacked the courage to commit."

"I don't know that it was courage," Eleanor admitted. "I could not hold still. And—"

"Dear heavens!" Phoebe said, staring past the shop they had just exited.

Three more carriages had discharged passengers onto the pavement. This group appeared to be predominantly male, the relatives, Eleanor assumed, of the ladies marching forth with placards hoisted high.

For the first time in her life she actually gawked. Well, maybe she'd gawked once before. She seemed to recall that seeing Sebastien completely undressed on their wedding night had been an eye-opener, too. But a nice one. In fact, she still loved to look at him. He was a magnificently built man.

"They're coming for the Masquer," Phoebe breathed. "I wonder if they know where he is."

Eleanor glanced around in chagrin.

The placards waving in the air pleaded for her to turn herself in. Instead, she turned in the opposite direction. A grandfatherly gent doffed his hat and held it beneath her bosom.

The mob had found her.

"Penny to save the Masquer, my lovely young lady? You shall be my prettiest contributor of the day."

"I—"

Phoebe stuffed several bank notes into his hat, then yelped as the grandfather's heavy-set wife trod on her foot and demanded he keep moving.

"I don't like large crowds," Phoebe said in a quavery voice. Her face whitened. She made a little fish mouth. "I feel as though I'm going to be stampeded by elephants."

Eleanor grasped her by the waist. "Oh, no. Not now. Didn't you outgrow the vapors?"

Phoebe's eyes rolled back in her head.

"Where is the footman?" Eleanor asked in panic. "Burton—"

He motioned wildly from the doorway of the linen-draper's across the crowded street, indicating he couldn't reach her. Muttering under her breath, she half-carried Phoebe back toward the glovemaker's shop.

A poster begging for Masquer mercy stared down at her from the plate glass window. There was no escaping herself.

The shop owner and his assistants poured out onto the sidewalk to witness the excitement.

Phoebe wasn't the only person fainting. It was like a contagion that spread through the crowd.

Only one establishment appeared to offer asylum from the hysterical excitement of the gathering throng. Not until Eleanor had shoved and elbowed her way there, dragging Phoebe along like a doll, did she realize that there were footmen standing guard outside this shop.

And they weren't friendly by the look of them, either.

"Ooh," Phoebe said, suddenly not a fainting-bone in her body. "This is Madame Devine's shop. I've been dying all my life to come here. How brave of you, Eleanor. I take back everything I said—you aren't dull at all. You're still a giggle."

Eleanor approached the Georgian-design brick building with trepidation.

She'd never visited the shop, but she remembered Sebastien explaining that Madame Devine catered to fashionable wives, mistresses, and courtesans alike. He might have been hinting that she make an appointment. The price for a private fitting was exorbitant. She spotted a young buck with two ladies on either arm, the footmen efficiently ushering them inside. Under other circumstances she wouldn't have been seen entering such premises.

Now she a felt certain prurient curiosity. After all, she'd been inside a brothel. She had made love on a floating one, too. She might as well make a full descent into moral decline.

What would Sebastien think if she surprised him with some provocative attire?

"Let's go inside," she said in resolve, although Phoebe had already forged ahead as if to charge the door.

The footmen stepped forward in practiced grace like a pair of crossed swords. "Your names, mesdames?" one inquired with a critical appraisal of Eleanor's comfortable shawl and bonnet.

"Lady Phoebe Haywood," her friend said before Eleanor could reply.

The footmen glanced at each other, unimpressed. Eleanor could have smacked the pair of them stupid with her unfashionable bonnet. "Lady Boscastle," she said offhandedly. "And I do not wish to shop here, anyway. I—"

"Lady *Boscastle*, of course."

"An honor."

"A privilege."

"Please forgive us. Your name must have been omitted from our list of today's customers."

Eleanor felt a peculiar rush of power. She liked it. The holy name of Boscastle. Why hadn't Sebastien taken advantage of it before? Did he resent his relatives that much? And what sort of women in his family held influence over an exclusive shopping district? Perhaps she wouldn't like them. Then again, perhaps she would.

"That clerk should be dismissed," the first footman said.

The other looked down at his list and said, "Ah. Here it is. You have an appointment right now. So sorry for the delay. We'll—"

A crowd of half-hysterical women knocked Eleanor into Phoebe like a wave.

"You shall have a divine appointment with my foot if you do not let us inside," she said, straightening her bonnet.

Within moments they met Madame's personal assistant, who rushed them through an unimpressive candlelit interior and up a flight of stairs.

Another assistant joined them in the upper hallway. Admiring the color of Eleanor's hair, her family connections, her unique eye color, she led them into a small chamber where only one other customer sat sipping Madeira and discussing her winter attire with Madame Devine.

The woman, dressed as modestly as a vicar's wife, glanced up. She caught Eleanor's gaze for less than a second, smiled politely enough, then resumed her conversation.

Phoebe drew what sounded like a dying breath.

Eleanor thought she herself might faint.

She nodded to Mrs. Watson. The courtesan nodded back without looking up again.

And that was that.

"Would Lady Boscastle care for some libation?" another assistant inquired, a black silk corset slung over her arm.

"Bring the entire bottle," Mrs. Watson said with a low, inviting laugh. "We shall have to wait for this atrocious mob to go away. We may as well shop to prove to our protectors that we aren't wasting their precious time."

"What a clever notion," Phoebe said, divesting herself of her cloak and gloves. "My husband will go into shock if I come home with a scandalous costume."

"As will mine," Eleanor said in resignation. Although she guessed it would be for a completely different reason.

Sebastien stared out the rocking carriage at the sea of gentlewomen who filled the streets, morning dresses swirling to the march of delicate slippers. He'd witnessed quite a few disturbances in the past. He had initiated frays in the public squares and on the docks of France. He had blown up ships. He had disguised himself as a farmer and protested taxes.

But he had never encountered such an intimidating mob in his life. Being comprised primarily of sympathetic, well-mannered women, they parted when his coachman Tilden asked them to move, and allowed his carriage to pass.

Even then, Tilden had to park a mile away from the shop where Sebastien had promised to collect Eleanor and her friend. He could not pick the ladies out in the crush. His beleaguered footman Burton explained that they had disappeared into Madame Devine's premises. Burton had been instructed to wait outside.

Sebastien's brows shot up in speculation.

Eleanor shopping at this Cyprian's modiste? As talk went in his club, the dresses and undergarments designed by Devine could arouse the carnal proclivities of a stone statue.

He wasn't made of stone.

He studied the poster in the window. He thought of Eleanor wearing risqué corsets that laced up front, undressing slowly for his private entertainment. Given a choice of his wife bedecked in trousers or tantalizing underclothing, well, there really wasn't much of a decision.

"My lord," Burton said, hovering behind him while glaring bravely at the other footmen. "Shall I clear the way for the carriage while you fetch the ladies from this place?"

Sebastien pulled out his pocket watch and pretended to reflect upon the time. At least he knew she was safe inside that shop. "There's no hurry. I wouldn't mind walking down to the bookseller's for a few minutes. I'll need something to read in the country."

Although if her ladyship enjoyed the fruits of an afternoon in adventurous shopping, Sebastien would not read a single page all winter long.

Chapter Twenty-nine

❧❧

At the last minute, neither Sebastien nor Eleanor wanted to leave for Castle Eaton. Teg had run away the night before and gotten into a brawl with three gutter dogs. He returned home in such pathetic condition that Eleanor had to stitch up his ears and scold the gardeners for leaving the back gate open.

One of the housemaid's aunts died of mysterious causes the morning of their departure. She left her niece all her worldly possessions, which didn't amount to enough for an early retirement from service, but the girl was so inconsolable that a crowd of strangers—law clerks and hot-chestnut sellers—gathered at the curb to offer sympathy, roasted nuts, and legal advice.

"At least," Sebastien confided to his wife, "it isn't a mob of do-gooders searching for a certain fabled mischief-maker."

She pivoted on her heel and left him standing alone on the pavement.

She could not find her traveling cloak. Nor her costume for the masquerade at the castle. She and

Mrs. Bindy, the housekeeper, searched high and low before they located the large portmanteau that contained both items sitting beside the bed. It had obviously been there all along, Sebastien said. A bag could not move by itself.

Then *his* traveling trunk came unstrapped when the coachmen leaned down to lift it.

All of Sebastien's clothes, his smalls, silk cravats, nightshirt, and books, tumbled into the gutter for London to behold.

"I refuse to believe in omens," Eleanor said, and wondered why she felt so sick to her stomach that she couldn't even finish her usual pot of tea.

"But you believe in fortune-tellers," he reminded her, when he knew he shouldn't have said anything at all.

"That's different," she said. "I only believe in the good things he predicted."

"There were the bad ones?"

"I knew you were superstitious."

Sebastien looked from his wife sitting resolutely in the carriage, to Mary standing on the front steps with an expression of black doom that could have stopped the sun from shining.

Superstitious?

Had he been a sailor about to embark on a voyage, he would have pulled his boat back to shore and waited for calmer seas.

But he knew that Eleanor was resolved to deliver this last letter to the duchess. Therefore, come heaven or hell, he intended to help her keep her promise—and keep her safe at the same time.

After their auspicious departure, Eleanor could not shake off her dour mood. She studied the metallic sky through the window as if waiting for the clouds to unleash calamity upon the earth. She kept wondering whether she had forgotten to do something before they left.

She complained that the carriage interior smelled unpleasantly of ashes and vinegar, the very concoction the footmen always used to refresh the squabs. She noticed a smudge on her glove and refused to believe Sebastien's reassurances that no one would care.

"Take my word on it," he murmured, not looking up from his newspaper, "no one who meets you is going to notice the condition of your gloves."

She laid her head against his shoulder. "The duchess is right. You are a rogue."

"I take umbrage to that accusation," he said mildly. "Even if it is true. Which reminds me, when am I going to see what you purchased at that naughty dressmaker's?"

"When it's delivered to our Sussex home."

They lapsed into a comfortable silence. The carriage rumbled past Apsley House with its multiple chimneys puffing smoke into the surly November sky. Bustling London would soon fall behind.

"We've almost escaped," he said, putting his paper aside. The relief on his face made her smile. But then, lately, she had only to glance at him and feel an incredible lightness come over her.

"Her grace is leaving in another week to go to the country with the children," she said, restraining herself from taking one last look at the mansion that the duchess loved. "I think she'd have gone sooner but Bellisant asked for a few more days to finish his sketch."

He smiled grimly. "I ought to finish him."

"I'm glad that you have restrained yourself," she teased, enjoying his possessive streak.

"Barely."

"By the way, she was grateful that you retrieved Mrs. Watson's letters without causing another uproar."

He smiled. "They practically fell into my hands."

"The duchess dislikes being in London for Guy Fawkes night," she said, changing the subject. "Of course the boys adore every moment of it. I cringe every time I hear one of those Roman candles set off in the street. Last year Will and I were returning home from a play when a carriage was overturned by a drunken crowd. It started in fun. Then someone threw a burning effigy at a gentleman walking to his club, and his coat caught fire."

"How fortunate I shall be close by to protect you from those vulgar people. In fact"—he tugged at one of the tiny white bows that adorned her bodice—"I'm close by right now."

"Yes. And you're always unfastening me one way or the other."

"I'm sorry."

"No, you're not."

His laughter filled her with poignant warmth. "No. I'm not."

She gave a small sigh and closed her eyes, the creaking of the coach wheels, her husband's deep voice, relaxing her. "I hope Teg doesn't get out again while Burton is walking him."

"I think you frightened the staff into vigilance."

"Mary did seem flustered when we left." She opened her eyes as she felt his teeth sink lightly into her earlobe. She struggled to remember what they were talking about. "Will," she went on, distracted by the dark head that had nestled between her breasts, "was quite put out, too, until he received that invitation to the castle."

His head lifted. "What invitation?"

"I think it came from the earl himself. He's apparently asked Will to give a few readings at the party. Will is very excited about it."

"I was excited about finally having you to myself."

"Does that mean he can't stay with us over the winter? I know his heart is set on it, but if you want me to rescind the invite—"

"You didn't."

She chuckled. "No. Only teasing—" She glanced up at the light pinging from above. "Is that rain?"

He listened. "I don't think so."

"A good downpour tomorrow night would put out all those awful bonfires."

His mouth thinned. "Pity it wouldn't put out conspiracies at the same time."

❧ ❧

Chapter Thirty

Castle Eaton's historical notoriety had existed for centuries before its current owner began hosting his popular masquerades. Beneath the castle keep lay a torture chamber that boasted five oubliettes. Inside these hidden cells, medieval prisoners had moldered, having been forgotten after months of interrogation. These heartwarming premises now served as a stage for the Earl of Eaton's opening entertainment.

The lords and ladies of the ton loved a good scare. The earl's midnight tours of the oubliettes, complete with a display of genuine torture instruments and servants moaning behind the walls, guaranteed that at least one guest would faint dead away.

Lord and Lady Boscastle made only a token appearance at this uplifting spectacle on the evening they arrived. Eleanor provided all the uplifting that Sebastien required. He, in turn, could make her faint dead away without even leaving their room.

Mr. Will Prescott, however, arrived in the nick of time to give a candlelight reading from Othello in the banqueting hall. Sir Perceval had accompanied him from London, having been employed by Lord Eaton to tell fortunes in the torture chamber and lend an air of mysticism to the party.

Unfortunately the fortune-teller dropped his crystal ball in fright when a beheaded ghost popped out of a trapdoor to greet the other guests. Sir Perceval read palms afterward in an aggrieved mood.

The next morning, Sebastien and Eleanor lingered in their bedchamber to brace themselves for the formal breakfast and the rigorous demands of intermingling with the other guests. Eleanor had become more at ease in this situation than was her husband, who'd never had much patience for parties to begin with. After all, she had pulled the wool over the eyes of an entire town. Still, it was Sebastien who received the first invitation for a social connection.

A chambermaid brought a message to the bedchamber from a gentleman who'd asked to meet Sebastien on the beach after breakfast. He had not given his name, but claimed that he and Sebastien were acquainted.

"It could be a hundred men," he said, hunting for his coat.

Eleanor handed his coat to him. "I'm coming with you."

"No. It might be news concerning the plot against Wellington."

"It might be another woman," she said tartly. "I know perfectly well what goes on at these parties."

His mouth pursed in objection. "This could be my

personal contact. I don't want you getting involved in my work."

"I didn't want you involved in mine, either," she reminded him.

He curbed his impatience. "You don't understand. Some matters can only be dealt with by a man."

"I've been a man," she said. "I think I understand quite well."

"And I'm supposed to explain that to another agent?"

"Of course not. You may introduce me as your wife. After all, a good operative should be the last person one suspects."

The castle perched upon chalk clifftops that eclipsed a bay. They walked down to the beach, he in his long black coat, Eleanor wrapped in a red cloak that reached her ankles. Their breath huffed out in the cold. Where the mist met the water on the horizon, fishing boats sailed in defiance of the unstable sands and storms that often arose without warning.

They waited over an hour for Sebastien's anonymous contact to appear. He never did. The only persons in sight were another couple who had sneaked from the castle to stroll along the beach.

"I knew it," Eleanor said. "It was another woman. When she saw me with you, the hussy lost her nerve."

He shook his head amusedly. "Then it is a good thing you came."

"Does that mean I can come with you the next time?"

"Absolutely not."

Her teeth were chattering as he guided her to a sheltered spot between a crop of boulders. She plopped down in the sand, her cloak drawn around her.

"Well," she said, with enforced cheer. "Here we are." She picked up a piece of driftwood and drew a castle in the sand. "Isn't this a nice day to contract a lung ailment? Are my lips blue yet?"

He grinned at her. "I'll revive you when they are."

"How long are we going to wait?"

A gust of wind blew across the boulders. He shielded her from an onslaught of wet sand, glancing up at the cliffs. "Another minute or so. The sea is best this time of year. There's no one else around."

"I don't wonder why. The sensible people are sitting by the fire taking tea with—"

"I have a confession."

Confession. A chill chased down her spine. *Finally.* She schooled herself to look surprised, the driftwood slipping from her fingers. "Do you?"

"I meant it when I said I wanted us to start over," he began somberly.

She gave him an encouraging nod. "The truth is a good place to start."

He nodded, his gaze inscrutable. "When I was gone, I did things in my work I'd never done before, things I did not dream myself capable of."

"You've hinted as much."

He smiled without humor. "There were times when I realized what I'd become and wasn't sure that I should come back to you."

"What changed your mind?"

"For one thing, I could not live any longer without you."

She didn't speak. She was afraid he would stop.

"And for another, I realized what *you* had become and knew I was responsible."

He subsided into a long silence.

Suddenly she couldn't endure the suspense. "And that is all that you wanted to confess?"

He frowned at her. "I wish to make it perfectly clear that my confession concerns acts of love, not those of war."

"Love?"

His unflinching gaze gave her another chill. "The duke did not order me to interfere with his wife's affairs. I asked to be put in charge."

"Did you indeed?" she asked, swallowing over an unexpected tightness in her throat.

"I deceived you," he said simply. "And I did not know how to tell you."

She expelled a sigh. So much for making him suffer. "I know what you did," she admitted. "I have known for some time now."

He studied her in disbelief. "And you allowed me to go along feeling guilty?"

"I kept waiting for you to tell me the truth." She shook her head. "I didn't know the whole time."

His eyes narrowed. "And you weren't upset?"

"Because you cheated? Because you played your duke against my duchess?"

"Your work for her placed you in danger," he said. "I never realized how much until I returned."

"I assure you, I was never in as much danger as you are now."

"Then you forgive me?"

"I haven't decided."

"I think you have."

"Did the duke approve of this deception?" she asked.

"Well, he heard me out and didn't offer much of an opinion one way or another."

The sea breeze lifted the dark red strands of her hair. "But he didn't stop you."

"No." He smiled. "He didn't."

"Then in my opinion, the pair of you are—" She restrained the urge to vent her thoughts. While she might feel justified calling her husband names, she could hardly state that the duke was a stinker. The duchess would assuredly do that. "I hope you're sorry."

A grin crept across his chiseled face.

"You aren't," she said. "In fact, I think you're proud of yourself."

He didn't deny it.

"I won you back," he said, his voice strong and yet gentle. "It was worth the risk for that."

She felt her eyes mist. In a few minutes the sea would wash away her castle. The princess who stood on the battlement walk, waiting for her prince, would either pull him up beside her or watch him drown in the moat he had built to protect her.

"I have always been a faithful husband," he said with a smile that went straight to her heart. "And I've always loved you. The question, I suppose is, do *you* still love me?"

She shook her head at him. "I think I must."

"Aren't you sure?"

"Yes," she whispered. "I'm sure."

"Forgive me," he said, bending on one knee, the color of his eyes irresistible Boscastle blue, "I thought I'd lost you. I would have done anything to make you love me again."

"It's getting late," she said, not because she cared one way or another, but if they did not return to the castle, she would fall onto her knees beside him and stay until they were covered in kelp and kisses. "We've got work to do before the masquerade supper."

"I was late to my own wedding," he said with a rueful grin.

"And a wicked disgrace into the bargain. My aunt still mentions it every time she writes."

"What can I do to make it up?"

She shook her head helplessly. "Not get yourself killed over this conspiracy."

"I can't let Wellington be killed."

"I was afraid you'd say that," she whispered. "Why did someone try to lure you here today?"

"He might have mistaken me for one of the other Boscastles. Perhaps it was an innocent error."

A clap of thunder rumbled suddenly above the castle turrets. He glanced up at the sky and grasped her hands, rising from the sand. Then they were racing up the path to escape the rain with the other couple who'd been on the beach behind them. The four of them were drenched by the time they reached the drawbridge. Sebastien brushed a hand through her damp hair.

Their bedraggled appearance raised eyebrows as they attempted to sneak past the more dignified guests who headed toward the great hall for brandy and gossip.

"Quickly," he said, squeezing her hand before they disengaged. "That's Will and Sir Perceval coming our way. Let's avoid them until I find that last letter."

"And make a few inquiries about the man who wanted to meet you while you're at it," she said, hastening up the stairs before anyone noticed the puddles they had dripped everywhere.

Sebastien watched his wife's white shoulders disappear into the steaming hot water of her hip bath. Her genie costume lay across the bed—a coin-decorated veil and peacock blue headdress, a tapestry vest with a scarf that draped around her midriff. He wasn't sure what to make of the mysterious message he had received. The chambermaid who had delivered it could not be found. Nor did the majordomo remember a girl of that description in his employ. He suggested, as Eleanor had, that perhaps Sebastien had a secret admirer who had been hoping to meet him alone.

The whole thing disturbed him.

But probably not as much as the fact that at the party his wife would be wearing a pair of loose trousers almost identical to his. She was a genie. He was Aladdin.

She looked beguiling.

He couldn't look at himself in the mirror.

"I didn't realize that your costume was so revealing," he said, pacing around the room. "Do you have any idea how many men will ask you to make their wishes come true?"

"I wish *you* would cease pacing and complaining. It's wearing on my nerves. What happened to Sebastien, the spine of steel saboteur? You can't have been on edge every time you carried out your own assignments."

He sent her a dark glance. "I did not have a wife draped in veils to distract me then. At least not of which I was aware. Had I known what you were up to, I doubt I could have concentrated at all."

She stepped out of the tub, squeezing the water from her long rope of hair. Her breasts shone, her nipples dark and prominent. He stared at her glimmering form and thought of a nubile young goddess and naughty pleasures and starting a family.

"You don't need to worry about me," she said. "I

promise to remain inside the castle. Will can play the cavalier for an hour or so."

"It shouldn't take me that long." He wrapped the towel around her damp shoulders, promising himself he'd have her back in his arms before midnight. "Lady Eaton's suite is directly off the staircase."

"All the better for sneaking in and out, eh?"

"I wouldn't know," he said innocently. "Well, not the sort of sneaking you mean." He turned from her with a sigh. "Speaking of sneaking, I—what is that smell?"

"I beg your pardon. I just bathed. I thought you liked my lily soap."

"That's not soap. It's smoke. I smell something burning."

She pushed around him. "I hope it isn't the candle in my magic lantern. I lit it to see if the wick was still good. I thought I put it out, though."

He picked up the lamp that sat on the nightstand. "You did."

"Thank goodness. I wouldn't want to burn down the castle."

"Perhaps it's the bonfire being lit in the hall to celebrate Guy Fawkes."

"Bonfires make me uneasy. I believe one of my ancestors was burned as a witch."

"You have certainly inherited your powers of bewitchment from someone."

"Be careful, Sebastien," she said softly as he went to the door.

"You, too." He frowned at her over his shoulder. "And put on a cape over those veils. You look too appealing in that costume. I, on the other hand, feel like an idiot."

He would have searched and exited Lady Eaton's bedchamber in under three minutes had her ladyship not decided on a costume change at the last moment. A full-figured woman with frizzy orange hair, who displayed more of her assets than he cared to see, had likely realized she wasn't the only Venus to bestow her beauty on the other guests.

Luckily she caught him in the gallery *outside* her door, and not on the way in.

"Open sesame," she trilled at the top of her voice, gesturing at the closed door with her conch shell.

He did not turn to acknowledge the flirtatious invitation to enter her bedroom. He had one of her old letters tucked inside his costume. For all she knew he'd been admiring the crossbow collection mounted upon the hallway wall.

"Excuse me?" he said.

She lowered her conch with a coy smile. "There might be treasure in my cave." She gave him a little wink. "Treasure that I only share with *certain* guests."

He edged around her. "Where there's treasure, there is usually trouble."

"I've heard," she said, thwarting his passage, "that

where there's trouble, there's usually a Boscastle in the vicinity." She examined his costume closely. "Or would you rather I call you Ali Baba Boscastle?"

He grimaced. "That's quite all right." This was what came from wearing clothes that Will had borrowed from the theater. "To be frank, you have the wrong tale. As well as the wrong male."

She laid her hand on one of his gold arm gauntlets. "A sultan?"

"His son-in-law, returning home." What a preposterous conversation. "I'm Aladdin."

"Didn't Aladdin have his own harem?" she asked in a throaty voice.

"I don't believe so," he said politely, plucking her fingers from his becircled biceps. "However, I certainly don't." It was all he could do to keep his only woman from writing her own entertainments.

"Everyone gets lost in the castle at midnight," she whispered, giving him a nudge. "The servants extinguish all the torches, and we have to find one another."

"How frightfully exciting."

He decided right then that he and Eleanor would be locked inside their room by eleven. At daybreak they would be on the road back to London to send the staff off to Sussex, and if it rained hard, they'd make a detour and stay for another day or so on the coast.

"I know all the hiding places in the castle," the countess continued, not one to take a hint. "Would you like for me to find you if you get lost?"

"I think my wife has already done that, Lady Eaton, but your offer is immensely kind."

"You haven't heard yet what else I'm willing to offer."

"That might be best left to the imagination." Suddenly he wondered if *she* was the one who had tried to meet him on the beach.

She studied him in sour amusement. "I thought that you and your wife had been estranged for years. Surely you're aware that she has been seen in the company of other men at other masquerades. I saw her myself at the Aldephia with a most handsome portrait painter."

"Oh, yes, Sir What's—"

"Nathan Bellisant. He's not as interesting as you. I don't think he wanted to paint me. He liked your wife, though. Followed her around like a lost puppy."

He touched his right hand to his forehead and sketched a low bow. "I assure you that she is very much my devoted wife, as I shall remain a faithful husband."

At least the latter part of that statement would never be disproved.

As far as Eleanor's devotion, she had proven that too, which didn't mean he could take her for granted again, nor leave her alone for the duration of even one more party.

And when he saw her coming from their room at the opposite side of the gallery, he could not escape

Lady Eaton fast enough. There were guests going up and down the staircase, admiring one another's disguises.

None of them looked as enchanting as the tall genie with an unlit lamp and peeved expression on her face.

He saw Eleanor look past him to where he and Lady Eaton had been standing. When she glanced back up at him rather testily, he patted the letter he had hidden under his vest.

"That's it," he said, sotto voce, as they met. "We're finished. Shall we go home?"

She looked over his lean, spare frame. "You're missing something—your dagger. I hope you didn't drop it in that brassy woman's bedchamber."

"Of course I didn't. Do you want to read the letter I found?"

"No." Her eyes held his.

She adjusted the scarf that was stitched to her bodice. "Please put it in a very safe place." She ran her fingers up his arm to the gauntlet that encircled his hard muscles. "I might have to put you in a safe place, too. I noticed that Lady Eaton found a way to stand at your side during our tour of the dungeon last night."

He leaned into her. "I didn't notice," he said. "But then I was preoccupied staring daggers at the gentlemen who were staring at my wife, and if they do so again, I'll put them in their place."

"Daggers." She drew her hand from the gauntlet with a wistful sigh. "Hurry up and find yours. Will is insisting I accompany him on a tour of the torture chamber. He doesn't want to go without me."

"I know how he feels."

"Are you afraid of the dark, too?"

He grinned. "Not if you're with me."

When he returned alone to their room to hide the letter, he heard the faint clamor of bells ringing from the beach. The storm had worsened. He glanced out through an arched window at the fishing boats bobbing at sea. The sailors had ignored the warning to come ashore.

These plots usually blow over before they amount to anything.

Have you read them?

He felt a tug of curiosity. Eleanor had chosen to keep her promise. But he hadn't promised the duchess as much. Furthermore, he had pledged to serve the duke. And keeping an eye open meant examining everything that came one's way. Even old letters.

He hadn't been assigned to covert activities for nothing.

He unfolded the letter and studied the feminine scrawl. Dear, dear. For a countess, Lady Viola Hutchinson did employ rather foul language and—Eleanor was afraid of bonfires? She'd had an ancestress burned as a witch? He hadn't known that. Had they even spent a November together before? There wouldn't be any fires lit in the village in this rain. Good thing they were wearing light costumes tonight. They'd roast otherwise in the great hall.

He glanced down again.

I have met the most intriguing man named Lord Barry Summers. He was a member of the War Office who lost his position due to that bastard Wellesley's influence. I do believe he hates that ambitious bugger as much as I do. He laughed when I confessed I wished a plague upon Arthur's wife. He promised that if I waited and satisfied his desires he would satisfy my need for vengeance. Not that any of this will interest you, dangling an old earl on your finger.

He stopped. Wellesley had become the Duke of Wellington. The recipient of this letter was the lascivious Lady Eaton, who'd snapped up her old earl. He'd no idea what had happened to this Lord Barry Summers. It was a name to remember.

He put the letter away when he heard a knock at the door. He hoped it was Eleanor and prayed it wasn't Venus. It turned out to be a castle footman with another message, this time from a man claiming to be a family relation. The gentleman requested that Sebastien meet him on the drawbridge.

"Is this another prank?" he asked bluntly.

"I don't think so, my lord," the footman answered. "Would you like me to accompany you just in case?"

"No, thank you. I'll go alone." Which meant he wouldn't involve Eleanor.

But if it was a relative, it could only be Heath. Who else knew Sebastien was attending a party at the castle? What could be important enough for him to ride from Town in the rain?

The plot against Wellington. A woman scorned and a cabinet member with a long-standing grudge. He felt a quickening, anticipation, the chance to be back in the game. He wasn't sure, of course, that there was a connection. But it was a start, as Eleanor had said, and his instinct said it was a good one.

"Please let Lady Boscastle know that I'll be delayed a few more minutes," he instructed the footman before he closed the door.

He took the time to find his coat and throw it on over his costume. A secret agent did not need to be parading around as Aladdin. He wished that Eleanor had read the letters she had found, but perhaps now it didn't matter. He would simply explain the contents of this last one to Heath. That way his wife would not have breaking a promise on her conscience.

He hurried down the spiral staircase, managing to dodge the guests who had strayed from the festivities. He would have to return to London if he was asked. He strode through the muddied bailey, beneath the portcullis, a man who'd run through worse than rain to prove himself.

Eleanor would understand, a woman who had

proven her own loyalties in England and to him in some rather startling ways. As she had once pointed out, their children would benefit from their parents' penchant for intrigue—medals, titles, positions at court or in foreign lands.

Ambitious, he and his wife.

If Heath Boscastle had come all the way from London to enlist Sebastien's help, she would understand why he had to accept. His problem would be persuading her she could not accompany him.

To his surprise, the cloaked man standing on the drawbridge was not Heath, but his own younger brother Gabriel. He felt a pang of fondness, remembering the wicked hell they had raised when he and Gabriel were growing up. He had not only taught Gabriel how to shoot a solitary acorn from a tree, but also how to entice a barmaid into sneaking a handsome boy an ale in the stableyard. Indeed, there was no one like an older brother to introduce a sibling to sin.

Well, so much for his ambitions. "You," he said, clasping his brother's arm. "You were supposed to be Heath."

Gabriel eyed Sebastien's silk turban in amusement. "I won't ask who you're supposed to be. Heath sent me, actually."

Sebastien glanced down the drawbridge to the sea, his anticipation sharpening. "Why?"

"Because I can ride faster than he could in the rain."

"No one can ride faster than you."

"A skill I honed so I wouldn't be blamed for what my three elder brothers had done. I was usually left to look the guilty party."

"Boys in trouble learn to be fast."

It was the second time in years they'd faced each other. Sebastien had come to his younger brother's rescue last September in London when he'd been ambushed in an alley. Gabriel had not contacted him since, although Sebastien had hoped he might.

Still, for the previous decade they had pursued different paths. Sebastien had chosen his career with hopes of glory, a military promotion. Gabriel had fallen into heroism.

Gabriel glanced up at the raised portcullis. He might be wondering whether the iron gate would drop and forever divide them. He drew a harsh breath. Obviously he had ridden hard to bring this message.

"The conspirator has been traced to someone who frequents your house," he said. "Heath thought you ought to know and respond accordingly."

"My house?" His brow knotted. "When?"

"Over the past year." Gabriel wiped a wet streak of rain from his face. "The link to the plot was only discovered last night. Do you have any suspicions?"

Sebastien's heart pounded. The wind howled across the cliffs and castle battlements. A man's house was his castle, the fortress in which he guarded everything he cherished. But if that man left his castle undefended, whether he ranked as a duke or baron, he should expect that an enemy would try to find a way inside.

Who had visited his house while he was away?

The bailey had become a sea of churning mud and confusion. The castle standards fluttered in the wind, their direction elusive. Rain slammed against his back and blew into his brother's face.

Whoever had befriended Eleanor would presumably have used her to gain access to the duchess. Her grace trusted few people with true friendship, and while those she did received special favor, she also associated with a certain questionable element. Questionable, at least, in Sebastien's biased opinion.

"Nathan Bellisant," he said with grim certainty. "It has to be him. He talked her into staying in London."

"A Frenchman?"

"You wouldn't know it to meet him. He's a portrait painter who was a frequent guest at my house. Not one I would have invited, but my wife and her friends are wild for his talent."

"And he's still alive?" Gabriel asked, his blue eyes taunting.

Sebastien forced a smile. Amazing how they had been apart for years and yet their minds wandered in the same devious ways. "The duchess has commissioned him to paint her children for Wellington's Christmas homecoming."

"Ah." Gabriel's mouth hardened. "Perhaps he'll

have to finish his painting in the Tower. We cannot disappoint the grand duke."

Sebastien felt a jolt of fury. Bellisant. The portrait of Eleanor. To view one's wife through another man's eyes, to see her coveted and used. How could he summon mercy for the traitor? He could not. He would do what the Crown expected of him, and if there was a personal element of revenge on his part—what of it? He would be justified in seeing the coward brought down.

The duke had never sent him on missions of kindness.

"A painter," Gabriel mused. "What a perfect cover. And he made friends with your wife at the same time."

"That will be enough, Gabriel."

"He didn't paint her picture, did he? No. You wouldn't have let that sort of nonsense go on."

"I'm letting your mouth go on," Sebastien retorted.

Gabriel wiped his cheek with his coat sleeve. "Do we ride together, or should I go ahead to London?"

"We'll go together, then separate. Find Heath." Sebastien pulled his coat up around his neck. "I'll have to change anyway and make arrangements for Eleanor's cousin to take her from here. At least come inside and have cake and ale before we go."

"I'll see to my horse's needs," Gabriel said, grinning. "You see to your wife. And, Sebastien—"

Sebastien pivoted with an impatient look, backing away from his brother. "What?"

"In this weather and that garb, you might consider going by flying carpet. Of course the wind would blow off your turban. Still, all things being equal, I think it might be a blessing."

Eleanor couldn't decide whether the roast pheasant was off, or the beastly music of the wandering minstrels had given her a sick headache. Whatever the cause, she excused herself from the noisy revels and slipped from the hall, her veils battened down. Sir Perceval had just arrived to read fortunes. Will trailed her dutifully to the door, munching on a chicken leg.

"When was the last time you saw my husband?" she asked in a whisper.

"I spotted him in the passage screens a half hour ago. He appeared to be leaving the keep."

She looked back into the throng of costumed guests lining up to have their fortunes told. "You don't have to walk me upstairs. I'll wait in my room until Sebastien returns. Sir Perceval looks as if he could use a guard, though."

"Sebastien asked me to see you to safety." Which he did, looking doubtful when she dismissed him outside the door of her room. "Lock up after me."

"Thank you, Will." She hesitated. He seemed always to be such a lost soul. "I could have never done what—well, this past year would have been uneventful without your help. Perhaps you have already guessed, but the duchess has a reward planned for your services."

He nodded wistfully. "It's a shame it all has to end. And, Eleanor, I'm sorry if I was not the most efficient of partners. Sometimes I got carried away. You never really needed me. I think—well, I've always needed you. Good night."

She bolted the door, listening to his footsteps recede. How sensitive he had always been, an only child who from her earliest memories had enjoyed putting on costumes, staging plays, inventing characters to befriend.

She turned.

The chamber seemed dark and gloomy without Sebastien. A damp wind penetrated the shutters.

She lit her unmagical lamp and put on the warm pelisse Mary had insisted she bring. Sebastien's coat, the one he'd worn on the beach, was gone. Her cloak was still wet. She rubbed her hands together, wondering why he had vanished so mysteriously. If that unnamed mischief maker had lured him off again, she would be upset that he hadn't at least told her.

She curled up on the chair where his coat had lain. She knew he could take care of himself, and she had no desire to wander either the castle corridors or the windswept cove in search of him. Of course, if he did not return within a reasonable period, she would ask Will and a footman or two to help her find him.

A sharp cramp in the pit of her stomach distracted her. Damnation. Of all the times for her courses to come. She would have to change, or better yet go to bed with a book and her missing husband to rub her back.

She shifted to her left side, slipping her hands beneath the pelisse for warmth. The lamp flickered. She placed her hand absently over her belly. Was this her usual discomfort, or something different? Her last flow had been four . . . five weeks ago?

She looked up at the lamp, afraid to hope. Five weeks. Perhaps even longer. She smoothed the pelisse over her body. She felt some forgotten object in the pocket—no, whatever it was had been lightly sewn into the satin lining. She plucked the few loose stitches apart.

Not another letter? She thought the handwriting looked familiar.

She leaned toward the light, chuckling in realization. A message from dear-hearted Mary, written on Eleanor's own foolscap. Straightaway she recognized the poor penmanship from shopping requests Eleanor had dictated to her during tea. No doubt Mary wanted to remind her to take that foul-tasting cordial. How could she be cross when her maid only meant well?

But all these ink smudges and blotches, not like her tidy lady's maid. Could they have been tears?

Madam,
I know you will never forgive me. But I hope
that a woman who has lost a child will under-
stand what another has done to save one. I have

betrayed you and the duchess. I never knew that her precious children were at risk. I only meant to make a few pounds. God forgive me, but I have sold personal information about you and Her grace to persons I now realize mean the duchess and her family harm.

And now you and his lordship may be in danger.

She swore. The rest of the letter was smeared, unreadable.

A rapping at the door startled her. She swallowed the bad taste at the back of her throat. "Who is it?"

"It's Will again."

"This is not a convenient moment."

"I can't hear you properly. Let me inside."

"Why?"

"Because I wasn't supposed to leave you. And sometimes Sebastien scares me. I'd think he'd as soon toss me off a cliff as acknowledge we're cousins-in-law."

"Listen to me, Will. Find Sebastien. Find him."

"What?"

"There is danger. I'll explain afterward. Fetch him, please."

"All right. Danger, you say. Oh, God. Don't leave the room."

Mary, in whom she had confided and who had confided in her. Mary, who knew every secret her mistress kept, the faithful servant who had wept when Eleanor miscarried, the one who had sat beside her bed without sleep or complaint.

She refolded the paper, rising from the chair. The chamber had grown so chilly she felt goose pimples rising on her arms.

Eleanor. Eleanor Antigone, take a hold of yourself, girl. She had not thought of her father in ages. *Shock,* she heard him stating in his matter-of-fact voice. *We did everything we could to save your mother. She had a weak constitution. Perhaps she was too pure for this world. We shall need each other now, Eleanor.*

This impure world. Rats and cats, duchesses and dukes. Who would want to bring a child into this evil? Who would name their daughter Antigone? She dug through her traveling trunk, pressed a clumsy finger to the latch of the hidden compartment.

Letters that could change England's destiny. She would have to break her promise to the duchess. Was Will, too, part of the plot? Unimaginable. For what purpose would he play a part? To gain the duchess's trust, knowledge of her family's whereabouts? For fame? Not Will.

But he was an actor. One who'd sworn to make his mark in history.

She read the letter that Sebastien had just stolen. It contained several references to settling an old score, a promise of revenge that would be dealt in due time.

A scorned woman seeking to punish the duchess. A disgruntled politician with a long-smoldering vendetta against the duke. Thwarted ambition. Twisted desire.

Not a game, after all.

Wellington understood the risks. So did his wife, whose disdain for social functions derived from more primal motives than her critics understood.

The duchess's sons. What better revenge was there for a rival to take on another woman than through the children she had borne with the man they had both loved?

The lamp light burned low. She stared across the room, wondering vaguely how long the wretched storm would last until she realized that it wasn't thunder that she heard.

It was Sebastien demanding entrance at the door. Thank God. Playing at intrigue had been wonderful while it lasted, right up until this moment. She flew from her chair to answer him.

"Open the door, Eleanor," he said in a low voice. "Will said something was wrong."

She released her breath and lifted the heavy bolt. Her muscles shivered in relief when she saw him. "Where have you been?"

"On the drawbridge with my brother Gabriel." He pulled off his turban, glanced at the traveling trunk lying on the floor. "I'm returning to London. Will you promise me not—"

"You were right. There is a plot."

"Bellisant," he said without glancing at her. "Where are my boots? And where the hell is Will now? He was supposed to follow me up here. My brother is riding with me."

"Calm down, Sebastien. It is not Bellisant."

He shoved his feet into the boots she brought to the chair, his eyes glittering, his mouth white at the corners. "Do not defend a traitor to my face," he bit out. "I've no patience for pretty artists and the ladies who adore them."

"Neither do I. He's a talented man."

"Eleanor, I warn you—"

She folded her arms across her midsection, Mary's letter still clutched in her hand. "Is it jealousy that accuses him or logic?" she asked coolly, although the faintest doubt flickered inside her.

He threw her a disgusted look. "Is it desire that comes to his defense or truth?"

"It is truth." She shook her head. "I do not believe anyone except Sir Perceval could have predicted this."

"You have been misled," he said without inflection. "Why do you think Bellisant wanted the duchess to stay in London?"

"He has no wits for a conspiracy."

He came to his feet, impassive, unflinching, a god of vengeance, until she held out the letter that she could not bear to look at again.

"It is not Bellisant," she said again, her voice shaking. "It's Mary. Oh, Sebastien, I have been misled."

He glanced down, blinking, her implacable lord. "How do you know?"

She swallowed. "She's written a confession. She betrayed me for money to give to her son. I trusted her implicitly, and she sold information that would be used—"

"—to assassinate the duke or abduct the duchess," he concluded slowly.

She drew away. Their eyes locked in mutual respect. "No. Neither. It's little Arthur and Charles. I don't know if they're to be ransomed, or worse."

He took the letter from her, shaking his head as he scanned it. "And you are convinced that Bellisant is not involved?" he asked gravely. "Think. He is an intimate visitor to their home as well as to ours."

"He might as well be a boy himself. If I am wrong, then I do not understand human nature."

He slid his hand down her arm. She had never felt closer to him than at this moment. "But you understand why I suspect him?" he asked in a low voice.

"Yes."

"I will show him no mercy if he is involved."

"Nor should you," she said. "They are children. Don't let anything happen to them."

He nodded tersely. "My brother and I are riding straight to London. Do not ask to come."

"I wouldn't go even if you insisted," she replied, giving him a reluctant smile.

He studied her in concern. "Please tell you are not keeping an illness from me. Or is this at last a healthy common sense?"

She bit her lip. "Neither, my lord. Your child is making its presence known in a rather uncomfortable manner. As much as I love both you and the duchess, there is no power on earth that will persuade me to risk a rushed journey."

He went still. She wondered if he understood what she had said until he held her away from him and a grin of unguarded joy broke across his face. "A girl or boy?"

She laughed. "I don't know. Ask Sir Perceval."

He lowered his head. "Now I don't want to leave you."

"Just come back soon." She clasped his hand. "Come back."

He nodded, turning from her in resolve.

She reached out to brush off the rain that glistened like teardrops down the back of his coat. She pretended not to notice as he covertly tucked two pistols into his belt alongside his dagger. Not the London gentleman he had appeared to be, but an officer and agent who would let nothing interfere with duty. She followed him to the door, her heart tight with worry.

He took pause. "Try to be good, Eleanor."

"Only if you return soon. I'll get into mischief if you're not back to keep me occupied."

But she knew now the only thing that could separate them this time was the unthinkable. He would help hunt down the conspirators, chase them across the Channel if necessary. He had no choice.

A knot of emotion constricted her throat as he

drew on a pair of gauntlet leather gloves, his brow furrowed in thought. "There is no one reliable at the Sussex house. The servants will be distressed over what Mary has done. Perhaps I'll ask Heath to send one of my cousins back to fetch you."

"Will could take me to his mother's house in Dover," she said decisively. "I would stay there until you come back. It isn't far. The road is decent, and neither I nor your child should be jostled over-much."

"I love you," he said, kissing her briefly before he opened the door. "Both of you."

She remained in her room for only a handful of minutes. Waiting for him to return was unbearable. She was almost glad to soon be in the midst of a frivolous masquerade to take her mind off what could happen, although she feared that if one more hand tugged at her veils, she would strangle the perpetrator on the spot.

And where *had* Will disappeared to? He knew there was trouble brewing. It was unlike him not to get involved. Was he off somewhere in the castle entertaining a private party? She had been keeping watch for him when she noticed Sir Perceval gesturing at her from one of the great hall's passageways. She rose from the table where she had been half-heartedly engaged in conversation. She crossed the hall and exited the passage to discover Sir Perceval in great agitation. He motioned her covertly toward him.

"What is it?" she whispered, very much suspecting that he'd made one false prediction too many, and was now paying the price. As the Masquer, she knew well that a man who did not live up to his name could get himself in thick trouble with the ladies.

"I cannot find your cousin," he said worriedly.

"Neither can I," she said slowly, her apprehension rising. Will wasn't the sort of person to vanish without a trace. "Where did you see him last?"

He motioned vaguely. "In the torture chamber, my lady."

She stared past him into the torchlit corridor. Lord Eaton had illuminated the stone stairs leading down into the oubliettes with skull-shaped silver sconces. A macabre touch, she thought.

"Why would Will go to the torture chamber?" she wondered aloud, her attention transfixed on the shadow that she had noticed upon the wall.

It was not hers.

Nor did it belong to Sir Perceval.

It was, however, one she knew well. In puzzled silence she looked up at the man who stood in the recessed alcove adjacent to the dungeon stairs. His gauntlet-clad hand lifted in a furtive gesture. She felt a rush of anticipation arise from the very soles of her feet.

"He might have gone there to prepare for tonight's entertainment," Sir Perceval said behind her.

"I don't believe you," she said, revolving slowly to regard him.

He shook his grizzled head. "Lady Boscastle," he said in a condescending voice as he produced a flintlock pistol from the depths of his blue robes. "I am flattered that you and that foolish duchess ever did believe me. Please continue down the stairs to join your cousin."

She swallowed a surge of anger. "I will personally carve you up to feed to the crows if you have hurt Will."

He reared back slightly at this unladylike threat, but his reaction wasn't nearly as satisfying as the stark panic on his face when he heard Sebastien speak over his shoulder.

"I would not challenge her talent, Sir Perceval. You see, I've witnessed her dexterity with a scalpel. The lady has nerves of iron. Quite impressive."

"Dear Sebastien," she murmured. "How good of you to say so. I am moved."

"Then move out of my way, sweetheart."

"For God's sake," Sir Perceval said in scorn. "She's only a woman."

"That's what you think," Sebastien said with a laugh.

She descended a step, her heartbeat quickening as Sebastien forced Sir Perceval to the wall with the tip of his dagger.

"She doesn't flinch at the sight of blood, either, a trait I find oddly endearing."

Her gaze lifted to his hard face. His eyes held hers in a fierce intimacy that sent her heart racing all over again. She managed a smile. "You never told me that," she said.

"I don't think I appreciated your unique abilities enough," he replied.

And before she could respond, he turned swiftly and grasped Sir Perceval by the wrist. The pistol clattered down the stairs into the darkness.

"Will is nursing a concussion in Lord Eaton's room," he said without looking at her. "You might wish to visit him. I'd prefer you leave me to deal with the traitor."

She knew better now than to argue. "Anything you ask."

"I shall take you up on that promise later."

"And you'll be too late," Sir Perceval said, then fell silent as the tip of the dagger touched his throat.

"Please go, Eleanor," Sebastien said in a voice of quiet authority that made her skin prickle.

She climbed up around him, then hesitated. "Who shall I send to you?"

He gave a nod in the direction of the passageway. Eleanor stared up in surprise. How long had that handsome black-haired man been standing there? What was it about his chiseled profile that compelled and felt disconcertingly familiar?

She did not recognize this man and yet she did. The raven-haired stranger stepped forth and bowed, his blue eyes assessing her in hooded amusement. For an alarming instant she thought she might be suffering from a delusion. *Did* Sebastien have an evil twin?

"My brother Gabriel," Sebastien said, walking Sir Perceval down the remaining steps. "He will see you upstairs."

"The resemblance is—"

"Unfortunate." Gabriel straightened with a charming grin. "I have to ride with Sebastien back to London. Now that I have made your acquaintance, I do understand why he is loathe to leave."

She laughed, welcoming the release. She could not decide whether the pair of them looked more like demons or avenging angels. But this charming rogue would be her child's uncle. All of a sudden she realized that a large family loomed in her future. The Boscastles ruled London.

Sir Perceval gave an indignant grunt of objection as Sebastien nudged him rather urgently down the steps. Soon after, the clank of an iron door echoed through the underchambers. She stole a glimpse at her husband's hard, beautiful face. His smile restored her spirits.

She would forgive him for interfering in her work. And she fully expected that he would apologize for calling the duchess's mission a "teacup" affair. She would not gloat, however. Sebastien had earned her deepest respect for employing his devious mind to put together what she had not even realized was a puzzle.

The cat, and the rat who'd chased her, had worked well together. It was almost a pity that they would be retiring from service to devote themselves to the next generation.

Well, that was as it should be.

Thus, closing that chapter on her life, she took Sir Gabriel Boscastle's arm in gratitude and left Sebastien to whatever dark acts he might be required to perform.

Chapter Thirty-one

❧ ❧

In her drawing room, the Duchess of Wellington took a light breakfast of kippers on toast and sifted through a slew of trivial correspondences. A creature of the night, Sir Nathan had consented to come at an early hour to capture the boys in their best light.

To Kitty that meant wielding all methods of bribery in her mother's arsenal to coax her beloved hellions into washing behind their ears and not dirtying their crisp Irish linen shirts. The nursemaid had awakened the children at the crack of dawn. She and the duchess hoped they would soon be tired enough to sit. While Kitty relished the energy of her sons, she understood Sir Nathan's frustration. How did one distill their boyish energy into a portrait that would be regarded in flattering terms by posterity?

She stared out the window into the garden where Sir Nathan had asked the boys to pose. An odd choice, she reflected, considering the uncertain November weather. Yet her eyes misted with tears as he walked the children to the garden wall. In a few years her sons would attend Eton. She could not abide an empty home. She would adopt more children and her husband could serve as ambassador on the moon should he desire. He would find other entertainments to keep him from family duties.

And she would have her memories, a portrait to remind her of these precious years.

"Your grace," her secretary Loveridge said rather breathlessly from the door.

She sighed, wishing she could go an hour without interruption. And, goodness, what were the boys doing with that rope ladder on the wall? Charles would ruin another pair of twilled woolen trousers climbing. Why did Sir Nathan stand there encouraging their misconduct?

"*Your grace.*"

She whirled in impatience at Loveridge's anxious tone. "What is it now?"

He bowed, his wig askew, as he presented to her a letter on a footed silver salver.

Urgent.

The duke, she thought, her heart in her throat. Even in a world at peace, her husband walked among enemies. Resentful Bonapartists, the occasional lunatic, old adversaries masquerading as friends. The price of leadership. She should have been a country wife married to a plodding squire.

She fought a wave of lightheadedness.

"Don't tell the boys yet," she said as she reached for the letter.

"No, your grace," Loveridge said with tears in his eyes.

If the news were dire, let them be immortalized by Sir Nathan on the last day of innocence they would ever know.

While the two Boscastle brothers pounded north toward London, a branch of messengers carried warnings to every conceivable port and custom-house in England that might be employed for escape or concealment. Humble clerks and widows, as well as ferrymen and shipmasters loyal to the grand duke, tumbled from their beds and went on the alert.

Sebastien galloped alongside Gabriel's black Andalusian, impressed by his younger brother's skill in the saddle. Two fresh horses awaited them in a coaching inn at Sevenoaks. A pint of small beer later, they cantered over the dark village green, joined at the abbey ruins by four red-coated outriders. Another detachment headed toward the moonlit coast road and Lord Eaton's castle. Sebastien felt easier knowing Eleanor would be under guard until he returned to her.

By the time he and Gabriel rode into London, church bells pealed and shutters opened onto a gray, misty day. Sweeps and milkmaids jostled between carts, grateful that last night's storm had passed and they could take home a few pennies.

A secret cadre comprised of former British officers had been called out on their way to cabinet meetings or coffeehouses. More than one valet had hurriedly knotted a neckcloth or left a chin unshaven as his master received a message marked *Urgent*.

The House Patrol scoured the city outskirts, the mews and the museums, pistols and cutlasses worn beneath their blue coats. Watchmen scrutinized the streets from their huts, forgoing the usual luxury of stolen naps. Turnpike keepers questioned travelers who aroused suspicion. Tavern owners and their wives watched for customers who begged a trundle for two young boys.

A chain of vigilance had been formed not only by the elite but also by the iron links of ordinary English citizens, some hoping for reward, some merely desirous of protecting the Duke of Wellington's sons.

Sir Nathan Bellisant wondered as he did at every point in a portrait why he had become an artist. Yet how else could a man of his unstable nature make a living? Could he have survived as a bank clerk? A spice merchant? A farmer who tilled from dawn to dusk? He had not slept for two days. This work tormented him. Still, he knew his doubts would abate after—*if*—he had rested and produced the definitive sketch of his young subjects that eluded him.

He doubted it would happen today. He had lost his concentration. Or rather his concentration had followed Arthur and Charles to their amusing game at the bottom of the garden. He glanced up at the rope ladder hanging over the wall.

"How did that get up there?" he demanded, his own childish imagination piqued.

Charles shrugged. "It just came. Can we climb it?"

Arthur, the duke's heir, yanked his brother by his jacket sleeve. "It's a trap. They've come to get us. Prepare to fight, men."

Nathan narrowed his eyes. "Who are we fighting? Are we outnumbered?"

Arthur turned to assess him with a look advanced far beyond his eight years. Nathan could have wept. *There* was the image he needed to capture. The veiled arrogance, the intelligence, the thirst for adventure—all imprinted on Arthur's unformed features.

But suddenly, as he turned to his sketching easel, the garden swarmed with Coldstream Guards. The red-jacketed guardsmen converged on the two children who stood in joyful terror at the wall.

The duchess ran out into the garden, her face as white as ash. Disbelieving, Nathan watched—well, what the blazes *was* he watching? A regimental parade through the house toward the park? A political celebration no one had thought to mention?

A victorious shout rang through the air. "You saved us, Boscastle!" Charles declared at the top of his voice, hefted onto the shoulders of a guardsman. "We were all but done for until you brought reinforcements!"

Nathan pivoted slowly, shaking his head in abject surrender. He stared at the dark figure advancing on him with a pair of pistols raised. He made no move to defend himself. He hadn't dreamt that a man could be arrested for being infatuated with another man's wife.

Boscastle clearly wanted blood. Nathan was going to die just like his father.

"I give up," he said, lifting his charcoal-stained hands into the air. "Shoot me now. I'm innocent, by the way. Not that it matters. And you didn't need a battalion to arrest me. My paintings are hardly a threat to home security."

"Get inside the house," Sebastien said, stepping around the sketches that the guards had trampled into the grass. "And for your own protection don't come out again until you are told."

"You mean—you aren't going to shoot me?"

"Not right now."

"Well, thank God, but—you don't mind not stomping all over those sketches again, do you?"

Government spies caught the rest of the conspirators who'd plotted to abduct the duke's sons that same day. Two had been waiting to spirit the boys away in a fashionable coach on Hyde Park Corner, accompanied by an attractive woman posing as a governess. She later confessed that her name was Viola Hutchinson and that she'd been in love with Wellington years ago. Three other members of the conspiracy surrendered on Queenhithe Dock. Four were arrested by the Coldstream Guards outside Apsley House.

Ashamed of her unwitting part in the plot, Mary

Sturges complied with the quiet-spoken Crown agents who came to the town house to question her. She admitted the plotters had first approached her at market and later bought information from her. Only recently had she learned that Sir Perceval was part of the conspiracy, and it was he who had threatened her and explained the gravity of what would be done. She broke down when Sebastien arrived, and begged his forgiveness. She swore that she loved her mistress, and no, *no,* the cordial had not been poisoned.

The Mayfair Masquer was never mentioned.

Lord Barry Summers, the instigator of the thwarted abduction, was taken into custody in an inn near Falmouth that evening. He might have escaped to France had an astute serving girl not overheard him reminding his wife to burn his documents.

The girl tipped off the good-looking officers on patrol downstairs in the taproom.

The village hailed her as a heroine. Libations were on the house.

By bedtime the duchess had taken a tipple or two herself and restored her household to its comforting routine. The boys had been allowed an extra hour of play before retiring, and two portions of almond cream pudding for dessert.

They claimed it had been the best day of their lives.

Sebastien slept at his cousin Heath's town house before setting off alone in the dark before sunrise the next day. Heath had his hands full with the Home Office. Gabriel galloped back to his wife.

Sebastien found Eleanor anxious but safe in Castle Eaton under the care of his cousin Lord Devon Boscastle and his wife Jocelyn. Most of the other guests had departed.

After being told of the failed abduction, the lords and ladies who had remained at the party found themselves suddenly eager to return home and spend time with their own children.

Chapter Thirty-two

❧ ❧

Sebastien strode across the castle's great hall to the bench where Eleanor sat engaged in an animated conversation with his younger Boscastle cousin, Lord Devon, and Devon's wife. His heart quickened as Eleanor glanced up and noticed him. His cloak and boots bore heavy mud stains. He had not shaved and had but washed in cold rain water before entering the keep.

She rose slowly, her smile both a balm and an enticement. Numerous servants flittered about the hall, tending the fire, bringing refreshments. He would have preferred that they were alone, but the lack of privacy did not stop him from taking her in his arms. Nor would he deny himself a long, passionate kiss. His grip tightened around her waist.

He needed to hold her, to reassure himself that she had remained safe while he had been gone. And that this time, nothing had happened to their child.

Her smile told him enough.

He kissed her again for good measure and for

making him a father. He couldn't atone for the last time. But he would be with her through this.

"There are people watching us," she whispered in breathless happiness against his mouth.

His eyes glittered wolfishly. "I noticed. And I don't care. Do you know how good you feel?"

She slipped her hand inside his coat, her fingertips exploring his chest, his muscular flanks. "No wounds?" she asked in an undertone.

"Sore muscles from hard riding." He captured her face in his hands. "Nothing that a bath and a few days in bed won't fix."

Her mouth curled in a knowing smile. "As a physician's daughter, I think that is splendid advice."

A meaningful cough intruded their reunion. Sebastien suddenly realized that he had not even acknowledged his younger cousin Devon for rushing to the rescue. He grinned at the tall lanky Boscastle who stood behind Eleanor, his blue eyes devilish and friendly.

Devon had been a rambunctious boy when they'd last met. The playful cousin. He looked every bit as full of mischief now. Sebastien gripped his arm. He was glad Devon hadn't changed. "How can I repay you?"

"I'd be insulted if you tried." Devon stared at him in respect. "I heard your efforts met with success. Well bloody done."

There followed the common ritual of manly shoulder slapping and another round of thanking each other until Devon's wife, Jocelyn, arose from the bench to join them. She wore a plum woolen gown, and her dark golden hair in a bejeweled knot on her nape. After Devon had introduced her to Sebastien, she took Eleanor aside.

"From what I understand, the Boscastle family hasn't seen your husband in years."

Eleanor smiled wistfully as the men walked toward the table to continue their conversation. "Until recently, neither had I."

The two ladies stood observing their husbands quaffing cider and catching up on family news. The servants brought in platters of fresh bread and two roasted turkeys. Lord Eaton, his wife, and his two older sisters appeared for the meal. Eleanor and Jocelyn soon joined them. Eleanor's appetite had grown enormously in the past two days.

An air of festivity enlivened the chilly evening. Good had triumphed over evil. That villain Sir Perceval, who had been a linchpin in the plot, had sat at this same table. Now the hero of the hour, Sebastien Boscastle, sat in their midst, deflecting the praise heaped on him with modest shrugs. Most of his truly dangerous assignments had been carried out in secret. So he stared at his pregnant wife and waited for the subject to change—regretting when it did. To her.

Or rather, to her secret identity.

"I'm of a mind not to return to London at all after this," one of Lord Eaton's sisters remarked.

Lord Eaton frowned at her, rubbing his beard. "No one is going to abduct *you*, Prudence."

"Well, what about the Masquer?"

Her bespectacled sister gave a snort. "He goes after the beauties. And he's never hurt anyone."

"If I woke up to see him standing at the foot of the bed with his scarred face, I believe my heart would give out, although if he begged my understanding—"

"I don't think anyone understands that poor monster," Jocelyn murmured.

"And you do?" Devon asked, laughing in amusement.

She lowered her custard tart. "I would merely like the chance to be alone with him for a brief time."

He frowned at that. "What for?"

"Just to tell him that beauty does not count for everything. And that if he removes his mask and reveals his true nature, he will find someone who loves him despite his flaws."

Devon made a rude noise in his throat. "Unless he really is a monster underneath, and then what would you do? You wouldn't offer a beast your affection."

"I would hope to tame him," Jocelyn said with a defiant grin. "Besides, you were wearing a mask when I fell in love with you."

"Well, I don't consider myself tamed."

She laughed. "Then I've done a good job."

He glanced at Eleanor. "What would *you* do if the Masquer appeared in your bedroom one night?"

"I should offer him solace," she said slyly.

"Solace?" Devon glanced from her to his wife as if they both had windmills in their heads. "I'd shoot the blighter in the bollocks."

Jocelyn's lips curled. "Nobody shot you when you were the Kissing Bandit."

"But that was a joke, wasn't it?"

"Perhaps the Masquer was having us on all along," Jocelyn said, smiling pensively. "Somehow I suspect the strange fellow wasn't who he seemed to be."

Sebastien took a drink of cider. Eleanor bowed her head, hoping the guilty twinkle in her eye wouldn't give her away. She sensed that she could trust the Boscastles with her secret.

But not yet. For now the Masquer and his motives would remain a mystery.

Chapter Thirty-three

❧ ❧

The ton agreed that the Little Season had ended with enough gossip to tide them over until next year. An abduction plot had failed. The waggish Masquer had vanished into the autumn mists, and while no one knew what scandals would hibernate over winter, everyone hoped the entertaining rascal would return. An editorial in the *Times* asserted that having been unmasked, however, he might have lost his impetus.

To which Sebastien muttered, "And about time, too."

Frankly Eleanor doubted the unfortunate fellow would ever appear again in his former guise.

She could barely squeeze into her comfortable gowns. She hated to admit it, but the costumes hidden at the bottom of her wardrobe would never be worn so dashingly again, if at all. At the rate her modest curves were expanding, even the carriage doors would have to be let out.

Her winter wardrobe was due to arrive any day. She hoped that Madame Devine designed with comfort in mind, as well as romantic appeal. And that the seams could be altered to accommodate her pregnant figure. For now, she would suffer for appearances' sake and not fasten her corset all the way.

On this, the first evening of December, she and Sebastien had dined en famille at the Kentish home of the Marquess and Marchioness of Sedgecroft. Sebastien had recounted Heath's warning that the London Boscastles could overwhelm those quieter beings unaccustomed to their charisma. Thus advised, a woman not as demure as she appeared, Eleanor passed through the crested gates of the estate with her guard raised, and her appetite piqued.

Two days later, fortified by the culinary offerings of three French chefs and the warmth of a family who embraced her to their collective bosom, she walked contently up the stairs of her husband's modest country manor in Sussex.

"Well," Sebastien said, unraveling his neckcloth in their musty, unaired bedchamber. "That was my side of the family." He glanced down meaningfully at the bump that barely showed beneath her cloak. He caressed it at least a dozen times a day. "Let's see what the cauldron produces next."

She sighed a trifle sadly. The house seemed so empty and cold. "I had always thought Mary would be here for my lying-in. What will happen to her?"

He took her hands, kissing her tapered fingertips. "Nothing dire, I promise. She betrayed you personally. She had no knowledge of the conspiracy. Her conscience, I would guess, will be punishment enough. Heath has asked for leniency."

She lifted her brow as he knelt to remove her shoes. "The Duchess has written to inform me that you're to be made a viscount. You must have known. Why didn't you announce it over supper last night? Your cousins would have celebrated the event."

"I thought titles didn't impress you."

"That was before I realized that a child would change everything."

"Having grown up with three brothers, I think that is an understatement." He tucked her shoes neatly under the bed. She thought again how well they balanced each other. "What else impresses you?" he asked.

She padded to the windows. He hung his coat up in the wardrobe. "Let me think," she said. "Husbands who come to one's rescue at the last moment."

His Hessian boots hit the floor, to be lined up beneath the desk. "Excellent. Do continue."

She pursed her lips as he removed his waistcoat and unbuttoned his lawn shirt. "Husbands who are passionate. And who hang up their clothes."

His neckcloth joined his other garments. "Yes. I thought I should assert my place."

"Faithful husbands," she said with a smile.

"Are there any other kind?" he asked in a velvet voice.

She glanced around.

He stood shirtless before her, a wicked baron, soon to become a viscount, one whose well-muscled beauty quite took her breath away. "And—oh dear, what were we—"

Her gaze moved past him, lifting from his tempting attributes to stare at the portrait on the wall. "That's Bellisant's painting of me," she exclaimed. "How did it end up here?"

"I had it sent ahead as a surprise," he said, leaning his arm against the mantel to admire it.

"I thought you didn't like his work."

"The subject of this particular piece intrigues me. And reminds me of a promise I have made." He smiled up briefly at the painted lady who stared across the room in artistic detachment. And then he walked forward to give his full attention to her earthly embodiment.

Her pulses beat erratically. "A new promise or an old one?"

"A little of both. On one hand, I have promised to place my family above all else." His hands encircled her waist, drawing her against him. "On the other, I have promised the lady in that portrait that I shall remember she is a person never to be taken for granted. Or left alone for any unreasonable period of time."

She turned into his arms. "I fear I should envy her then. You seem to have fallen in love with a shadow lady who does not exist."

He closed his eyes. "If either of us wear another mask, let it only be to confound the world, not each other."

"Agreed," she whispered.

He caught her chin with his thumb, lifting her face to steal the first of endless kisses in the night. Shivers melted her spine. If the child inside her had softened her body and rendered her more vulnerable, Sebastien had grown all the stronger. She sought the closeness of his arms around her at every chance. It was true they had both wandered astray since their wedding day. Certainly a budding family would impose limits on their dangerous pursuits.

Three heartbeats now.

And the Boscastle line, in all its passion and infamy, continued.

Acknowledgments

A huge thank-you from my heart to everyone at Ballantine Books, for all the hard work and behind-the-scenes brilliance that deserves recognition.
This writer is grateful to each one of you.

Read on for an excerpt from

The Wicked Duke Takes a Wife

by
Jillian Hunter

Published by Ballantine Books

It had taken Miss Harriet Gardner two years of intensive training in the social graces to become that mysterious creation known in polite Society as a gentlewoman. It took the stormy young Duke of Glenmorgan less than two days to undo months of discipline, of tears and sweat, to reawaken every gutter instinct Harriet had learned to subdue.

He stood in the doorway, silent, his presence so imposing that Harriet felt as if time had stopped. Suddenly the butler, the footmen, the maid bringing another platter of sandwiches for tea, seemed at a loss as to how they should proceed. They stared at Harriet, awaiting her direction.

But she was staring at the cloaked duke who must have wondered whether he'd arrived at a house of eccentrics. Raindrops slid from the brim of his black silk hat and ran into the faint lines carved into his cheeks. He glanced back at the carriage parked in the street. She studied his profile. He had a sharp blade of a nose and a cleft in his chin. When he turned again, his blue eyes cut straight to Harriet, riveting her to the spot.

He's young, she thought. *And he looks a proper beast.*

He wrenched off his sodden top hat. The thunderclap that accompanied this impatient gesture deepened the tension holding his audience spellbound.

"Is this or is this not Lady Lyon's Academy for Young Ladies?" he demanded.

His voice, the deep, lyrical lilt, reminded Harriet of her duty. He was bringing his niece from the Welsh–English border to the academy in preparation for her presentation at court. Only a genuine peer claimed that honor. "Your grace," Harriet said, sinking into a curtsy, "we are called the Scarfield Academy now. And—"

She lowered her gaze in embarrassment. The butler was bowing, the two footmen followed suit, and the maid dipped so deeply that her sandwiches slid to the edge of her tray. Harriet cringed. They must look like a collection of windup toys whose springs had gone askew.

"Well, whatever this place is called," the duke said over Harriet's head, "I hope that my aunt and niece might be allowed to take refuge from the storm."

Harriet glanced up from his black mud-splattered Hessian boots and straightened instantly. Through the curtain of rain that shimmered in the open doorway, she could see his coachman conversing with the academy's stable master. From the carriage, a silver-haired lady was waving a lace handkerchief at the house like a naval officer flagging a ship down in distress.

"I do apologize, Your grace." She darted toward the door. "I shall bring them in straightaway."

He stepped in front of her. "Have a footman attend to the task. With umbrellas if possible." His disgruntled gaze seemed to absorb every detail of her appearance. "I'm in no mood to hear another lady complain that the wretched rain has ruined her hair."

A test, Harriet told herself. This was one of those social trials that sooner or later a woman in her position must face. She would remain unmoved by his curt manner. She would stand, in her mentor's words as, "a beacon of civility when battered by a storm of rudeness."

What misfortune that Harriet had loved thunderstorms since her earliest years.